NEEDLES & NIGHTMARES

Stories from Saforia

Dani's Duet: Part 2

By: A. R. Lines

For more information, email: authorarlines@gmail.com

CONTENTS

Dedication

To those who'd rather live in a fantasy world because reality is a dumpster fire.

Plus, having magic would be dope.

Author's Note & Content Warning

This is an omegaverse book. This means that a large part of the story is based around scents, heats, adaptive body parts and knotting. Omegaverse is an alternative universe where the creatures and humans involved fit into three categories: Alphas, Betas, and Omegas. They have animalistic characteristics regardless of what kind of creature/shifter/magical being they are. Relationships are mainly driven by the sexual beast-like connections that Omegas form with those they regard as their pack.

This is a world where it is common for one female (Omega or Beta) to end up with multiple mates. They consider this their pack, their family. In this world magic abounds and there are many types of creatures, or beings, but they all fit into one of the three categories or designations. They will still exhibit characteristics of what they are on top of their designation.

There will be references involving sexually explicit scenes (consensual). These characters enjoy intimacy and a large part of omegaverse surrounds this aspect. Anxiety, as with anyone or anything, exists, and the characters will exhibit signs of worry and tension. This is not all sweet and fluffy and throughout the book you will encounter scenes of violence and injuries to more than one of our MCs.

Because of the genre, there will be scenes with spankings/domestic discipline, light degradation, biting/marking and a breeding kink. Our MMC's really like the thought of offspring (or they just enjoy trying).

This book is steamy, and the focus is on their Omegas. There is a good deal of MM and a bit of FF. Our FMC will add mates to her pack as she goes.

Also, this is high fantasy, a whole new world and while some creatures and animals will be familiar, there are others that exist unique to this place.

But, if you do find any spelling errors or grammatical issues please don't report it, send me an email at Authorarlines@gmail.com and I will be more than happy to fix these!

Glossary Of Certain Terms:

Piemel - Flemish for penis

Dowan - Coffee-like drink

Schatje - Little Treasure

PROLOGUE

Unknown

My shaggy muzzle lifts into the air, scenting something rotten on the breeze. Naargeestig forest's dense foliage usually acts as a barrier against the outside world. I spend my days in peace, surrounded by the lush woodland, feeling the soft earth under my feet. But today, something has intruded on my solitude.

A sneeze tickles my nostrils at the ugly smell, and I turn away, refocusing on digging a new chamber in my den. Whatever it is doesn't concern me. I find all I need within my woods, and I want nothing to do with the world beyond. Being alone suits me just fine, and the rest of Saforia feels the same way.

Wildlings are uncommon. Those few who are discovered typically face apprehension, and in many cases, overt hostility. It's what my mother taught me after my father left us. Apparently, he didn't know what she was when they mated, and she was pregnant before he found out. The way she always told it made him sound like an absolute wretch. How could a male just abandon his mate and child?

It shouldn't matter what they are, only how they treat each other. I scoff. No, I need nothing from outside my forest. My mother moved here before giving birth to me. She was a strong female and always did everything she could to take care of me.

Even while heavy with child, she traversed the thick woods to find a suitable den for us. These ruins became our perfect home. She raised me on the scents of lush growth and fresh air. I learned to hunt in my Wildling form, the same as she did. Tracking, traps, cooking, cleaning — my mother was a fount of knowledge.

Her loss still aches in my heart. She was an incredible female to do all of it alone. But eventually the mate sickness caught up with her. At least I had her for twelve years before she passed.

At first, it was lonely and frightening in the dense forest, but I learned to adapt. Now, I'm an accomplished hunter. I know the texture of each tree trunk and the smell of every blade of grass like old friends. These woods hold no secrets from me.

The scent of rot in the air grows stronger, and my inner Alpha grows uneasy. Sure, there's always the normal smell of decay from leaf litter, dead trees and the animals that have passed on, but this rot is different, like nothing I've ever smelled before. There's something *wrong* with it.

With a huff, I stop working on my den and shake out the dirt from my fur. No one else is around to investigate, so I guess I have to. Leaning down on all fours, I move into an easy lope and follow my nose towards the unsettling scent.

Even as I travel through my woods, I argue with myself about going to poke around. Something in my gut is telling me this is a bad idea. But... the rot is only growing more powerful and soon it may encompass my entire forest. I cannot live with that smell permeating every inch of my home.

The mossy ground cushions my paws as I hurry toward the source of the awful, putrid scent. The sound of loud stomping feet reaches my ears, and I slow my pace. Whoever it is, their movements betray them. They crush every dry leaf and brittle branch with each step; the sound echoing through the stillness.

The usual song of the forest has fallen

silent. I halt, cocking my head to listen intently. Unease threads through my body as I try to decide if I should just turn around now and pretend this scent and sound aren't infiltrating my woods.

My hesitation costs me. A loud coughing bark echoes through the trees to my left, and a monstrous form crashes into me, sending us both onto the loamy ground.

A snarl rips from my chest, and my teeth sink into whatever body part is closest. A high screech pierces my ears as I tear chunks out of the attacking beast. Finally, it backs off and I get my first proper look at the creature.

Everything about it is wrong. It resembles a monstrosity, a twisted creature pieced together from the shattered forms of several animals. A Gator's head sits atop a Bear's bulk, with Wolf's paws and a Scorp's stinger completing the monstrous form. What kind of wretch would create this abomination?

This thing is an insult to the Goddess. An insult to nature itself! I pity the animals that were destroyed to make this creature. Silently, I vow to end its pitiful existence.

I launch myself at the beast, aiming for the vulnerable throat, and sink my teeth into the soft flesh. With a swift turn of my head, the taste of tainted blood explodes on my tongue as I tear through skin and cartilage.

Normally, when I make a kill, it's to feed myself, and I make sure I use every part of the animal. But, I want nothing to do with this monstrosity, so I let the chunk of flesh fall from my jaws and send up a prayer to carry the souls of this beast to Sanctuary.

Before I've even finished my thought, another three abominations crash through the brush and surround me. Snarls and eerie growls create a cacophony in my normally quiet forest. Rage unlike anything I've ever felt before boils my blood.

Who dares to defile my woods with this black magic? Before the thought is complete, the measured steps of a presence echo, almost swallowed by the beasts' discordant howls.

"Well, well, well, what do we have here?" A male's nasally voice drawls. There's a long pause before he shouts, "QUIET!"

All sounds cease. Even the monsters' bizarre noises were not as unsettling as the oppressive silence.

"Much better. Now, this one looks strong. My Master will be pleased with this addition," the male continues to speak to himself.

"What even is it? Not a Wolf... Not a human... Maybe it's one of the Master's beasts already? No, no, I would feel it. Doesn't matter. Its parts will create something powerful."

My head cocks as I watch the male stroll into view. He's just as wrong as the surrounding animals. His body is stitched together from different beings; the lines crossing his face are stark against some of the pale patches. He is a terrifying nightmare that should not exist.

Ending this creature would be a blessing to the Goddess. My lips lift into a snarl. Anger pulses through me as I watch him control the abominations surrounding me. He's to blame for these poor beasts? It will be a pleasure to end him.

As I sink onto my haunches, readying myself to leap at the male, black smoke slithers through the grass like deadly snakes, startling me. What the fuck is that?

It follows me as I try to back away. Only remembering there's a beast behind me when claws rake down my back. I release a loud howl of pain and leap forward, right into the insidious smoke. Twining around my wrists and ankles, it slithers up my body, and the last thing I see is the manic grin of the patchwork *piemel* in front of me.

◆ ◆ ◆

My head aches as if I've consumed copious amounts of fermented berries. I only had to do it once to regret ever tasting the potent fruit. Why does my head ache if I don't remember indulging? I try to roll over, but every inch of my body hurts like I had to fight off a sloth of Bears.

Goddess, what happened? I finally pry my eyes open, only to be greeted by thick blackness. I blink a few times, as if that will clear my vision, but it does nothing. Am I blind? Or is it just very dark in here?

Where am I? This isn't my den. The scent is all wrong. Putrid rot and the smell of taint is everywhere. I can hardly scent the dirt below my body.

I wiggle my fingers and toes, easing the pain away so I can try to figure out what the fuck happened. Eventually, I sit up with a groan. It's slow going, but I'm determined to stand.

Although when I do my head bumps against a rocky ceiling causing dirt and small stones to fall all around me. Shit. This is bad. Blindly, I feel around me to map out my space.

More roughly carved stone behind me. In front of me, my hands collide with solid metal bars. Fear shocks through me, and I take slow measured breaths to control it as I continue to feel around.

Bars on three sides and stone behind and above. I've been caged. By who? And why? No one even knew I lived in Naargeestig forest, so why would someone even bother to find me?

Nothing makes sense.

My body jolts as memories race through my mind. The same rotting scent in my woods. Investigating. Abominations. The patchwork *piemel.* Black snaking smoke attacking me.

Shit. This has to be the work of a black magic User. Still, that awful smell of rot... it's not black magic. I remember the male muttering about his master. What is he?

Terror unlike anything I've ever felt before permeates my body, freezing me in place. Goddess, what do they want with me? Am I going to be torn apart to create more of those abominations?

My breath hitches, the walls seem to close in, and I can only think of the darkness that awaits me. This is it. The end. There's no way out. I slump down onto the dirt floor and take slow breaths.

Don't give up yet, Tev. My mother's voice echoes through my mind. *You're stronger than this.*

CH. 1

Lianis

A large, terrifying dragon glares down at me and my pack. I barely notice the rhythmic thud of a male's feet as he walks along the dragon's scaly back. It's only when he speaks that my tension eases.

"Lia! My mate will be thrilled to see you again," Rafe says jovially and sticks a hand out for me to shake as he comes to a stop in front of us.

"What are you doing here? Not that we don't appreciate the help, but... how?" I ask, arms crossing after greeting the male.

"Ahhh, right." Rafe rubs the back of his neck and glances back at the watchful dragon. "So our son is a Seer, and he told my Kitten that her friends needed help or we'd never see you again. Of course she pleaded so prettily, and Gin here caved to her desires, as usual."

At those words, the dragon lifts his head, snorting a puff of smoke in Rafe's direction. The heat of it washes over us, and I shiver, fear trailing up my spine. *Fuck.* Gin is one scary being. Thankfully, they're on our side.

"Wait, you have a son? Did I miss Luella's entire pregnancy? How the hell did that happen?" Surprise makes me flinch, eyes widening. Was the Omega with child while in Banell? I ought to have scented that! She shouldn't have been anywhere near the danger we put her in!

Rafe's laughter booms, startling the sweet Pixie next to me as well as Eram. That male is wound tighter than a boghag. I wonder when Eram will finally relax enough to let Dani in?

"Oh Goddess, no. I think if she'd been pregnant when she was taken from us there would have been no stopping Tawson and Gin from actually destroying our world. Luckily, cooler heads prevailed, and Tawson only blew up the gate at Banell." Rafe chuckles, a fond twinkle in his eye as he tosses a look at the fearsome dragon.

Gin snorts again, impatient, and shoves Rafe with his snout, coating the back of Rafe's tunic with black smoke.

"Hey! Dammit, Gin! Luella's going to be pissed that you ruined another one of my shirts! You know how much she likes our used clothing in her nest!" The ever cheerful Alpha complains loudly over the dragon's chuffing laugh.

"WAIT!" Dani shouts, startling everyone, even Gin jerks back before leveling a glare at the little Omega at my side. "You said Luella! You know her? Oh, fuck! You're part of the Elite! Shit, you're her mates! Wait, I recognize you from the market! Oh fuck! She's okay? Goddess, I need to see her so badly. Please tell me she's okay?" Dani's words tumble out so quickly it's hard to understand her.

The little female steps forward, no longer wary of the angry dragon, and grabs Rafe's hand, tugging on him with each question.

Eram jerks forward, wrapping his arms around Dani and lifting her into his chest with a low growl. I can't help the smirk that plays at the corner of my lips. Even I was uncomfortable with Rafe getting his scent on her, I'm glad he broke from his stoic facade and stopped that.

"Yep!" Rafe chuckles at Eram frantically rubbing Dani's hand over his cheek, covering Rafe's scent on her. "Luella was frantic when the vision came through and sent her strongest mates to come save you! She wanted to be here herself, but she's currently grounded."

The dragon snorts another puff of smoke at Rafe's words, the blackness sticking in my throat, making me cough. Eram was smart and put his back to the dragon, protecting Dani from him.

"Why is she grounded? What did she do? Are you lot not allowing her to go out?" Dani wiggles out of Eram's tight grasp, her voice growing darker with each word.

She's a vision of strength and menace. Coated in the gore of all the beasts she killed, standing tall against a fucking dragon and an Alpha. The light seems to shine down on her, reflecting off her pretty opalescent wings. Dani's hands fist at her sides, slipping through the folds of her dress only to come out with another fucking weapon. How many does she have squirreled away on her body?

The thought of patting her down, running my hands over her body to search for each dagger and sword, brings a sultry heat to my core. I can't wait to get to know her better; she's such a pretty little Pixie.

"No, no, no! Nothing like that, I swear!" Rafe holds his hands up, swallowing back the grin I know he wants to beam at her. "Honestly, Luella could ask us to do anything and we'd cave to her every desire but… Well, let's get you all to our Keep and I'll allow my mate to tell you about her adventures."

"Fine." Dani crosses her arms, a fierce glare leveled at the chipper Alpha.

"Great!" Rafe claps his hands, the grin he's been holding back beams at us, and he scans the cart and the rest of my new pack. "How about you two shift back and dress so we can see a dragon about an Omega!"

Costen and Hagon hesitantly step away from the cart, monitoring the dragon and the unknown-to-them Alpha. Costen is fast to relax, the Snow-Cat is not much for holding a grudge, but I can see Hagon resisting anything from Pack Foreastra. He's still wary of me, but he is due for another session under me, so I'll fix that.

Once those two are dressed, and Ily can hide behind Hagon instead of a blanket, they stand with Dani, Eram, and me.

"What do you want?" Hagon's gruff voice draws Rafe's gaze.

"Well, how important is the stuff in the cart? We can get you there in a few minutes if you're not afraid to ride the dragon." Rafe grins at our scarred grump.

Before Hagon can turn down the offer, Dani jumps up, her wings buzzing with her intensity as she cuts off whatever denial Hagon is about to give.

"Well, what are we waiting for? Let's go! I have a bestie to see!" Dani says, hands propped on her hips.

"Dani," Hagon starts, "we can't-"

"Hagon! Alpha, please? I need to see her. There's so much I have to tell her, and staying on the road any longer is dangerous. Jerrik and those undead beasts could be back at any moment. We're not safe. Remember what my mother told me? Getting to their Keep will protect us." Dani grabs Hagon's hand, pleading with him. She softens her tone, murmuring to him and rubbing her cheek against his palm.

I smirk as I watch emotions play over Hagon's face. It's fucking hard to deny that sweet Pixie anything when she gentles herself. Finally, the male settles on defeat and heaves a tired sigh.

"Okay, Menace. Whatever you need." Hagon brushes his fingers over her cheek before turning to Ilaris. "Are you okay with this, Sweet Boy?"

"Yes, anything for my Omega." Ily turns bravely towards Rafe and Gin. "C-can I bring a few things? Is... is he strong enough to carry all of us?" He shakily points at the dragon.

Gin huffs out an angry plume of black smoke, a low rumble vibrating the ground. Rafe guffaws, slapping his thigh.

"I'd take that back if I were you," Rafe jokes to Ilaris, who blanches and shrinks into himself, "and you! Quit that. What do you think your mate will say when she hears about your behavior?" The cheery male scolds Gin, and the moment he says 'mate' the dragon stops growling and slams his mouth shut with a glare.

"Oh, he's just a big grump. Don't worry about him, and yes, you're welcome to bring your things. Gin is a beastly dragon and can carry us. But I'll need everyone to be on alert for more of those putrid griffons. If we're attacked in the air, Gin won't be able to fight without dumping us, and I think we'd all prefer to actually arrive whole and unhurt." Rafe drops his smile, uncharacteristically serious as he explains our travel plans.

As I scan over my pack, Eram and Hagon's frowns mirror my own. The risk to our safety grows rapidly with every mile we travel on the road, but the skies don't seem like a secure alternative. I don't like the options we have, but I think, since Rafe said it will only take minutes to get there by dragon, that it's our best hope.

Dani and Ilaris scramble over to the cart, gathering blankets first. Dani also grabs her bag of weapons, forgoing her bag of clothing. My grin is bright as I withhold a laugh. She has her priorities straight.

Costen, the sweet Alpha, grabs one bag of clothing for each of us, and we all trudge over to the dragon's side.

"How do we... Get on him?" Costen falters, looking over the black and purple scales of the towering beast.

"C'mon over, friends!" Rafe waves us towards the front leg. He's already got one foot propped up on the limb. "Don't be afraid to grab onto him; you won't hurt him; these scales are impenetrable."

Eram goes first, his lips pressed together, brow furrowed in concentration as he ascends Gin's side and plants himself in between some deadly-looking spines along the dragon's back. Next we shuffle the Omegas up, followed by Costen, me and Hagon last.

We stuff our bags between each of us and the spines, while the Omegas huddle beneath their mountain of blankets, and Rafe hops up and plants himself at the front near Gin's massive head.

"All right! Our flight will be short, windy and probably cold. Keep your hands on the dragon and hold on tight. Alpha's, I'm counting on you to keep a lookout for danger. Just shout if you see something," Rafe says gleefully, one arm wrapped tight around a tall spine as the dragon rises.

The motion is unsettling, and my stomach turns with each step. It only gets worse as Gin's wings flap. As soon as his body lifts off the ground, I swear I'm going to vomit at the weightless sensation, but I hold it together.

A chorus of whimpers and rumbled protests sounds from my pack around me, but as the dragon's wings move faster, it deafens all sound. Wind rushes past my ears, and my eyes water at the sting. Fuck, it's going to be hard to monitor the sky like this.

I sweep the tears away and scan the blue skies. Nothing. Not even a cloud in sight as we travel over the forests and villages.

I send out a quick prayer to the Goddess, to protect us on our flight, and hope we all make it safely.

CH. 2

Dani

The flight is quick, but I have enough time to squeal joyfully at the wind rushing past my ears and the motion of the dragon flying beneath me. The sensation is freeing, and I vow to spend a little more time going for flights. I can't get as much height as a fucking dragon, but I don't exercise my wings as much as I should. Mostly, I use them to help me fight better.

We land at a massive Keep with an earth-shaking thump. The dragon roars, and the vibration below my ass has a squeal peppering the air. I will *not* tell my mates how much I liked that. Hagon especially would not take that well.

"DANI! LIA! ohmyGoddess!" A familiar,

heart achingly sweet voice shouts. "Get down here right now and hug me!"

A laugh bubbles up, and a cheek-splitting grin takes over as I swing my head towards the staircase and enormous doors leading into the Keep. But the moment I lay eyes on my best friend, all joy drops off my face only to be replaced by shock.

Luella, my bestest, prettiest, sweetest friend, is different. She has *wings!* Pretty brown fur covers most of her body, cute little kitten paws, a long swishing tail and those *ears!* What the hell happened to her? She's also surrounded by six other mates and a sweet little boy who clings to her hand. Goddess, she looks radiant.

The dress she's wearing is gorgeous! Who's been making her clothing? That fabric flatters her, and it's tailored to accommodate her new features. Dumbstruck, I stand atop the dragon and stare open-mouthed.

Shaking myself, I don't bother waiting for anyone to help me. I toss my pile of blankets at the nearest male and lurch down the side of the dragon. When I slip and fall, I shake my head at my idiocy and use my wings to glide the rest of the way down.

"Luella! Oh my Goddess! Look at you!" I can't stop the shriek of excitement that slips out as I hurry up the steps. "Who's all this? Introduce me! What a cutie! Hi! I'm Dani. It's very nice to meet you, young sir. What happened to you? You remind me of someone I met recently." Overwhelmed with enthusiasm, my words are a jumbled, breathless torrent.

Luella almost topples over with laughter, more than one hand grabbing her, keeping her upright as she giggles wildly. When she calms enough to stand up straight, she slams into me and crushes me in a powerful hug.

"Oh, Dani, I missed you so much! Still the same, although..." she steps back and her nose wrinkles at the sight of my bloodstained clothes, "what the hell have you been doing? I sent my males because Dai had a vision that you wouldn't make it here alive unless someone went to help. I'm so glad they made it in time, but... why are you absolutely filthy with blood and gore? Who're those handsome males with you? How did you come across Lia? Did you meet the Elves? What happened to you in Pekayan? Are your parents okay? Stupid Jerrik, why can't he just leave us alone?" Luella still rambles when she's nervous, and it soothes all the jagged edges of the fresh wound Jerrik caused during his latest visit.

She's still clinging to me when the rest of my pack and her two mates make it up the steps. Costen steps into my back, wrapping his arms around us, hugging Luella and me.

The crushing pressure is comforting, but a chorus of snarling growls sounds behind Luella. I lock eyes with her short, blue male. He shrugs with a grin and mouths '*Alphas*'.

"Please remove your hands from my mate. I'd rather not give you such a poor impression of us during our first meeting. But I cannot tolerate any Alpha scent on my Omega. I'm having enough trouble with another Omega touching her." A tall mint green Alpha steps forward, placing his hands on Luella's shoulders and gently guiding her back into his chest.

"Oh, quit it, Tawson! You know how worried I've been about her! You agreed I could hug her as much as I wanted. Wait-" Luella stops mid-sentence, her head snapping in my direction. "Omega? Did he say Omega? Dani, did you reveal late too? What the hell is going on?"

"Actually," I start with a forced laugh, "I have a *lot* to tell you. It'll explain everything but, first, I'd love to wash and change into something not crusted with blood. And, um... I left all my clothing, so could I borrow something?"

After the reminder of all that's happened, all the excitement and wonder at seeing Luella again, I'm having trouble not breaking down. I haven't had the chance to mourn my foster parents, and it's hitting me now that I'll never see them again. I can't believe Jerrik killed them.

Never hear my mother nagging me to sit up straight and not to curse like a heathen. Never hear my father's quiet words of encouragement to learn more sword work. Never learn more stitches from my mother, her pride in my seamstress work glowing in her smile.

Unknowing of my current struggle, Luella chirps at her Alpha's to get us a room and bring everyone a set of clothing.

"There's a large bathing tub in every room, so you can wash with your entire pack," Luella winks, nudging me with her elbow.

I force a smirk and shake my head at her, trying not to let her clue in to my inner turmoil. Costen, Hagon and Ily can all feel my grief through our bond, and my sweet Omega shuffles up to my side and wraps an arm around me as we follow Luella's pack through the massive stone Keep.

Luella tosses a smile at Ily and me, her eyes asking all the questions she's trying to hold back. '*Who is that? Is he a male Omega? How did you meet? Why are your Alphas okay with another Omega touching you? What the hell is going on?*' Even voiceless, my bestie is overflowing with rambunctious energy and dying to pepper me with questions.

I just need a moment to grieve my foster parents before I can find my usual spirit. Pack

Foreastra leads us into an enormous room with a massive circular bed in the center. The far wall has a balcony, and the windows reach from ceiling to floor, but I can't see a door anywhere.

"We'll leave you to clean up; someone will stop by with a handful of clothing." The Gargoyle steps forward. "When you're done, you're welcome to get some sleep, or you can join us for dinner. We'd love to have you." He sweeps into a short bow and with a grin ushers his mate out the door.

The silence in the room is oppressive. I need to get clean, so I trail off down the hall and open doors until I find the bathing room. Luella was right; the tub is massive. Gorgeous carved stone and looks as if it could fit my entire pack.

Clothing drops to the floor carelessly as I strip. The blood has dried and crusted over, making the fabric stick to me. My lip curls at the sensation, but I just rip it off. A weight in the pocket startles me out of my daze, and I pull out the necklaces of bones, placing them both on the edge of the bathtub.

It doesn't take long to fill the tub with steaming water from a tap in the wall. I'm amazed at the odd system; it's very similar to what I saw in Banell.

As I sink into the water, my thoughts finally plummet into the sadness of losing my foster parents. I reach for the gruesome necklaces. Tears drip onto the bones as I weep, biting back any sobs.

For some reason, I don't want my pack to see me break. I'm not that person! I'm not a weepy, sensitive Omega. With a silent snarl, I dash the tears away and let my anger push the sadness down.

Burning fury builds in my gut, and the longer I stare at the bones of my foster parents, the madder I get. I hate them! Why did I even keep these? I don't need a token of my parents to remember them, especially one so morbid.

My fists clench over the macabre jewelry. With a death grip, my knuckles whiten, the pressure so forceful that I can hear the grating of bones. My hands shake, and I pull my arm back and throw them as hard as I can.

"AHHH!" Costen shouts as the horrid things smack into his face.

"Oh Goddess! Costen, I'm so sorry! I-I didn't mean to hit you." I cover my mouth with my hands, guilt riding me hard. For hitting my Alpha and for throwing the last bit of my parents, hoping for them to break.

"Oh, Dani… I'm so sorry, Pix. I didn't know them, but I know you, and they must have been incredible beings to have raised someone so fiercely protective. Can… can I join you? Please?" Ignoring my shameful apology, Costen's voice cuts through my guilt, addressing the deep ache in my heart.

With tears welling in my eyes, I nod as sorrow swamps me. I need my Alpha. I need the feeling of his sweetness surrounding me. Costen is full of warmth and compassion; the bond lights up with his sympathy and desire to care for me. Those emotions hit me in the heart, and more tears fall, leaving salty tracks down my cheeks as I reach for my first mate.

My jaw trembles with the force of holding back loud wails of pain. The moment Costen slips into the water and pulls me into his hard body, I break. Everything I've been holding back and pushing down comes rushing out of me in a torrent of mournful keens.

Costen is the perfect male. He doesn't offer weak platitudes, just honest, comforting strength flowing through our mate-bond as he holds me. One hand rubs my back; the other cradles my head against him.

I let his scent permeate my body. The crisp mountain breeze is like a cooling balm to my pain. It seems to cleanse the dark ache infecting me as it brushes against my soul. Carrying the scent of pine, fresh earth and a hint of snow provides all the comfort without forcing me to speak my agony. Sharp wind leaves a tingle against my cheeks; a feeling of connection melts into me. The natural essence of Costen calms and centers me, a grounding presence.

After what feels like hours of harsh wails and soul-wrenching sobs, I can finally take a deep breath. Pulling back from Costen's comforting arms, I peer up at my Alpha with reddened, puffy eyes.

"Would you let me bathe you?" Costen whispers, brushing wet hair off my cheeks, saying nothing about the mess that I just cried all over him.

My throat is tight, making it difficult to speak, so I nod instead, appreciating him all over again.

Our bath is quiet, but comforting, with the sounds of water sloshing a soothing background. I don't feel the need to speak, and my Sweet Snow just hums as he smoothes soap over my skin, not lingering on any one spot. When he gets to my hair, Costen scrapes his nails over my scalp, sending shivers of pleasure down my spine, and a hushed groan slips out.

I don't know why that feels so fucking good, but with each brush of his fingers through my hair, the pain inside me lessens bit by bit. Until finally, I can breathe again.

Once I'm rinsed, Costen rushes through his own wash, waving me off when I try to help with a soft smile.

We dry off quickly, wrapping the bathing sheets around our nudity before leaving the peacefulness of the bathing room.

CH. 3

Hagon

Dani's pain filters through our bond, driving my Alpha mad with the need to fix it for her. But I know it isn't something I can mend. I wondered how long she could suppress those feelings after that undead piece of shit made light of the torture and murder of her parents.

My Menace, my tough, take-no-shit Omega, is strong. Stronger than any Omega, than any female, I've ever met. But she's not made of stone. Though she kept a stoic face, I knew she hurt. Before she blocked it, I felt a sharp stab of immense pain that ripped through the bond.

When she wandered off alone, my body had followed without thought, knowing she needed me, but Costen boldly stood in the way and clearly drew a boundary. I'm impressed with the male. I didn't think he had it in him, but he cares for her more than I think even she knows.

Plus, he is the right Alpha for the job. I'm not soft enough, and her tears gut me. Even the Alpha female appeared helpless. Although she only has a bond with me at the moment, meaning she can't feel the horrid, soul-deep pain cutting Dani.

Ilaris nodded at Costen's insistence that he go comfort her alone. My Sweet Boy would have been excellent with her delicate emotions, but Costen has known her longer, and he has an amazing intuition with our Pixie.

Eram, when I glance over, looks as though he's sucking on lemons. I snort, drawing his attention off the hallway to the bathing room.

"What?" he snarls at me.

"You need to work on your facial expressions. Every emotion that passes through you is clear as day on your face." I wave a hand lazily, taunting the male. He needs to let out some aggression, and I'm the perfect male for the job. "You look like you're sucking on something sour, Err."

His face reddens as he presses his lips tight and his brows dip in a furious glare. The absolute insult on his face only amuses me more. Hmm… Maybe this is why Lianis enjoys taunting me.

Shaking off the thought, I refocus on the uptight male. Eram's lip curls in a sneer before he marches towards me, violence written on every inch of his tall, thin body.

"Take it outside, boys." Lianis steps in between us with an amused smile. "Let's not wreck the nice Keep. We wouldn't want Tawson or, Goddess forbid, Gin to take offense and remove us."

Her words make sense and only deepen my frown. Everything she does irritates me, even when she's speaking reason.

It will take a while for this mismatched group to find its rhythm as a pack. A bunch of strange Alphas thrown together will always have a learning curve while we find where we belong in the hierarchy. Most packs form when Alphas are young. Usually with our childhood friends or siblings so the hierarchy asserts itself, and each male already knows where they belong.

Our peculiar pack, with two Omegas, will face arguments and physical aggression before we find our place together. Lianis especially irritates my Alpha since her dominance is stronger than ours. But, she has already mentioned she has no interest in leading, so I should be fine around her…

With a snort, I shake off those thoughts and focus on dragging Eram outside to the practice ring. I'd noticed it on our arrival — a large sandy space, fenced in with a shed full of weapons. The male needs to loosen up and learn some proper fighting techniques. I'm happy to be the one to teach him.

My feet pause at the door, and I toss a hard look at Lianis. "Behave. Take care of Ily, please." The please gets stuck in my throat, and I wince, grimacing as I force the word out.

I don't know why I can't settle my angry emotions with Lia. I kind of like her, but the thought of her with my Ily or Dani just grates on my nerves.

"Of course, Pooki." Lianis snorts. "Our Omegas need comfort, not lust. I know how to treat a mate properly," she sasses, hands propped on her hips, one brow raised in challenge.

I swallow all my irritation and refocus on Eram. The male's glare burns into the side of my face with his sullen outrage at being hauled around. Ignoring his sulkiness, I pull him through the halls and out the first door that leads to the practice ring.

We pass a male that lives here, and the tall mossy green Orc follows us with a wide chilling grin. Maybe it's the imposing curve of his tusks, or perhaps his aura that gives him such a frightening air.

"What'cha doin'?" The Orc speaks with a strange accent that I've never encountered before, and no matter how badly I'd like to ignore him, I know I shouldn't.

"Releasing some tension." The words come out gruffer than I intended, but I shrug it off when the Orc just grins bigger.

"Aye! Tha' sounds fun! Can I join ya? I could use a good workout! The name's Brenth." This male is much more cheerful than I expected. My feet stutter a step before I straighten myself.

"Uhhh, sure?" I don't know why it comes out as a question, and I huff out a tired breath.

"Well?" Brenth asks, keeping pace with my quickened steps.

"Well, what?" I grump.

"He wants to know our names, Hagon." Eram rolls his eyes at me, trying to tug his arm out of my grip.

"Oh... Uh, I'm Hagon and this is Eram." My voice is hesitant, and my feet slow as I glance at Brenth. I was so wrapped up in my irritation that I missed what the stranger was saying to me.

"Aye," Brenth smirks at me, "it's nice ta meet ya. Why the need to release tension? I get it, but I sense something deeper nagging at ya." The

Orc is unusually astute, and I spare him another searching look.

"This one needs some sense knocked into him. He's been postponing taking our Dani as his mate even though it's clear they are fated," I reply with a grunt. Brenth is a stranger to me. He does not need to know all the details of our lives.

"Hmm, aye, that is one issue. But there's more." Brenth crosses his arms and cocks a brow at me. Those tusks make his grin more sinister than intended.

"Well, yes, I have been hesitant because of my sister but there's a bigger problem right now and right before your pack-mates rescued us, our mate, Dani had just been told some devastating news and now she's sobbing in the bath and her pain and misery is filtering through the bond to everyone else and it's driving each of us mad with the need to fix it. But it isn't something we can fix." Eram steps forward and blurts out the source of my irritation.

Except now all I want to do is pound his face into the sand and teach him not to spout our business to strangers. Luckily, we're in the practice ring, so I'll be able to vent my frustration.

"Huh, I didn't expect all that. I just assumed ya needed to work out your hierarchy properly. Since you're all strangers that have been tossed together by your mates, it takes a little time to find your place. I would know; my brother and I were late additions to our pack. But, since the pack was mostly settled, it didn't take too much effort to fit in," Brenth replies, his smirk turns knowing as he leans back against the fence. "Well, don't let me stop ya from working out your aggression. But I'll take the winner. I could use some exercise."

My head shakes at the casual slump of the fearsome Orc, and I refocus my full attention on Eram. After going over what he knows of fighting, we begin.

His defenses are weak and he's easily distracted, so my hits have him in the sand more often than not. But, Eram keeps getting up, and that alone is impressive.

"Don't take your eye off your opponent, Err," I coach; I'm less agitated after getting to let off some steam, and I'm now focused on educating this male. "Keep your fists up, yes, a little higher. You want to protect your face from hits. That's better."

We go a few more rounds before Eram is puffing hard and coated in sweat. Finally, he taps out with a limp wave and shuffles to the side of the ring to sit in the sand.

"My turn?" Brenth steps forward with a bright grin. "I'll give ya a challenge."

"Alright, Orc. Let's do this." I swipe perspiration off my brow and settle into a defensive stance.

Brenth moves faster than a being that large should, and I'm put through my paces. His advance is calm and thought out; each hit is like blocking a hammer, and I'm backed almost into the fence-line. Finally, I spy an opening and throw a few hard punches to his stomach and side, gaining a few moments to breathe.

We trade blows, growing more confident as we learn each other's moves. Brenth is an excellent opponent. Finally, he lands one punch too many, and I hit the sand in a puff of dust.

"Alright," I wave a tired hand, "I'm done. Brenth, you make a fair opponent. Thanks for the workout."

"Aye, t'was a good match, Wolf." The Orc offers a hand to pull me up. "I look forward to another fight."

Taking his help, I rise to my feet and dust off the sand before heading over to haul Eram up. We both need a wash now, but I feel more centered, and Err looks far more relaxed than I've ever seen him.

"C'mon, Err. Let's get cleaned up and see how our Omegas are doing." I toss an arm over his shoulder and march him back towards the keep. “Thanks, Brenth,” I say with a wave over my shoulder as we leave the Orc to his continued practice in the ring.

CH. 4

Dani

Costen, my Sweet Snow, takes such good care of me. Helping me dress and cuddling me tightly every chance he gets. Eventually, the pain lessens enough that I can take a full breath.

It's almost dinnertime, and I feel ready to speak to the rest of my pack. I appreciate that they've given Costen and me some time together, but I want my whole family around me. Especially, Ily. My poor sweet Omega is anxious because our Alphas have kept him away from me while I worked out my pain.

The clothing that Lulu lent me is soft against my skin. I pause, needing to inspect the fabric itself. What the hell is this gorgeous dress made of? It's smooth and luxurious against my cheek. Like velvet but not as heavy. I'm going to need to find out where she got this as soon as possible. Just imagine what I could make with this!

"Are you okay, Dani?" Ily's tentative voice breaks through my contemplation.

"Ily!" I rush over to my Omega and toss my arms around him. As soon as I reach him, he's crushing me to his body.

My sweet boy has been so worried about me. "I'm sorry, Ily. I just needed a second, but I'm okay. Don't worry, I have no plans to be anywhere but with you," I murmur to him, nuzzling into his hair, inhaling his slightly sour cherry scent. His anxiety turns his normally sweet smell tart.

The longer we stay in our embrace, the sweeter his scent grows. My Omega must have been frantic.

"It's fine. I understand needing some time to deal with that," Ily mutters, arms tightening around me as if he's afraid I'll disappear. "My Omega gets a little antsy when I haven't been able to scent you in a while."

"Where is everyone?" I ask, peering around the massive bedroom. I don't see Hagon or Eram; Lia's also missing. At least Costen is here, sitting on the couch near the entrance reading a book.

"The two meatheads went out to deal with some things," Lia's sultry voice echoes through the room as she strolls out from the long hallway to the bathing room.

"How're you feeling, Pretty Pixie?" The female Alpha strolls over, slinging an arm around my shoulders and tugging me into her spicy, addictive scent.

I soften into her, appreciating her strong embrace and nuzzle my face against her chest. Pillowy breasts cradle me, and I have a moment of pause. I've never been with another female, but Lianis wraps her other arm around both Ily and me, pulling us both into her.

"Better now with your arms around me," I reply softly.

The strength of her hold and the softness of her body comfort me in surprising ways. Ily snuggles tighter against my back, and the three of us relax. My lips find any bare skin to kiss, sneaking in a lick here and there. I want to taste her, to drink down that spicy, dark dowan scent.

Ily mirrors me on the other side of Lia, and we work together to pull her shirt off. The Alpha female yields only when she chooses. Once her shirt hits the floor, she's quick to disrobe both Ily and me.

My lips and hands move toward her chest. The softness of her breasts is a contrast against her muscles. The moment I get my lips around one of her nipples, she presses me down into the bed.

"I've been waiting patiently for some time with you, little Pixie," Lia purrs.

"I want a taste!" I demand.

"Don't worry, pretty thing, I can make that work." She grins before drawing Ily down for a deep, licking kiss.

Lia positions herself above me, facing Ily so we can all taste each other. The moment her cunt is above me, I dive in and groan at the spicy tang of her wetness. Ily's moan mirrors mine as Lia wraps her lips around his cock.

I hold nothing back, licking and nibbling her lower lips and tangling my tongue around her plump clit. Whenever I can get a moan out of her, a thrill of delight darts through me. I'm proud that I can give my alpha female pleasure.

My tongue dives deep into her wet cunt, and I thrill at the taste and sensation of her walls contracting over me. I want to make her cum as hard as I do when my Alphas tend to me.

Every now and then I peer up at her plump lips wrapped around Ily and groan at the sight of them together. Her pink against his deep tan is such a gorgeous match. Is that what we look like together, too?

"Oh, fuck! Pretty Pixie, I'm going to cum all over your talented little tongue." Lia pulls off Ily's cock long enough to praise me.

It encourages me to work harder. Reveling in each twitch and moan I gain from her. I pull my tongue from her pretty pink pussy and move back to her clit, sucking the little nub into my mouth with a harsh pull.

Lia screams around Ily as she cums, taking him along for the ride and drinking down his orgasm. I rest my head back against the bedding and grin, wetness decorating my cheeks and chin.

"Come here, my darling Omegas," Lia purrs, tugging us both down to cuddle with her.

I feel closer to her. We finally had a moment without the Alpha's butting in on our time together. A pleased grin stretches my cheeks and I take a moment to wipe my face clean.

The door bursts open, the sound echoing through the room startling Ily, and me; we untangle ourselves to see two filthy Alphas swaggering in, the stench of sweat and dirt filling the air.

"What happened to you guys?" A slight smirk curves my mouth as I speak; my eyebrows raise in amusement.

At least it seems like Hagon and Eram have worked out some of their hostility. Eram's serious face now bears a smile, and Hagon is less grumpy than usual.

"Just getting some exercise," Eram replies, making his way over to me, "are you okay?" His brows wiggle at me and a knowing grin spreads over his face.

His breath caresses my skin, sending ripples of goosebumps down my spine. His scent—musky, earthy, and utterly captivating—always goes straight to my head and my core, leaving me breathless. The mere sound of his voice is all it takes to have wetness building in my cunt.

"Yeah," I sigh into his neck, the sweat glistening on his skin, deepening his already potent scent, "I'm fine. You smell... so good." My head is growing fuzzy, and my instincts scream to build a nest and drag this Alpha into it.

Eram laughs and eases me back into Ily's arms. "I need to wash off the sweat and sand from our sparring. Are we going to meet your friend's pack for dinner?"

"Hmm," my head feels funny and it's hard to think, "y-yeah? Yes. I really need to catch up with Lulu, and it'd be nice to meet her pack properly." It's a struggle to pull myself together, but I straighten up and switch my focus to Hagon.

"I'm fine, Menace. But tomorrow you should join us in the practice ring. I know you've been wanting to work out more. Being on the road is hard, but we've got some time to relax. At least here we're close to Varough and can easily slip over to pay the King a visit." Hagon's deep rumbly voice soothes some of the tension in my core.

These Omega instincts are getting louder, urging me to nest and gather their scents, but the moment one of my Alphas comes near or even speaks, they settle. It's strange, but I'm excellent at pushing away inconsequential things.

"Okay! A fight sounds so good," I chirp excitedly, "now you two go wash so we can find the dining room and I can hug Lulu more."

We get lost in the maze of hallways trying to find Luella's pack. Finally, we find a maid, and she laughs when I explain where we're trying to go. The sweet female guides us back and into a sumptuous dining room. Velvet hangings drape the walls, and a gorgeous chandelier makes the smaller room cozy.

Luella jumps to her feet when we appear and rushes over to us — at least she tries to. But one of her massive males snags her and deposits her on his lap.

"Little One, you need to be more careful," the big dragon rumbles to her, "no jumping around or running, you could hurt yourself or the bean."

My head cocks and my brows furrow as my nose scrunches. What the hell is he talking about? She wasn't doing anything dangerous...

"OhmyGoddess!" the words rush out on a harsh exhale. "Lulu! Is it true? A baby? Come here! Oh, Goddess, I'm so happy for you! A little bean!" My wings flutter with joy, lifting me off the ground to hover. A light buzzing sound emanates from me as I sway from side to side and vibrate with delight.

Luella may not have ever said it in so many words, but she's always wanted a big family. One where everyone is happy to be together, with youngens laughing and running around. This news only adds to the conversation I need to have with her about our mother.

"Relax, Menace." Hagon huffs out a laugh, wrapping a hand around one of my ankles, keeping me from flitting around the room with elation. "Maybe if you come back down, her mates will allow you both to hug?"

Hagon's words penetrate through my excitement, and I have to focus on slowing my heart rate and wings. Steadily, I lower back to the ground and work to keep my wings from taking off again.

"Lulu!" I beam at her and open my arms, waiting for her mate to release her. "Please can I hug her?" I direct the question at the big male cradling her.

It's sweet how they are gentle with her. Especially since she's with child. I can only imagine how overprotective her Alphas will be now that she's pregnant. Hopefully, they can see that I am no danger to her. I've heard how crazy Alphas can be when their mates are expecting.

The big Alpha releases his grip, and when he sets Luella on her feet, she leans into him, murmuring something quiet and nuzzling her cheek against his, scent marking her Alpha.

The big guy takes a deep breath of Luella before shooting a glare at me and rumbling a low growl in warning. Pffft, like I would ever hurt my bestie. He has nothing to worry about.

All four of the Alphas in my pack take offence and return his snarl, the sound loud in this small room. I meet Luella's eyes and roll mine with a smirk. She grins back brightly and walks over to me, tossing herself into my arms at the last second with a wild laugh.

"Luella!" the big male roars, only to silence

himself when she just chuckles harder.

“I’m fine! I’m not an invalid; my body is fully capable of functioning even while carrying a child! I’m an Omega. We’re literally made to carry life,” Luella scolds him with a sassy eye roll.

Pride fills me! She never would have talked back in our home village. My gentle bestie has grown so much, and it brings a tear to my eye to know that she’s finally found the family that she’s always wanted. Especially because these males take excellent care of her.

“Lulu, I’m so happy to see you again! Look at you, you’re fucking glowing!" I beam, resting my hands on her shoulders.

“I know, right? Being an Omega and having such wonderful mates is everything I’ve ever hoped for,” Luella replies, equally excited. She’s always been good at matching my enthusiasm. “Plus, pregnancy really agrees with me. Oh! You have to meet my adopted son, Daison. He’s with his grandparents right now, but tomorrow I’ll introduce you properly.”

Right, I forgot about the sweet little boy that was hiding behind her Alpha’s legs when we first arrived. He’s absolutely adorable, and it’s just like Luella to adopt a foundling.

“I have so much to tell you.” I calm my high-pitched tone to something more reasonable as I remember Bassanai's words. "Um, so maybe we should sit down. I have some pretty crazy news to tell you."

We finally release each other, and my pack follows me to the table. This will be an interesting conversation.

CH. 5

Jerrik

Master was not pleased with me. I failed to grab the Pixie, and the castle wards sent a wave of searing pain through me. My jaw clenched, the taste of grit and resentment thick in my mouth as I glared at the encroaching day. For three days, I huddled in that cliff-side nook like a rat, and the time allowed me to contemplate. I'll figure out a better way to take that Omega. Neither she nor her pack will stop me.

Luella will be mine, a gift from Master, and it won't be long now. That deformed, winged female will become my toy. She will obey me and no one else. She will have no other choice.

My cackle echoes off the cavern walls. The

sound only adds to my manic joy. My face twists into something dark and terrifying.

A surge of rage courses through me as I flex my unfamiliar limbs. The phantom sensations of my former self constantly and infuriatingly remind me of what was done to me. Master has done such a good job knitting me back together after those beasts left me in bits littered all over the forest floor.

But I am better than before. He fused together fragments of Alphas, combining them with my weak Beta designation. Now I am *more*. So long as his magic endures, I am a being of immense strength, nearly invulnerable. Because he is a divine being, his existence will continue for as long as he desires.

I sit in Lash's old room. Still filled with books and silly things that my predecessor used to entertain himself. What a fool he was. It is fortunate that my soon-to-be bride obliterated him.

Luella's power should have frightened me, but Master vowed to strip her of her Demi-Goddess magic, leaving her as vulnerable as a kitten. I am strong, but I cannot compare to the power of Gods and Goddesses.

Thankfully, the filthy little Pixie still cannot access her magic. She remains weak and powerless. Once I get my hands on her, I am going to make it hurt. She has thwarted my attempts for the last fucking time.

Emerging from that hidden spot in the cliff, I became mist to investigate the castle's wards. They are numerous and profound. Countless generations of rulers have strengthened the defenses, making them nearly impenetrable, even to Master.

It is up to me to find and exploit any weaknesses. I will *not* fail my master again. With his promise hanging over me, I *need* to complete this one measly little task.

After days of meticulously examining every part of the castle's defenses, I found its weakness. My laughter escapes, reverberating through the space and catching the notice of a few of my masters' hideous creations.

A bird-like head pokes into my chamber, chirping curiously. I despise those repulsive things. Beyond the stench of decay from half of them, the rest were a revolting sight. I don’t understand how master can love them so much. At least they are useful.

Reaching out, I grab the book and throw it with force at the bothersome thing. It squawks and then scurries away, its many spider legs carrying it across the ground. The noise sends a shiver down my spine. While I'm not fond of insects, I must admit that I can understand the practical benefits of merging the legs of one onto a beast. The spine-chilling sound of the creature is enough to send beings fleeing in terror.

Even though I despise them, I recognize my master's wisdom in continuing to produce those things. They will do us well in taking over Saforia. All beings will have to submit to our masters' power. They will see. They will all gaze upon his fierce power, bathed in his majestic glory.

The idiotic beings who live here will soon learn their place, and the females, Alpha's, Beta's, and most of all the Omega's, will know their duties. We will return to the traditions of the past. Those were the better days, when the air was thick with unspoken rules, and a male's word was law.

If only things had been like this the first time I saw Luella; this whole mess wouldn't have happened. She would have surrendered to my desires immediately, and we would have been married in a matter of days.

With a wistful sigh, I exhale the past and concentrate on the present. Soon enough, we will all be able to enjoy that life, with its joys and simple pleasures. Master has an excellent plan.

Together we will smother this land with his nightmares and dominate the beings until they comply.

Yes.

The time is nigh.

We will govern with an iron fist of fear and power.

CH. 6

Ilaris

Seeing my sweet Omega so happy brings a smile to my lips. Her friend Luella is so soft compared to Dani. I'm actually surprised that the two of them get along so well. I've been told my whole life that Omegas don't like other Omegas in their space, but from the first moment I met Dani, I needed to have her by my side or it felt like I couldn't breathe.

Apparently, it's not true for these two either, and I don't feel aggressive around the strange Omega. I slip past Eram and steal the seat beside Dani. The Alpha releases a low, good-natured rumble as he settles into the seat opposite her. Hagon sits next to me, the warmth of his body radiating against my side, Costen next to him, and Lia beside Eram.

Dani leans forward, elbows on the table, resting her chin in her hands. This will be interesting. I wonder how Luella and her pack will feel about the revelations Dani has to share.

"So… before I start, I just need to say, Lulu, you are fucking gorgeous, and who knew this is what you were hiding under that sweet little human guise, but it also helps confirm a few things." Dani chuckles, grinning brightly at the other Omega.

"Thanks, D," Luella replies, a dark blush staining her cheeks as she brings one of her paw-like hands up to hide behind. "Yeah, this was quite a surprise. Especially the wings! I'm still trying to figure out how to use them. When I first changed and was filled with rage, it was second nature, but now I just flop about. Plus, these guys are all overprotective with me being pregnant."

"I'm not surprised, Lulu. I can only imagine how crazy my pack would get if I was pregnant too!" Dani says with a laugh, but it's overshadowed by the loud snarls from each of our Alphas and my own light purr.

Just the thought of her carrying one of our young has my cock hardening so fast it aches. I reach down, trying to subtly press a heel into it. Fuck, I can't wait until she's ready for us to breed her.

"Oh, shut up! I'm nowhere close to ready

for young! We have too much adventuring to do, plus we have to figure out how to get rid of Nyurel," Dani says with a wave, but she's silenced again by a loud chorus of furious growls from Luella's pack.

The sound is a terrifying, booming echo that fills the space. My shoulders pull up near my ears as the rest of my body shrinks in fright. I reach my hands up to cover my ears, trying to lessen the vibration ringing through my body.

Hagon's warmth wraps around me and drags me onto his lap. The comfort of his scent and strength sinks into me, helping to ground me in the here and now. My Alpha knows how to keep my head from the dark thoughts that haunt me.

"ENOUGH!" Lia shouts, her chair scraping against the stone floor as she shoves it back to stand. "All of you need to calm the fuck down. Can't you see what you are doing to the Omegas? Goddess, it's like dealing with a bunch of children."

Her words have me peeking at the table, scanning each being. Except for the enormous, dark male whose face is a mask of simmering anger, most of Pack Foreastra wear expressions of deep chagrin, their faces downcast.

"Sorry." One of the light green Fae speaks up. "We have... history with that foul God, and it is upsetting to be reminded of our unfortunate encounter." The diplomatic response brings a slight smirk to my lips.

Clearly, this pack has a couple of discerning Alphas. I raise my head off Hagon's shoulder and brave the tense air to observe Lianis scold this pack like pups.

"I don't care if you have history! Tawson, of all these Alphas, you should know better than to bring your emotions to a table of strange beings. My pack has history too, but you don't see us losing our shit over words." Lia slams her hands on the table, the cutlery rattling with the force. "Now, can we all sit down and have a civil discussion? My Omega has important shit to tell you."

Silence reigns through the cosy dining room; the only sound is Lianis settling back into her seat with a huff. Everyone stares at the female Alpha with shock and appreciation, except for a few of the other pack's Alpha's. They glare.

"Thank you, Lia." Dani leans over Eram, murmuring warmly to Lia. Eram doesn't appear to be upset with the position as my sweet Pixie's breasts rub against his hands. If the blush on our stiff Alpha is any indication, he's as hard as a rock. Maybe he'll finally give in tonight?

"Okay!" Dani sits back with a loud clap, drawing all focus back to her. "As I was saying,

Nyurel is hunting me because he wants to steal my dormant power just like he tried to do to you, Lulu. Apparently, Bassanai is our mother," Dani finishes softly, her eyes fixed on Luella.

"Why is-" Luella starts before she shoots to her feet with a gasp. Her pack of males all startle. The big one jolts to his feet, his brow furrowed in concern as he pats her down, seeking the cause of her distress. The Omega eases his hands away, only for him to pick her up and place her on his lap. She meets Dani's gaze with a roll of her eyes and a huff of laughter before shrugging and sitting back against her mate.

"Are you saying what I think you're saying?" Luella breathes quietly.

"Yeah, hun. We're actual sisters, and I couldn't be happier to know that we are actually family," Dani replies, a warm smile creasing her cheeks.

The two share a focused look; I swear they have an entire silent conversation that the rest of us miss. Luella taps her male, and he releases her with a grumble. Dani rises gracefully. A wave of emotion washes over the room as the females meet, their embrace a symphony of sorrow and relief.

No one interrupts their reunion. Clearly, they're closer than any of us really knew. I should have though, I'm an Omega. One of our inherent abilities is to sense emotion in others, but I am a little broken…

My eyes water at the deep emotion, but I suck back the tears. It isn't right for me to distract them with my weepy tears. I need to let my mate have her moment with her sister. They have been apart for months.

Finally, they break apart and return to their seats. Luella, hopping into the big one's lap instinctively. Even I can see that he's wound up so tight, like a bowstring stretched to its limit.

"Continuing on," Dani smirks, still brushing tears off her cheeks, "we're actually sisters, different fathers." She recounts everything we've been through; the weight of her tale settles heavily, a cloak of sorrow woven from our arduous journey and the Goddess's brief visit.

Pack Foreastra stares with shock and discomfort when she mentions Jerrik and what happened to the male. Luella looks a little green, one hand cradling her stomach.

"Holy shit!" the ochre Alpha exclaims, eyes wide. "You've had one hell of a journey. I'm so glad Daison told us to go get you. My Kitten almost lost the only family she has!"

Dani smiles, focusing her delight on Luella, but the big one is striding from the room with the small Omega cradled in his arms. I frown at his retreating back, Dani mirroring my confusion.

"Where is he going? Why is he taking my sister away? I still have so much catching up to do!" Dani questions loudly, perturbed that after their tearful reunion her sister is being taken away again.

"Easy, she's got morning sickness and did not want to puke in front of our guests," the green Fae replies, Tawson, I think his name was.

"Oh…" Dani mutters, still staring off after Luella.

"So, Nyurel has found a new minion and fresh prey for his obsession with power," Tawson remarks, scrutinising my sweet Pixie.

"I guess so," Dani replies absently before her head whips back to the table, staring at the green Fae.

"What do you mean, a new minion? No, forget that. New prey? I'm not fucking prey!" she protests, crossing her arms with a grumpy frown.

I doubt she realizes how adorable she is when enraged. Like a spitting, growling pup. I can't stop staring at my mate; I'm captivated by her beauty, and I'm sure my eyes are sparkling with adoration.

"Sorry, but Tawson isn't wrong," the other

vibrant green Fae speaks up, "it isn't the most flattering term, but it's fairly truthful. Nyurel, that foul God, hunted Luella for months, even kidnapping her once and infecting her with a black magic curse. At one point, the God had even captured our entire pack!"

"Calm down, Alec." Tawson pats the male on the shoulder and takes over the explanation. "Nyurel hunted Luella across the land, but after she shattered the barrier preventing her from her true form, she eliminated the black magic User, though Nyurel disappeared before she could do anything to him."

"Okay," Dani breathes, leaning back into her seat, "that's a lot of information, and you kind of skipped over the fact that my fucking sister *was kidnapped!* And then cursed! If this *God* can capture and hold your pack, what chance do we have to survive? We can't stay here for the rest of our lives, never leaving the safety of your wards." Her hands wave and flail with her irritation.

She stands again and paces, muttering about shitty Gods and Goddesses. The rest of us watch, no one speaking until Eram grunts and stands, snagging Dani around the waist and hauling her into his lap.

She snuggles in with a heavy sigh before turning her focus back to the green Fae. "I know

I need to find the rest of my pack and exchange claiming marks, but we had more than one reason for traveling this far."

"We'll do what we can to help. You are family, all of you," Tawson says, his tone softening. I get the feeling that he doesn't do animated or tender for anyone other than his Omega.

Dani wiggles, trying to get up again, and I have to suppress a laugh at their struggle. Eram is determined to keep her there, but my Omega is stubborn, and a muted, hissed argument ensues before Eram relents.

She hops up, leaning both hands on the table and leveling a contemplative glare at the other pack.

CH. 7

Dani

Tawson assured us they'd do everything in their power to aid us. Should I ask him about our other reason for coming this far? I mean, they are the Elites, so it would make sense that they know the King. They could probably get us a meeting quicker than if we went on our own.

"You're willing to help?" I ask the green Fae and, without waiting for an answer, I push on. "Maybe you could explain to us why so many Omegas are being abused and forgotten about. Why the King's decree has done very little to help those stuck in dangerous situations."

I know I'm unfairly targeting the Elites, blaming them for neglecting the Omega population's needs. It's a disregard I've seen echoed across the land. But they're one of the King's primary packs, sent out to protect Saforia. How could they have missed it? How could they have not seen the state of things and done something about it?

Tawson frowns at me, the other males on that side of the table mirroring his confusion. "What are you talking about?"

"Omegas!" I roll my eyes, cross my arms and shake my head. "The fact that Omegas are being abused and forced to do things they don't want. You and your pack have been all over the land; you can't tell me you haven't seen the neglect! In my travels to get here, I met two abused Omegas!" My words are harsh, but I'm annoyed at their continued silence.

"Please explain," Tawson grits out, his face an emotionless mask. I can see the tension beneath the surface. My words have deeply upset him.

Before I can criticize them more, Luella comes back with her beast of a mate. She stops in the doorway, tuning into the agitated state of the dining room.

"Uhhh, what's going on?" she asks, her wings flutter as she moves forwards again, her head swivels between Tawson and me.

“I was just asking your pack why they've allowed Omegas to be abused,” I explain, a frown marring my face.

“What?” Luella halts again, staring at me hard. Her mouth gapes open, eyes wide as she searches my gaze for the truth. When she sees how serious I am, she switches that shock to Tawson.

“Sweetheart, I swear, I do not know what she's talking about. If we'd known that Omegas, our softest designation, were in danger, we would have done something,” the Fae clarifies, his tone so gentle with Luella.

“Please,” he turns back to me, “please explain what you mean.”

Before blurting everything out, I check with Ily, who nods, but he shutters his emotions behind a mask of indifference. I know this conversation will be difficult for my sweet boy, but it needs to happen. Next, I glance at Eram, making sure he'll be okay with me telling them about his sister, Allista. My soon-to-be mate nods, his face set with serious determination.

“Ily, you don't have to be here for this. Why don't you and Hagon head back to the room and get ready for bed? We'll join you soon,” I offer my Omega an out, so he doesn't have to relive his trauma again, but Ily's already shaking his head.

"No, I'm okay, Dani. I'd rather stay." My brave, sweet male.

Turning back to Luella and her pack, I jump into what I've learned. How someone caged and abused my Ily. How Allista was forced into an unwanted bond and fled with her brother. An attempt to get away from cruel Alpha's.

By the time I'm done, Luella and her entire pack are vibrating with rage. Even the gentle blue Beta has a fierce frown, eyes swimming with outrage on behalf of my mate and Eram's sister.

"What... Why... How has this been happening for so long?" Luella stutters out. "Why hasn't Seren done something about this? Tawson! If you hadn't claimed me, that could have been me! I could have been the one used and abused or forced into a bond I didn't want!" The longer Luella speaks, the angrier her mates grow.

Until the quiet Orc snaps her up into his arms and hunches over her with a silent snarl. The other members of Pack Foreastra are not doing much better. Tawson, their Lead Alpha, pushes his chair back with a screech and stands stiffly.

"Dani, tomorrow, I will take you to visit the King. I'd like you to tell him *exactly* what you just told me. He is *not* aware of these abuses, and he *must* do something. If he *doesn't*, I promise you, *we will.*" Tawson moderates his voice, working hard to keep his fury contained.

Based on their reaction, I truly believe they were unaware of the dire needs of the Omegas. I uncross my stiff arms and give him a nod. Excellent.

There's no reason to delay our visit to Varough; I should be just as safe there. I'm glad I was correct and that the Elites know the King well enough to use his first name. I'm quite surprised they told us. But when I see the King tomorrow, I'm going to use his name as well. He doesn't deserve his title because of the neglect he's allowed. I don't give a *fuck* if he is our King.

It takes a while for everyone to settle down after that tense conversation, and Luella's mates pass her between them, her feet never touching the floor as each male reassures themselves that she's safe. It's pretty adorable. These big fierce Alphas acting so soft towards her.

My bestie, my *sister*, deserves all of this, and it brings me such joy to see her being cared for so well.

Peering over at Ilaris, I check to see how well he's handling everything after I spilled his horrible past to these practical strangers. My sweet Omega is tense, but Ily's putting on a brave face. Hagon has one hand on his thigh, fingers digging in. Compared to Ilaris, Hagon isn't handling this very well. That brings a grin to my face.

Our poor grumpy Alpha. We'll make him feel better as soon as we get back to our room.

Finally, we sit down and eat. Conversation turns to less stressful topics, and after I watch my sister for a while, happiness washes over me. She's a different being now, a far cry from the meek, quiet female she was when she lived in Pekayan. I've always hoped she'd find this kind of life. I'm so glad these Alphas claimed her. That she turned out to be their fated only makes it better. This is the life she was always meant to have.

Dessert is brought out, and I instantly know my bestie made the cake. A decadent chocolate monstrosity, decorated with beautiful dark chocolate frosting in such gorgeous swirls and flowers. How did she pull this off?

"Lulu! This is amazing! You've really grown in your baking. How did you make these frosting flowers?" I exclaim, my eyes trained on the delicious chocolate. I'm sure I'm drooling, but I don't care.

"Thanks, Didi." Luella laughs, her joy contagious, and my grin mirrors hers. "My wonderful pack has been buying me all the ingredients and baking pans I could ever want. Plus, I've been teaching my new mother-by-mating how to bake. It's only encouraged me to try more complicated things. And every time I slip into the kitchen here, our staff cheers because they get to snack on all my discards." Her joyous laugh has each of her males smiling at her, adoration shining in their eyes.

I envy the way her pack anticipates her every need, showering her with subtle touches and devoted attention. The way each mate circles around her, needing to be in her orbit. I'm so fucking happy for her.

But glancing at my males and female, I notice the lingering awkwardness as we navigate this new dynamic. Since most of my mates didn't know each other before joining our pack, it's clear that we need time to build the same strong bonds and easy communication that Luella's large pack enjoys.

Heaving a tired breath, I refocus on my sister. Just thinking the word brings a thrill of excitement that bubbles in my gut, and a smile returns to my face. Regardless of the fact that I've had a very trying journey, just knowing I truly do have family here means the world to me.

The rest of our evening goes by in a whirl of desserts and polite conversation, all of us avoiding the hard subjects, keeping it light before we retire for the night.

I'm eager for tomorrow. We get to see the King and plead our case. As I settle in to sleep, surrounded by my pack, a slight smirk tickles the corner of my mouth. I say 'plead our case' but in reality I know I'm going to go in there and yell at the male for failing our designation. Omegas don't deserve to be forgotten and left to suffer. The horror stories that Ilaris and Allista lived through aren't going to be the only ones. If it happened to them, it's definitely happening to more, and they should not be without hope. If I have to, I'll travel the world rescuing Omegas in need. I know my pack will join me without complaint. It's a noble cause, and we all believe in it.

Snuggling down into Ily's arms, Costen wrapped around my back like a clingy vine, Hagon, Eram and Lia reaching a hand over to touch both of us Omegas. I sigh with contentment and let sleep take me.

CH. 8

Eram

Morning light trickles in through the large window over the balcony. I wake slowly, the warmth of my pack around me encouraging me to stay asleep as long as possible. But, I know once Dani is awake she'll be springing up with all the energy of a sprite and fluttering around to dress and ready for our journey to Varough.

Hopefully, I can slow her down for about an hour so I can claim her. I refuse to wait any longer. I've put it off enough, and I know my continual pleas to wait have hurt her. Well, no more. I don't want to venture into the busy capital without my claim visible on her pretty pink skin.

The bed bounces a little as Lia rolls off. My

eyes slit open to watch her, and she catches me with a grin and a wink as she kicks Hagon in the ass, earning a furious snarl as the male shoots upright.

Everyone jolts awake at the sound, and I can't stop the laughter that erupts from me, earning a shocked, wide-eyed stare from each of my pack-mates. It only encourages more chuckles to spill from my lips.

"Is Eram okay?" Dani whispers loudly to Ilaris, watching me with a sparkle of warmth and delight in her eyes.

"I dunno," Ily replies sleepily, his words running together as he tries to figure out what's happening. I don't think he's much of a morning Wolf.

The chuckles trail off, and Lia meets my eyes with a subtle nod as she leans down to whisper into Ily's ear. Whatever she says has his cheeks burning a bright red as he scrambles out of the bed and jumps into her arms.

As soon as he's up, Lia marches off towards the bathing room. Hagon growls, the sound vibrating the bed before he's stomping after them, leaving Dani and me in the messy bedding.

My Omega watches me, her joy fading into a wary stare. I may not have mated her yet, but I swear I can feel her closing her heart, waiting for me to postpone our bonding again.

Not this time. I do something very unlike myself and launch my body at her. She squeals as I tackle her backwards into the middle of the bed. I wrap my arms around her petite body, caging her in, letting her feel the heat of my body, the need pulsing through me into my thick cock.

The moment she feels that bar of desire pressing into her center, she goes from laughing to breathless. Her eyes half-lidded, and those plush lips purse before her tongue slips out to wet them, drawing my gaze.

Without thought, I press a demanding kiss to her lips, and she surrenders. I expected more feistiness from her. She's a fighter and not much for the softer urges of a traditional Omega, but I forgot she gentles herself when her Alphas grow demanding.

Dani's fingers run through my hair before she grabs a fistful and tugs hard. I grunt at the pain and pull back, a question in my eyes. *'Do you want me to stop?'*

But this tiny Pixie never fails to surprise me.

"If you stop, I will castrate you," Dani snarls, an Omega growl underlining the words.

I fight to keep my face neutral. That was

the cutest sound, and I know if I laugh, she's more likely to gut me than grin.

"No, Dani," my voice is a little breathless, "not this time, sweet Pixie. You're mine, and I intend to place my claim on your skin. I want my teeth to mark you deeply, so everyone that sees you will know without a doubt. *You. Are. Mine.*"

With each word out of my mouth, her eyes grow hazier, the glassy look of lust filling them as she searches my gaze for the truth. What she sees must be good because she wraps her legs around my slim waist and presses her slick cunt against my cloth-covered cock.

There's no more talking. We wrestle, rolling around playfully, nipping and kissing as we sink into each other. Her hands rip and tear my shirt and light pants until she reaches skin. I help her pull the clothing off, hurrying to remove her underthings so we're skin-to-skin.

Her gorgeous pink against my dark brown is a beautiful contrast. That, and those fuck-me curves, have my mouth watering and my teeth aching to sink into her. This little Pixie, with the sharp mouth and pointy swords, is my mate. Fated to me by the Goddess. I will not squander this bond.

My fingers trail over her skin, pressing into her, making sure she'll feel me for hours after. The moment my hand reaches her thighs,

I'm greeted by copious slickness. The sticky, slippery substance covers her thighs, guiding me to her center.

Pressing a thumb into her perky nub, I revel in the way her eyes grow hot and her body squirms. My Dani can't decide if she needs to get away or move into the pressure.

I help her out by sliding three fingers into her heat, savoring the sound of her sultry moan. The way her body squeezes down on my fingers is painful but only drives my desire higher. Just the thought of that same pressure surrounding my cock has my breath catching and my fingers moving faster inside her.

Dani moans and pleads with me for more. But I work her until slick coats my hand, dripping down my arm. I don't let her cum though. That will only happen around my cock.

Pulling my hand back, I lift it so she can see how much she's coated me in her scent. Before she can beg me to return to her cunt, I run my tongue down my arm, catching all that slick in my mouth. Her taste sinks into my very being, into my soul, changing me on a fundamental level. I'm forever changed, and I am thrilled about that fact. A wave of exhilaration washes over me, the future stretching before me like a boundless, sunlit ocean.

My mate. My fated one. The only being in the

world that was created perfectly for me.

Why did I wait so long? Why did I think I needed to hold back in order to protect my sister? I could have had this all along and helped my charge.

Shaking my head, I refocus on the gift below me with a devious grin. She matches my energy, flashing her own sharp teeth as I move in for a consuming kiss.

We battle for dominance, lips clashing, tongues dancing and teeth nipping. It's feral and delicious. My sweet little Pixie is not a submissive Omega, and I'm starting to appreciate that fact.

Her hands roam over me, nails digging in and leaving trails of red. Not quite breaking through the skin but enough that I know she's leaving her mark on me. My own fingers move over her softness equally desperate. Cupping her breasts, pinching her peaked nipples, enjoying the high-pitched groans she releases.

Finally, Dani has had enough of my teasing and clamps her thighs tight against my sides, her arms around my shoulders, and flips me onto my back. The breath rushes out of me as my body lands, but before I can orient myself, she impales herself on my rigid length.

"Fuck!" I shout, fingers digging into her

hips as I tug her harder onto me.

The sensation of her wet, tight heat surrounds me, and my brain goes fuzzy. I'm all instinct now. The tight grip I had on my savage Alpha side is gone in an instant, and I snarl at her, baring my teeth in vicious need.

This pretty little Omega just grins wildly and rocks her hips, causing me to lose whatever feral ideas were just swimming through my mind. Heat boils in my core, and all thought ceases.

Our bodies move together, hips grinding, hands clawing, leaving crimson trails as we devolve into our base parts. Just Omega and Alpha. Male and female. Doing a dance as ancient as the Goddess. Passion escapes us in moans, snarls and whines.

The feeling of my Dani is everything. My Alpha has had enough waiting and strikes as we force our bulging knot into her sweet heat. Teeth sink through skin like butter; her blood wells up and sends a cacophony of flavors over my tongue. I close my eyes and make sure my teeth are deep enough to leave a good scar and to embed my scent thoroughly in her soul.

Dani doesn't wait; she rushes forward, snapping her sharp little teeth into my neck high below my ear. My little mate wants to make sure *everyone* knows I am taken. That sends a ripple of pleasure through me.

Her possessiveness arouses me, and I fear I may be a tad obsessed now that I have marked her as mine. Finally, I pull my teeth out of her pink skin and lap at the blood. This will scar beautifully and warn any Alphas to stay away unless they're looking for a fight.

She releases her bite and tends to the bond mark on my skin. Her little tongue brushing over the sensitive wounds sends a shiver of desire through my blood.

"If you keep that up, my knot will stay put for the entire day," I growl at her fierce grin, grinding my cock inside her channel, enjoying the way she clenches over me.

"What makes you think I want to stop?" Dani retorts, savage glee written on her pretty face.

The way she rolls her body against me has my eyes fluttering shut. Fuck. She's a Goddess, a beautiful troublemaker sent to draw me out of my stubborn, standoffish shell. I think I understand Hagon a little better now.

We spend the rest of the morning fucking until she's drained every bit of seed from my body. Her eyes, bright with joy, and the proud, almost arrogant tilt of her smile, fill me with happiness.

My mate is an ethereal Demi-Goddess and I count my lucky stars that she didn't give up on me.

CH. 9

Costen

Our breakfast with Pack Foreastra is a little awkward without Dani. Her friend Luella pouts when we inform her that Dani is busy. The moment the sweet winged Omega begins to tear up, her terrifying mates crowd around her until the big dark one snaps her up into his arms and marches out of the dining room with a feral snarl. The usually chipper male, Rafe, frowns but rushes after them, joined by the other green Fae and the short blue male.

We're left to dine with Tawson, the two Orcs, and the Gargoyle. The silent Orc sends a scowl at the doorway, and it's quite scary. I don't know if it's the impressive tusks or his unnerving silence, but the tall, muscular male's presence fills me with a sense of unease, his very stillness radiating tension.

"Good morning!" Lia says cheerfully loudly. "Quit your pouting; that shit is for your Omega. Now I don't remember if you've introduced yourselves properly to the rest of my pack. Tawson, Brenth, Brynd and Fen." She motions to each male as she names them.

"Oh! Uh, hi! I'm Ilaris, but most call me Ily," Our gentle male replies shyly, hiding slightly behind Hagon's broad shoulders.

"Hagon," The scarred Wolf grunts, crossing his arms and glaring at the other pack.

"Um, I am Costen," I say quietly, "it's nice to meet you."

"Sorry about that. I'm sure you understand the need to be near your Omega... Omegas all the time. It never gets easier," Tawson says, waving us to join them at the table. "It's especially difficult because our mate is pregnant and her emotions are a little wild. She'll be fine in a moment."

"Thanks, Taws," Lia replies with a smirk and fills two plates. She expertly ignores the savage glare Tawson levels at her for the nickname.

I already knew Lianis liked to stir shit up, but she's braver than I thought, challenging this male. There's a frightening amount of power and dominance radiating from him.

The smiley Orc belts out a hoot of laughter at the sour look on Tawson's face and slaps him on the back.

"Aye, this is more entertainin' than I expected. It's quite fun having visitors." Even though Brenth's delight is genial, his grin is still fierce, and I'm unsure how to act.

I've always been a little awkward, but when Dani is around, the tension in my shoulders disappears. Perhaps her presence gives me strength, helping me become a better Alpha. Just as I think this, my wonderful mate sends a shot of courage and pride through our bond. Straightening my shoulders, I give the Orc a small smile and take my seat between Ily and Lia.

There isn't much conversation until Luella returns with the rest of her mates. The feeling of dominance immediately saturates the air, and the room feels smaller. Even though I'm an Alpha, and have my own dominance, the weight of theirs still presses down on me hard, and for a moment it's difficult to breathe.

Someone clears their throat, and suddenly, air flows faster, and I gasp quietly as I suck down oxygen. Whoa. That was strange.

"What... what was that?" I brave the question, my words tripping over my tongue.

"Heh, sorry, that's what happens when

you get our pack going with worry for our pretty little Kitten," the cheerful Rafe replies.

"Yes. We apologize. I forget that most can't handle our collective power when we all react so strongly," Tawson adds, "it's also exacerbated since our mate is pregnant."

"Hmph," Hagon grunts, crossing his arms with a salty glare. "You should work on that."

Lianis bursts out with a howl of laughter at Hagon; a few of the males on the other side of the table join in, and I peer around in confusion. Why are they laughing? I mean... Hagon was a little rude, but I don't understand what's going on.

Ily's brow crinkles and his nose scrunches as he watches the female Alpha lose it. At least I'm not the only one confused. I reach toward Ilaris beneath the table. He grabs my hand with a light squeeze and meets my eyes.

"Do you get why that was funny?" Ily leans over and whispers the question to me.

My head shakes, and I try to smooth out the frown, but I'm still lost. At least my sweet Omega is with me. Having this pack gives me such a sense of home and comfort. They don't poke at me or mock my stupidity. I know I love Dani, but I think I love Ily and Hagon too. They're so sweet to me, and Hagon is surprisingly patient when he's teaching me things.

"Sorry about that." Fen, the Gargoyle, cuts through the group's laughter. "I don't know what's wrong with them, but let's move on. How are you this morning?" The male's voice is smooth and friendly, lightening the weight that was sitting on my chest.

"Oh, we're just fantastic!" Lia says brightly. Her smile hints at the laughter she's working to suppress.

"Good bed," Hagon adds, his tone forever gruff.

"It was a very nice room. Thank you for putting us up in such luxury," Ilaris says, his tone soft and a little shy.

"Yes, thank you. It's more comfort than I've ever experienced," I decide to answer as well.

My words have the room growing quiet, and an awkward silence stretches on. Only the shifting of clothing can be heard.

"Ye'r welcome!" Brenth booms, ending the stiffness in the dining room.

I pick up my utensils and return to eating, determined to keep my mouth shut for the rest of this meal. The moment I make a movement, everyone else breathes and returns to their meal. Soft chatter fills the hushed air, and I inhale deeply.

Why do I even bother? Sadness washes over me, and my shoulders slump as I pick at the rest of the food on my plate. This is why I was pushed out of my cluster. They hated my stupid questions. But... how am I supposed to know when I'm allowed to speak and when I should remain silent?

I need my Pix. Her understanding, support, and warmth chase away the shadows of self-doubt.

My mate bond lights up with ferocious strength, and my spine straightens as my shoulders relax. It dawns on me that it isn't Dani lending me her courage. The warmth of Hagon's resolve floods me, a beacon of hope that chases away the demons.

A smile stretches my lips, and I flick my eyes over to him, only to find Hagon staring straight at me. The grumpy male winks at me, lips quirking up before he returns to his meal.

I am not alone. These words repeat in my mind, and my grin grows as my hunger renews. Yes. I am lucky to have found such a wonderful pack and mates.

◆◆◆

We're all gathered outside the massive entrance to the Keep, waiting for Tawson and his brother Alec to meet us. With Dani tucked into my side, her head resting on my arm, and Eram clinging to her, the weight of their affection settles over me. It's nice sensing Eram in our matebond.

I expected him to be standoffish, yet he brought warmth and light to the bond. Huh, so he hides all this happiness beneath that frosty attitude. My lips pull up into a grin at the way he's following Dani around like a cub.

It's very sweet, and I'm happy for Dani. Each time Eram had put off bonding or even getting close to her, it wounded her. My Omega is fantastic at hiding beneath a mask of bubbly happiness. Even when her soul aches, she always wears a delighted grin.

"Alright, let's go," Tawson says as he marches down the steps of his home and strides past us. "We're fairly close to the capital, so it shouldn't take us longer than an hour on foot."

Hagon grumbles, crossing his arms as his eyes track the Fae as Tawson leans down to speak to his mate.

"Why aren't we taking horses?"

My Pix groans and rolls her eyes at the gruffly asked question. "Hagon! That's rude. It's only an hour's walk; we're fine."

"Dani, it's okay. We don't have enough horses for everyone or a big enough cart, so walking it is!" Luella chirps brightly.

"I'm not going, but I think at least half my pack are joining you. I know they have some business with Seren, too." The sweet Omega explains before grabbing the hands of two mates and heading straight for my mate.

Dani slips from my and Eram's hold. The two Omegas rush into a tight embrace, their hushed whispers and the tremor of their shared laughter filling the space before they separate, their faces alight with mirth. With a lingering touch, their hands remain clasped, the unspoken words of their conversation lingering in the air between them.

The big one, Gin, has finally had enough and snaps his mate up into his arms with a grunt. Hagon is grumpy, but this guy has perfected surliness. I'm glad our scarred Alpha isn't quite so bad.

Once Luella and her mates that are staying have disappeared inside the Keep, we're left with Tawson, Blue, Brenth and Brynd. They lead our pack down the long road from the Keep and out the main gate.

We're close enough to Varough to see the large city in the distance, and a thrill of excitement streaks through me. The sheer volume of beings is unlike anything I've ever experienced, and I'm eager to explore the castle.

It's not far, but hopefully Nyurel stays away from us. With the extra males, and devastating power leaking from Tawson and his packmates, I think we'll be okay. They can't be called the Elites for nothing.

Taking Dani's hand, we follow along behind Hagon and Ily, with Lia and Eram close behind. The two Orcs bring up the rear, the morning sun glinting off the sharpened axes strapped to their backs.

A sense of security settles my nerves, and I allow myself to relax with a smile. This is going to be fun!

CH. 10

Dani

The walk to Varough is short and pleasant. Despite the faint voice of caution hinting that leaving the Keep was a bad idea, the Elites' power should be enough to overcome any attacks. Luckily, it's a quiet walk in the bright morning light.

As we approach the front gate, the city's vibrant energy, a wave of noise and movement, shatters the peaceful atmosphere. The guards eye our group with furrowed brows. One of them turns and snags a messenger, murmurs something and sends the boy off at a run.

"Tawson," the other guard greets the Fae with a nod. "The King is expecting you."

"Thanks, Faylon. Anything unusual to report?" Tawson asks, pausing beside the guard.

"Everything has been quiet. Is there something wrong? Should I be wary?" Faylon straightens his stance, concern washes away his aloof expression.

"Maybe. Just be watchful for any black magic or bizarre behavior. Send a runner for me if you notice any purple or black mist," Tawson replies. He pats the guard on the shoulder before heading into the city.

My mates and I follow, their gazes mesmerized by the sights, sounds, and smells of the vibrant, crowded streets; chattering beings of all kinds, and the tantalizing scent of exotic spices hanging in the air. I fight to keep my jaw from dropping; the unique architecture and unfamiliar smells are unlike any village I've ever experienced.

Captivated by the sights, we slow our pace, the scent of exotic fruits and vibrant wares filling our senses. As my eyes land on a stall draped with gorgeous fabric, I stop sharply. Costen crashes into me, wrapping his arms around my body, stopping me from tumbling into the dirty street with a muted '*oof*'.

"Sorry! But look at that shimmery bolt of cloth. I could make such a gorgeous dress with that," I mutter, my eyes trained on the textile stall.

"Hey! Hold on a moment, we've lost Dani to the market!" Costen shouts at the rest of our group.

Lia chuckles before urging the rest of our pack to wait for me to finish cooing over the pretty fabric.

My fingers itch to stroke over the array of cloth, but a small Indaral interrupts my gaze. I've never met one before, and my excitement grows as I restrain myself from pouncing on them and blurting out all the questions rattling around in my head.

"Can I help you?" The Indaral asks, with a glint of avarice in their eyes.

"You're an Indaral!" I exclaim before slapping a hand over my mouth. A few beings behind me release muffled laughter, and I stare up at the sky for a moment and berate myself for my impetuous mouth.

"Sorry, ignore that, please. How much for this gorgeous shimmery fabric?" I sigh inwardly, praying my foolishness hasn't offended them.

"Ah, it's fine, child." The Indaral chuckles at my burning cheeks before gesturing at the cloth I'm eyeing. "This is cashmere. One of the softest fabrics I've ever had the joy of finding. It is rare and difficult to obtain. A bolt is quite expensive."

My hands trail over the shimmer reverently, and I sigh at the price the Indaral names, my shoulders sagging. It's silly of me to want it so badly. I don't currently have a home, and without a workspace, I cannot work on creating something beautiful.

The clink of coin pulls me out of my daze, and my eyes widen when they land on Lia paying the Indaral.

"Lia! You don't have to do that. I don't need it," I cry, hurrying over to her, trying to stop her from dropping so much money on me.

"Pfft, my Omega wants the pretty cloth, my Omega is going to get it." Lia waves off my concern with a smile, taking the entire bolt and tying some rope around it so she can wear it like a pack on her back.

The tall female grabs my hand and drags my gawking body away from the textile stall. Costen follows close behind with a light chuckle, and as soon as we join the rest of the group, everyone resumes the trek towards the towering castle in the distance.

"You didn't have to do that!" I hiss at Lia as she continues to hold my hand, pulling me along beside her.

"Nope. I didn't have to," the Alpha agrees, her tone cheeky, "but I wanted to get something for one of my Omegas. I have a feeling that neither Ily nor you have been courted properly." Giving Costen, Eram and Hagon a piercing look.

Ily's got both hands over his mouth, attempting to hold back his laughter at the wide-eyes on each Alpha. Costen leans over, whispering to Hagon.

"What… how are we supposed to court them? Do we buy them gifts too? I thought we're supposed to make them happy… They look happy," his whisper is loud enough that we all hear.

What a sweet, pretty kitty. Costen is a little clueless at times, but I find it endearing, and I think our entire pack would agree. The way Hagon's grumpy scowl softens at the question. How Eram's cool stare warms. Ilaris beams at our pale kitty. Lia's piercing eyes turn from accusing to understanding. Each member of our growing family finds our Costen adorable in his innocence.

I shake off Lia's hold and rush towards my Sweet Snow, launching myself into his arms. My mouth finds my claiming mark on his neck, and I smother it in kisses and nibbles, earning a chuckle that quickly turns to a moan. I ought to know better; the crowded, chaotic streets of Varough are not the right place to start something.

"Yes, Costen," I pull away and meet his searching eyes, "yes, you make me deliriously happy, and I truly don't need more than that." My lips meet his for a soft kiss before I step away and grab Lia's hand again.

With our growing pack, I want to make sure I'm paying equal attention to each of my mates. They're all important to me, and each fills a hole I didn't know I had in my soul. It's sort of like... I hadn't known I was missing a piece of me until I found each of them, and I think I might burn the world down if something happened to any of them.

I shake off my murderous thoughts and focus on what's ahead of us only to come to an abrupt stop when I realize we're at the gates.

The dark obsidian wall, imposing and endless, towers above, casting long, sharp shadows that slice across the uneven, worn cobblestones underfoot. A shiver of unease slithers through me. Something in my gut is shouting that everything will change if I step foot inside that castle.

I don't understand what danger lies ahead, though. We *have* to see the King. It's imperative that he know what's happening in his Kingdom. And if we don't go in there and tell him, who will? I have a burning desire to shout at him for losing touch with his land, for letting Omega's be used and abused. No, I'm going to ignore the warning, and storm into his throne room, to let loose a torrent of furious accusations at the King.

With my mind made up, I march forward, dragging Lia with me past the guards. They turn and eye me with suspicion, but Tawson steps forward and gives them a brief explanation. Just his presence along with his pack-mates soothes the guard's irritated edge. They move back and allow us onto the castle grounds.

The two Orcs earn tense glances from the guards, but they do nothing as our group passes into the courtyard.

My anger takes a pause as I revel in the beauty surrounding me. There's so many different kinds of flowers, and they overwhelm my senses with their floral aroma. The plants and trees are vibrant colors that send joy through me. Green, purple, blue, red and orange surround my body as I drift away from Lia and into the flourishing garden with a spin.

Wings buzz as I flutter and dance through the brilliant nature, and a wide grin takes over as I throw my head back with a laugh.

"What a gorgeous creature you've brought me, Tawson." The resonant voice halts my feet and wings. I spin towards the sound, a scowl already plastered to my face as I prepare to snarl at whoever disrupted my moment with nature.

CH. 11

Seren

There's a Pixie in the royal gardens. A vision of pink and shimmery colors that dances and flitters from flower to tree. Her short pink hair sways with her motions, catching the soft breeze from her gorgeous wings.

My eyes are stuck on her as she prances away from the female Alpha who'd been holding her hand. Either she doesn't realize she's in the royal courtyard or she doesn't care. Either way, I'm enchanted with this ethereal beauty. Her tiny stature makes her look vulnerable and submissive; I want her fiercely. My cock hardens in my trousers, and I shift in place attempting to hide my reaction to her.

As I try to conceal my attraction, I tear my eyes off her joyous form and find Tawson observing me quietly, in his way. So, I blurt out the first thing that comes to mind.

"What a gorgeous creature you've brought me, Tawson." I watch my old friend closely, catching the tiny tick at the corner of his lips suggesting he's laughing at me. I miss the Pixie spinning towards me, but the rest of the group with Tawson watches the tiny female with amusement.

"Excuse the fuck outta me?" Her voice is sharp and cutting. She stands, hands on hips, with a scowl to rival one of Gin's.

She's adorable when angry, and I get the sense that if I laugh, I may regret it. So I bite my cheek and force my face into a frown instead.

"What a mouth on you," I reply and turn towards Tawson. "Well, I'm sure you've got a story for me. Let's retire to my sitting room, and you can tell me why you've brought strangers to my home." As I watch the Pixie from the corner of my eye, ignoring her, I feel her fury like a palpable vibration, her pink skin darkening to a deep rose as she flushes with anger.

Without waiting for an answer, I stride towards the monstrous doors leading into my castle. Meeting Ward's eyes, I smirk and raise one brow in question. My oldest friend and head of my security bites his lip, laughter dancing in his eyes.

This will be a fascinating meeting; I can feel it. Ward will be on his toes, waiting for the feisty Pixie to do something. There's no doubt in my mind that I infuriated her, and the way she was glaring at me contained an unequivocal insult.

As I stroll through the pristine halls of my home, I let my thoughts wander. I haven't felt such an attraction to any female in ages. It's almost... strange how strongly I reacted to her. Her beauty is so striking that I barely noticed the rest of Tawson's companions; all I could see was her radiant smile and the way the sunlight caught her hair. At least, before I interrupted her joyful frolic.

The sound of footsteps echoes off the high ceilings as their group trails after me. Guards open the heavy oak doors to my sitting room, and I toss myself into the hardback chair that signifies I'm hearing citizen complaints. Although since it's Tawson, I waive formality. My old friend knows me well and would have sent a runner if this were something more.

"Please take a seat." I lazily wave a hand towards the scattering of chairs throughout the room. "I'm looking forward to hearing your story, Tawson. Who are your friends and why have you brought them to my home?" Though I'm looking at Tawson, my focus is on the pink Pixie flitting at the edge of my vision, her iridescent wings catching the light as she stomps over to a chair.

With a loud, ear-piercing screech, she drags the heavy object along the polished marble, leaving scratches in its wake, seemingly oblivious to the destruction. There's no hiding my smirk. This tiny, gorgeous creature is fascinating. The opulent surroundings and suspicious guards intimidate most who penetrate this far into my castle. But not her; she doesn't seem to give a shit about my status or the surrounding luxury.

Finally, I drag my attention off of her to survey the rest of the ragtag group finding seating. The statuesque Succubus intrigues me; they rarely leave Lowleaf. Most of Saforia is wary of them because of the rumors and stories that surround their kind. Rumors that make them seem like soul-sucking demons come to ruin lives. But that isn't the truth. Sure, they replenish their magic through intimacy, but they do not suck souls. *Just orgasms*, I think with a smirk.

The pale Alpha is fascinating. I don't know if I've seen his kind before. The white skin with black stripes has my fingers itching to stroke over him to see if it feels different from the rest of his body.

Curious.

The Elemental gives off a cool, untouchable air, but I can see his tension. The male is tightly wound, his muscles coiled and ready to snap. He will be interesting to play with.

Then, my gaze snags on the scarred male. That one's witnessed more combat than most. His successes line his body with pale stripes of honor. The scowl on his face is telling, though. He is not one for foolishness. Unless it's the tiny Pixie. It seems she fascinates everyone, not just me.

The slim male sticking close to the scarred one catches my attention. He continues to hide behind the bigger male. A shy, uncertain frown mars his pretty face as he scans the room. Hmm… male Omega? Is it possible? I haven't had one make it to Varough in at least sixty years. They are quite rare. The desire to get closer, to catch his scent and confirm my suspicions is strong, but I push it down and finally focus on Tawson.

My old friend is laughing at me behind his stoic facade. The tiny twitch of his lips gives him away. That and his eyes dance with amusement. I roll mine at him and let my exasperation show before urging him to step forward and explain why my sitting room is filled with strangers.

Once everyone settles, I relax into my

chair, one leg thrown over the armrest and my back slouched onto the opposite side. My eyes scan the odd group of beings in front of me, pausing on the Pixie and the male Omega.

"Tawson, explain." It's not a bark, but it is full of dominance. In order to hide my curiosity, I plaster on an impatient air and focus on my old friend.

"This is..." Tawson pauses, gaze searching the Alphas. "I don't think they have decided on a pack name yet. But they have a few grievances to air." The Fae smirks, poorly hiding his amusement from me.

"Grievances? What grievances could you possibly have?" the question slips out, and I hide a wince at how much of an asshole I sound.

"Excuse me?" the little Pixie snarls, standing from her seat, hands on her hips and fury twisting her features.

I'm taken aback by her rage-filled tone, and my brows shoot up, but I maintain my casual air. Curiosity about this female only encourages me to poke at her. I shouldn't treat my citizens like this, but there's something about her that inspires my bad behavior. Or maybe it's the fact that Tawson is here and I've never been able to maintain my kingly air around him.

"Now listen here, you overgrown, meathead, Alpha! How you're not aware of what's been happening in your own damn kingdom eludes me, but don't worry, I'm here to help," the Pixie snarks as she marches towards me, finger pointing accusingly at me.

Ward, my personal guard and closest friend, steps in her path, blocking her from approaching my person. He's only doing his job, but I want to snarl at him to get out of her way. The surprising urge sends a jolt of tension through my body, catching me off guard.

Am I attracted to this tiny, pink, Pixie? Hmmm... fascinating. It's the first time in ages that I've found a female intriguing. Most of the Beta and Omega females that hang around the castle are whiny, annoying and only after me for the crown. I haven't bothered with finding a mate among them because they're all wrong for me.

"Get out of my way, you beastly lump!" The female's shouting draws me out of my thoughts, and I can't stop the wide grin when I see her berating my guard. "I have some important info for the *King,* and you need to step aside so I can inform him of how badly he's lacking!"

The way she sneers king has my hackles rising. What have I done to offend her so badly? My gaze searches each face sitting in front of me. Tawson seems curious but not fully clued in. The male that I think is an Omega, trembles as he sits in the scarred one's lap, his face hidden in the Alpha's neck. The pale Alpha watches the Pixie with a dreamy smile.

The Succubus meets my eyes with a toothy grin. No help at all from anyone. I return my focus to the tiny female scolding Ward and cock my head.

"Ward," I call his name. He knows I want him to step aside and allow this pretty Pixie to come to me.

My guard tosses me a wide-eyed look over his shoulder, as if asking, *'Are you sure?'* At my nod, he steps aside, cutting off the angry female mid-sentence.

"Thank you!" she shouts before resuming her march towards me. I shift in my chair, finally sitting up properly to meet her accusing eyes.

There's no opportunity to speak before she's laying into me, her voice full of fury and condemnation. I have to focus on her words, but she's gorgeous in her anger, and my eyes drift over her curvy form, laced into a pretty green and blue dress.

"How dare you!" The shouted words jar me, and I refocus on her face as she screeches, "You make all these rules about Omegas and then just fuck off? Where's the authority? The kingly leadership? You just trust that Alphas will obey? Are you fucking serious? Alphas are a bunch of meatheaded idiots, you included!"

The insult has my lips twitching, but if I allow my amusement to break free, I'm pretty sure this little female will stab me. With her wildly flailing arms, her scent drifts over to me, and as soon as her sweet, sugary Omega pheromones hit my nose, I lose my mind.

"Mate!"

CH. 12

Dani

The King's deep rumbling growl vibrates through the room and my entire body, sending slick leaking down my thighs. He snarls one word and snatches me off my feet mid-tirade.

"What are you doing? You barbarian!" I screech as I'm grabbed up and pressed into a hard chest.

When his scent reaches my nose, my eyes roll back and, embarrassingly, I moan loudly. Rich, frosty, juicy berries. Fruit is one of my weaknesses. It's a pure, natural sugar I crave. Full of sweet juice that fills my mouth and quenches my thirst. It's not just a desire. It's a need so strong that my body is moving without my mind's consent.

"Oh Goddess, why do you smell so fucking good?" I press my face into his neck, rooting around for where his scent is the strongest.

My teeth ache with the desire to bite into his pale, grayish - white skin. I wonder if his blood will taste as sweet as frost berries?

I have had them on the rare occasions when sellers brought them to the market. But they are difficult to come by as they grow only on the highest mountains in the bitter cold and snowy landscape.

For this male to smell like one of my favorite treats must mean he's fated to be mine. Just like Bassanai said. I want to hold on to my anger, to continue to berate him for failing Omega's, but, Goddess, he smells so fucking good.

"*Mine.* My mate. My pretty little Omega," the King rumbles out, his words short and full of dominance and power.

"Finally! Where have you been hiding? Why have you taken so long to come to me?" he questions in between sniffs and nuzzles to my head and hair.

Those demands come out loud in the silence of the big room, and I'm finally jarred from my intense need to bite him. Shoving at his chest, I fight his hold and try to regain my feet. As well as some space from this potent male.

The King refuses to release me, growling at my attempts to get away from him. Over my shoulder, I see his guard hovering nearby with bewildered eyes, wide and surprised, while his mouth gapes and his hands hover in the air, unsure what to do.

My pack all stand from their chairs, Hagon turning a furious red as Ily mutters something in his ear and hangs onto his arm. Costen is confused, glancing at each of our pack-mates for an answer, while Lia just grins brightly and gives me a wink. Eram, on the other hand, is tense, his hand resting on his sword, ready to pull it out in my defence but wary of the guards in the room.

I take a deep breath, instantly regretting it and loving it in equal measure, because his scent makes my head hazy and my body pliant. But I fight that desire and lean as far away from him as he allows.

"Listen here…" I pause, not remembering the King's actual name and turn to flick a look at Tawson. The Fae stands there with a wide grin and a relaxed demeanor. His Orc pack-mates peer around the room in confusion but make no move to do anything.

Tawson chuckles before mouthing the King's name, '*Seren*'. I heave a sigh and turn my eyes back to the barbarian clinging to me.

"Seren." The moment I say his name, I regret it.

The King's chest switches from growling to a bone-melting purr. I feel my body losing all tension, and I melt into his muscular chest, rubbing my face against him, scent marking the King.

"Say it again, mate," Seren demands through his purr.

The moment he says it, making it sound like an order, my obstinate nature surfaces through the fog.

"No!" I force out between numb lips.

"I will never say your name again until you put me down!" I order the fucking King.

The Alpha stares down at me with a pout. The King of Saforia is fucking pouting at me. I struggle to comprehend what's happening right now.

"Mate?" Seren mutters sulkily, his brows raised and bottom lip pushed out. Confusion shines down at me from his icy blue eyes.

With a heavy sigh, I roll my eyes before softening my tone. The baser instincts of this Alpha have clouded his mind, and the higher-functioning King is a little lost in his head.

"Uh, My Liege... Your Majesty? You need to

put me down. I won't go far, but we need to have a conversation before we let our instincts have free rein, okay?" My hand rises to pat his arm. I'm no longer struggling to get away, knowing that I need to tread carefully. If I make any violent moves, I have a feeling that this Alpha will carry me off to an easily defensible space where he can claim me without interruption.

Most Alphas have evolved past that barbaric instinct, but we all know it's still there. Hidden deep within their psyches. Awaiting the right moment to seize control. To toss a female over their shoulder and carry her off to their cave.

The King grunts, eyes wary as he stares into mine, searching for something. The truth, maybe? Finally, he relents and places me on my feet, but he keeps one hand wrapped around my own. Clutching me like a needy youngling.

Turning to face the rest of the room, my pack, Tawson, the Orcs and the King's guard, Ward. Except for Eram and Hagon, my mates are mostly amused, but they admirably hold back all that Alpha possessiveness.

"Okay, so it appears we've got another problem to deal with," I start with a heavy sigh, "I just can't fucking deal with this shit. Apparently, the fucking King of Saforia is my mate? I can't mate the King! I'm the furthest you can get from a *'perfect'* Omega. This is unbelievable." Ranting out all my exasperation doesn't help the way I thought it would. Now, I'm even more frustrated.

Glancing down at his pale greyish-white skin against my soft pink, I follow Seren's arm up to his face. Only to find him staring down at me with desire and need. It appears the King has left the building, leaving us with only Seren's baser Alpha to contend with.

Inhale, pause, exhale, pause. I repeat the mantra and breathe slowly, pushing down my instinct to be angry about this turn of events. Unfortunately, all this does is drown me in his pussy-melting scent. I lock my knees, fighting the overwhelming weakness his scent causes, resisting the desperate urge to climb him like a fucking tree and bury my face in his skin; the smell is intoxicating.

Instead of devolving into my baser instincts, I turn towards the King's guard, Ward. This male knows the King the best, I assume, so I hope he can help us out.

"Uh, Ward, is it?" I call over to the male.

He's observing me and Seren with a frown. That expression sends unease through me, and now I'm not sure I should ask him anything.

"You have questions you think I can answer?" Ward's deep voice echoes through the room. It sends involuntary shivers down my spine, and my senses can't decide whether I'm intimidated or turned on.

"Well... Yes. Since the King is currently..." I trail off, unsure how to describe the de-evolution of Seren's mentality. "Why has he sunk so deeply into his baser Alpha self? Why did none of my other Alphas have this problem? Do you have any ideas? Isn't the King... I dunno, supposed to be the best of us?" There's no helping the sarcastic tint to my questions, and I watch Ward's face carefully, catching each minute flinch to my words.

Before the guard can answer, Lia steps forward, her tail swishing with her agitation. The beautiful Succubus stands as tall as Ward, and the sour pinch of his lips and furrow in his brow has me biting back a laugh.

"Okay, Ward." Lia's sultry voice is warm in the room's tension. "I can see you're having some trouble answering my pretty Pixie's questions, so let me help." She doesn't pause to give him a chance to respond, continuing on she turns to me, "Some Alpha's, if they've suppressed their Alpha tendencies for too long can have difficulty with their instincts when something big happens... Let's say, meeting their fated?"

At that, I turn and peer up at Seren. The

big icy male stares down at me with puppy-dog eyes, pleading for me to give him attention and scritches. It's enough that I almost burst into hysterical giggles, but I sink my teeth into my bottom lip to stop it. Unfortunately, I forget for a moment how fucking sharp they are and injure myself.

I hiss as blood wells up, but before I can suck my lip into my mouth, Seren releases a bone-chilling snarl and scoops me into his arms. He moves so quickly I barely have time to understand what's happening. Seren's pale, plush lips descend on mine, and he licks the blood off my skin with a deep, guttural moan before he dominates me with a mind-melting kiss.

My awareness narrows down to only him and me. It's as if the world disappears and Seren becomes my everything. His dominance pulsates against the walls I've built around my inner Omega, breaking them down, drowning me in him. Pulling me deep into my baser instincts as well.

Deep inside, a whisper of defiance tries to surface, though it's weak and distant. I'm sure there's shouting all around us, but we're in our own little bubble of reality, and nothing can touch us.

One moment I'm falling into Seren's kiss, the next my body is flying and I land on the softest cushion in the world. Finally, I look around and realize we're no longer in that big sitting room. We've moved.

I'm alone with an Alpha that I think has gone into rut, and my inner Omega is driving my actions. The rest of me is still there, just buried deep enough that I can sort of understand what's happening, but I cannot do anything about it.

This should be interesting.

CH. 13

Seren

My Omega. Mine. The sweet taste of her blood lingers on my tongue, and I'm feral for another drop. It's sugary with a metallic tang, and my mind keeps telling me it's the best thing I've ever had.

I need more. I need to bite. To claim. To breed.

My head shakes at these thoughts circling around on repeat. I need my Omega to make a nest so I can claim her properly.

"Nest." It's the only word that makes it past my salivating jaws.

The pretty little pink beauty blushes such a tantalizing color. I want to run my tongue over her cheeks to see if her skin tastes sweeter with that darker tint.

Her head swivels, checking out my bedding, and a cute little frown mars her face as she notes how few nesting supplies I have. My Alpha snarls at the fact that I've already let her down. My feet move towards my closet and the stash that I've been building for years while I searched for my mate. I hope she likes it.

My Pixie's head pops up from her diligent work making a base layer for the nest with my bedding, and her eyes widen with avarice at the armful of pillows and blankets I'm bringing her.

"Yes!" she shouts with glee and pops up to her feet. Those gorgeous iridescent wings flutter madly with her excitement as she waits for me to approach.

I'm hesitant to get too near, even my baser Alpha knows better than to encroach on an Omega's nest. But she growls when I pause too far away.

As soon as I approach the edge, she snatches the top pillow off my pile and rubs her face against it. Grinning, she pats the item into place with a cute little hum before repeating the action with the next item in my arms.

Determination flows through me. I will stand here as long as she needs me to. Since nest-building is sacred to Omegas, she deserves to take all the time she needs. Even though my cock is attempting to break through my trousers, I will hold her supplies until she deems it acceptable.

The rut pounds through my blood, my muscles feel as though they are bulking up, and my body is shifting to settle in for days of fucking. I have no perception of time as my mind devolves into the mantra: *rut, claim, breed.*

This precious Omega is mine, and I will keep her safe. We will not leave this room until I've claimed her deeply. My inner Alpha has waited long enough to find the one meant for him, and I have no desire to stop him either.

She's mine.

As I think this, a rumbling snarl vibrates from my chest, cutting through the room, and my eyes catch the moment it hits her.

Her hands fly to her stomach as it cramps, and the sweet scent of her slick fills the air, clouding my mind even further. But I don't have to wait any longer because her eyes meet mine, pleading with me to make it stop.

But I don't want it to stop. I want her messy and begging for my knot, for my teeth. She will know the full power of my dominance before we leave this room. She will bow before my Alpha and submit to me as my Queen.

I strip, handing her each piece of clothing, knowing she will want it in her nest. Even with the cramps, my pretty Pixie shuffles around on her knees, arranging each item where her Omega deems perfect.

When I'm nude, my cock throbbing with the need to be inside her, I approach the edge of the nest and wait. A low purring growl continues non-stop as I urge her to invite me in. This sweet pink Omega will never escape me. *She's mine.*

In the back of my mind, I know she has other mates, but my feral, rut-brained Alpha is sure we can fuck their memory right out of her head. When the haze no longer has me in its grasp, I'm positive I'll be less possessive and able to share her with her mates. This thought has my Alpha chuffing with laughter. He knows this is going to be a trial, but he's the most dominant, so who's going to stop him?

A light chirp, underlined by a sweet Omega purr, pulls my full attention over to my Queen. Naked, skin glistening with sweat, she's the most magnificent sight I've ever laid eyes on.

"Alpha, please?" The Pixie's syrupy voice has my chest rumbling in response.

My rut is affecting her, almost like a heat, but it will pass as soon as this daze is over. Her vocabulary is devolving into chirps, purrs and growls, similar to my own. Except my Alpha is intent on only purring or snarling until he can get inside this delectable female.

I take her plea as an invitation to enter the nest and climb over the soft barrier she's built around the edge. Each motion makes my cock throb harder. The sway and heft of it is a mesmerizing dance to the pretty Pixie waiting for me in the center. Her eyes track the way it bounces with my movement, and a continuous purr thrums in her chest, softening the aggression in me.

When I reach her, I scent mark her hair, each cheek and her chest with a low purr, encouraging her to do the same. It's delightful how our scents mingle together, creating a sugary dessert that I *need* to devour.

As soon as the scent marking is complete, I've reached the end of my patience and I manage one word.

"Present."

My voice echoes throughout the room with a snarl, and the sweet Omega scrambles into position. Her juicy cunt faces me, and her arousal sends my mind spinning. The plump, wet lips of her center entice me like nothing else. Everything blurs, a disorienting haze washes over me, and moments slip away unnoticed.

When I surface from the haze again, it's

to find my face pressed into her skin, my tongue reaching her depths, scooping out as much slick as I can. Blankets muffle her moans and screams, and her tiny hands clutch fistfuls of softness, which she's about to tear.

Good. I'm smug that I've reduced her to this mewling, wet creature. It's only right that she joins me in the depravity circling my hazy mind. I just wish I wasn't lost to the rut so I could remember every moment of this claiming.

Pulling back, I lick all the slick off my face. I can't wait any longer. I need to get my dick knot deep and sink my teeth into her pretty pink skin.

Grabbing her hips, I still her twitching form and place my tip at her entrance. The burning heat sinks into me, and I groan. My Omega has had enough, though, and dislikes the tease. Even with my grip on her skin, she shoves back hard enough and envelopes my cock up to the knot.

I wheeze at the incredible pressure, heat and slick easing my way in. My brain scrambles in the best way, and the fog takes me.

Flashes of our mating reach me deep in the rut. Her beautiful body fighting against my dominance, trying to take more than I am giving. Her fiery nature only encourages my Alpha. My Pixie's sweet, sultry moans are music to my ears, and I want more. And those dazzling, delicate wings just shout at me to touch and stroke. Every time my hands pass over the joints on her back, she squirms enticingly. But as my fingers trace over the edges, I earn sweet trills and moans.

Each orgasm is a gift, and even in my haze, I treat it properly. Praising my mate, encouraging her to give me everything. She wants my knot more than anything, but I'm waiting for just the right moment, when she's limp from too much pleasure and whining for me to take her.

Finally, after what feels like hours of mating, she's soft and pliable, purring and snarling in turns for my knot to sink deep. To plug her tight and breed her. To give her my claiming mark, and for her to bite me in return.

With how much slick she's covered us both in, it's easy to slip my knot into place. The sensation of her walls clamping down around it, the way it inflates even bigger, pressing into her O-spot, has my eyes rolling back. I cum. Harder than ever in my long life, my eyes are blind to everything but the pleasure. Even so, my teeth find her neck, high below her ear, and sink deep. My Alpha is sure that if we leave a good scar, no one will make any attempts to take my Queen from me.

Her blood is sweet, like the most decadent dessert, covered in spun sugar. The way it melts on my tongue and sends a wave of bliss through my entire body. I barely notice her teeth clamping down over my wrist, but when the bond lights up inside me, rapture like nothing else surges through me and I fill her with more cum.

My hand strokes over her skin, playing with her hard, pointed nipples. I grin at the way she shudders and twitches, before moving my hand down to rest on her stomach, bloated with my seed. The basal instinct in me is ecstatic that we have our mate and we are working on breeding her.

When her jaw releases the bite and her sweet little tongue laps at the mark, soothing it, tiny zaps of pleasure rush through my blood. This is everything I've ever wanted. My Omega, the perfect being to complement me. I can't wait until the rut passes and we can have a proper conversation.

My last thought vanishes as the fog grows thicker, pulling us both down into the intensity of my rut.

CH. 14

Hagon

What the fuck is going on? Where the fuck did that Goddess-damned Alpha take my mate? I don't care if he's the fucking King, I'll wring his fucking neck for stealing her away. And this beast of a male better get the fuck out of my way.

"I'm sorry, but I can't let you go after him," the guard states, again. Standing firm in front of the door and keeping my pack from chasing after Dani.

This argument has been going on for a while, and my restraint is waning. I'm just about ready to unleash my Wolf and maul this fucker.

"Hagon," Tawson steps closer to me, cautious of my fury, "you have to understand, Ward is just doing his job and protecting the King. You look about two seconds away from mauling every being in this room."

Even though his words make sense, I'm past reason. I want my fucking mate in my arms, and safe. I know Omegas choose their pack, but none of us were able to have much of a conversation before all this happened.

"Ward, Tawson, how has the King suppressed his Alpha for long enough to allow himself to go feral for the first sweet-smelling Omega?" Lia asks the questions we all want to know. "Doesn't he take in freshly revealed Omegas? How has he never lost it around them?"

The beastly guard shifts on his feet, avoiding my eyes as he huffs out an exasperated breath. He remains tight-lipped, his hesitation palpable; either he truly doesn't know, or the weight of royal secrets keeps him silent.

"Ward!" Tawson snaps, his patience at an end.

"Fine," the guard replies, equally annoyed, "Seren has been using a rune to suppress his instincts in order to do his job for these Omegas. But I think... I think finding his true, fated mate overpowered the suppression, and all those instincts came roaring back all at once, causing him to lose it. I've honestly never seen him act this way around anyone. But, I think you can rest easier knowing that he would never injure his mate." Ward turns directly to me for the last bit.. As if it will set my mind at ease.

Pfft. How could that possibly bring me comfort? No, I need to lay eyes on my mate to be certain. As the thought consumes me, my knees buckle under a wave of intense lust, a sudden, overwhelming heat that steals my breath, leaking through my mate bond with Dani.

When I can collect myself, first I check on Ily and find him clinging to Costen, eyes shut tight and a flush tinting his cheeks. Obviously, I'm not the only one who felt that. Costen's barely staying upright, with Lia's help. Eram is kneeling, head hanging, and a groan echoing from his chest.

"Uhhh, are you okay?" One Orc asks, hesitantly stepping towards us. Only to be stopped by Tawson.

"They're fine, don't you remember what it's like when Luella shoves her arousal through the bond?" Tawson questions, laughter in his voice.

"I guess you can take that as confirmation that your mate is okay," Ward says with a hint of smugness, and a shot of fury pushes past the desire, and I'm moving before I know what's happening.

My body collides with the big bastard, and I tackle him into the wall. His spear clatters to the ground, and everyone else steps away from our little fight.

His fist smashes into my side with a heavy thud, and pain streaks through me from the impact. I pull back and return the hit, aiming for his kidney, only to snarl angrily when he blocks me.

"We don't have to do this!" Ward shouts, trying to hold me off, but I'm past reason.

The beastly male shoves me, giving himself space to move away from the wall. But I recover quickly and I'm on him again in seconds. The room becomes a blur of motion as we trade blows, the sounds of our fists colliding echoing around us. I don't care where we are; I just hope my pack stays out of trouble and doesn't get in the way.

Fur sprouts on my arms, and my hands shift into claws. My grin is manic and full of fire as I stare down at Ward. His face is bloody, and bruises are already beginning to form, but he does not look afraid of my Wolfish claws, and that only infuriates me more.

"What the fuck are you smiling at?" I snarl in his face.

"A good fucking fight," is all he replies with as he stands and his own hands shift.

Aww, fuck, he's a Shifter? Well, this fight just got a little more interesting. My grin grows into something bloodthirsty, and he matches my energy.

Our bodies collide as we rush at each other, slashing claws and furry limbs flying. Time seems meaningless as sweat drips down my chest, my fur growing matted with exertion.

Snarls and deep bassy growls reverberate through the room. My body crashes into the chairs we had occupied before, sending shards everywhere. I'm quick to regain my feet and crouch, ready for another attack by this big bastard.

Ward's shifted paws are massive. He must be some hefty animal, and I'm kind of curious to know what, but I'm not ready to stop the fight just yet. This is the perfect release of all the tension that's been gathering since Ily and I decided to make this fucking journey.

He circles me, looking for an opening that I will not give him. Movement in the corner of my eye draws his attention, and I chuff at the idiot for looking away. With quick, silent steps I rush him, tackling him mid-body and sending us careening into the rest of the chairs.

My furry fists slam into his chest and body. Ward's got his guard up, so I'm waiting for an opening before I go for his face. He brings his feet up, slipping them under my guard before sending my body flying and slamming into the wall with a painful thud.

All the air leaves me in a loud '*Ooof*' and finally exhaustion makes me sluggish. I think I'm ready to end this fight now.

Ward moves into my blurry vision, reaching a hand out to help me up. He's not such a bad male. I take it and let him pull me to my feet. A groan slips past my bloodied split lip; it soon turns into a chuckle when I meet Ward's eyes.

Before long, we've devolved into manic laughter. Tears sting the cuts on my face, but I relish the sensation. That was the best fight I've had in ages.

"Thank you," I slap Ward on the back as we take in the room.

"Yeah, you're welcome," he replies, sarcasm lacing his tone, but the bright grin on his bloodied face gives away his amusement. "That was actually quite good. Since I assume your pack will be here permanently, we'll have to do that again but in the training ring next time."

When his words sink in, my grin disappears, and my scowl returns with a ferocity that settles over me like a cloak. But before I can snap at him, another voice interrupts our moment.

"Uh, you done?" Eram snarks, arms

crossed and a scowl to rival my own plastered on his face. "We're all worried about Dani. I just fucking bonded her this morning. You don't get to claim all the bitter worry. Now, Ward, what *can* you tell us?" He switches his focus to the male beside me.

"Right." Ward sighs, his shoulders slump as he scratches the back of his head. "Yeah, so the King, Seren, has been searching for his fated mate for decades. After a while, he realized she wasn't just going to march herself into his castle and fall into his arms, so he started suppressing his instincts. He could better attend to the Omegas that arrive here freshly revealed. He didn't want to lose his head to every sweet scent that showed up, although I must admit, none of them ever scented as good as your mate. I always told him it was stupid to use that suppression rune; his true mate would smell better than anything, and he'd lose his head regardless, but he was determined to do it his way."

The rest of my pack and Tawson's approach our exhausted, swaying forms as Ward speaks. I tug his arm down as I sit on the ground with a wince. We don't need to stand for this conversation.

Ward sighs but follows me down. My pack clears a small space, kicking debris out of the way so they can sit as well. With a shrug, Tawson and the Orcs follow suit.

"I may be just a Beta, but I could scent Dani's sweetness the moment I stepped outside. When my eyes landed on her beauty dancing in the garden, I lost my ability to breathe. She's absolutely the most gorgeous creature I've ever seen. Legitimately breathtaking. And I know the King felt the same. I've never seen him so mesmerized by anything," Ward pauses, his eyes dazed as he re-watches that scene in his mind. I want to snarl, but he's not wrong. Dani is fucking magical, especially when she's laughing and carefree.

"There was no way I ever expected him to react as he did, though. When she got close enough to touch, I observed the exact moment his Alpha rose inside him. He went feral so fucking fast. All those suppressed instincts came rushing back to him in a second, and Seren went into rut."

"Fuck!" I shout, angry all over again. This means that posh fucker is knotting my Omega right now. His rut has likely affected her and pushed her body into a heat-like state so she can last as long as his rut does.

"Well," Lia claps her hands, the sound sharp and cutting in the silence that has blanketed the room, "looks like our new pack-mate is the fucking King of Saforia. I, for one, did *not* see that coming." The deranged female is grinning, completely delighted by this possibility.

"Does that mean we can get some rooms? I think I'd like to clean up my Alpha and tend to his wounds," Ily pipes in, watching me with heat and censure. The mix sends a confusing blend of instincts coursing through me. My Omega needs me, but he's also upset with us. I want to purr and growl simultaneously.

"They'll likely be a few days…" Eram says, his voice scathing, lip curling in distaste. "I guess we should settle in. It would be nice if I could be near my freshly bonded mate." The hint is heavy and obvious.

Hopefully, Ward doesn't block us again. I understand that he's just protecting his charge, doing his job, but can't he understand that the King just fucking stole our Omega? Doesn't he realize what that does to our Alpha instincts?

I'm going to have to bide my time until the King and I can have a proper conversation about where he stands in the hierarchy of our pack.

I crack my knuckles as I stand, wincing a little as the cuts over my fists reopen at the motion. Huffing out a tired breath, I swing my gaze to Ward and wait.

"Yes, fine, I'll have the maid show you to some rooms in the royal wing. I recognize your need to be close to her. *But* there will be guards posted outside his door. Seren will be protected in his current, mindless state. You will just have to wait to see your Omega." Ward is firm with his warning, and I nod, an angry scowl tugging on my scars.

"Fine."

CH. 15

Lianis

After the excitement of watching Hagon and Ward tumble around the sitting room, brawling, I'm pleased to be shown to a pack room. I was hoping they wouldn't try to separate us. Although I'm only bonded to Hagon now, I do not want to be separated from my Omega and pack-mates.

The space is luxurious beyond imagination. I thought Tawson's Keep was swanky, but this place is opulent. The small sitting room, with its cushioned couches sinking invitingly under the weight of a body and crackling fireplace, promises warmth and comfort. Beyond the threshold, a gigantic bed suggests comfortable rest for all of us, and the attached bathing room showcases an enormous tub that gleams under the light. The air hangs heavy with the scent of expensive soap.

I can't wait to sink into a bath. Maybe I'll be able to convince Ily to join me. We can use this opportunity to become more familiar with each other. I haven't spent any time alone with him yet. Hagon is a bit of an Omega hog.

As I walk past Ily, about to sink into one of the cushy couches, I snag his hand and tug him along with me into the bathing room. Kicking the door shut behind us, my arms wrap around Ilaris and I give him a squeeze, rubbing my face in his shaggy auburn hair. Sweet syrup and tart, juicy cherries make my head fuzzy with desire.

"Would you like to bathe with me?" I ask, even though I've already begun to disrobe him.

"Hmm...?" Ily's reply is a quiet hum before he shakes his head. "Y-yeah, a bath would be nice. Maybe it will distract me from the arousal Dani is basically shoving through the bond."

A wide grin flashes my petite fangs at him, earning a blushing smile. I am going to take full advantage of the desire bubbling in my Omega. He will not leave this room without my bond on his pretty tan skin.

"Is that so? Good. Now let me get the water heated. Maybe you can help me undress?" With Ily now standing nude in the warm room, my eyes drink their fill.

He's so pretty. Short and lean, his body is soft the way Omegas are supposed to be. However, beneath that softness, muscles flex and coil. He is also a little underfed, and that is something we'll be fixing now that we're not on the road.

Hesitantly, his hands reach for the ties on my tunic, the air thick with anticipation as he moves into my space. I lean down so he can reach. It's hard being the tallest one in the room. Ily's hands tremble a little, nerves making him even shyer than usual.

"Easy, Sweet Boy, you're doing a good job." I let the praise hover in the air between us.

His eyes move up to mine, filled with a sparkle of lust and uncertainty. Although the moment that '*good job*' sinks in he brightens and his hands stop trembling, unlacing me with confidence.

As soon as my top is loose enough, I shuck it off and toss it on the floor with Ily's clothing. His hands hover over my exposed skin, hesitant, but I'm not having that. I press his palms into my chest and encourage him to explore.

Ily peers up at me, a question in his eyes, asking if he's allowed. I think he's got his Alpha in his head stopping him from enjoying this, so I do what is necessary to put my Omega at ease.

Through my bond with Hagon, I yank on him, insisting he comes to us. The response I get back is pretty normal for the grouchy male. But I can sense that he's making his way here.

While I wait for the Alpha male, I turn my full focus back to Ilaris. "Okay, Sweet Boy, your Alpha is on his way. I need you to know that this is okay, though. You don't need him here when I can protect you just fine. But I understand your attachment to him. He is fantastic in bed," I add with a playful wink, working to set his nerves at ease.

"I… I know, it's just, I've been with Hagon alone for so long, it doesn't feel right that he isn't here with us. I know he can be… kind of an ass, but he's my ass." The adorable male defends his mate, and I cannot stop my bright grin at his words.

"You're right. But he's *our* ass now. Remember? He carries my bite as well. It's only fair that you are marked by me as well," I pause, thinking for a moment, my eyes roving over all the skin on display. "You don't have Costen's bite yet?"

"There just hasn't been time for us…" Ily replies with a sigh, eyes cast down. "I really want his mark on my body too. It's just been a little crazy."

Lifting his chin with my tail, I bring his

gaze to mine. He needs to see that I am telling the truth.

"That is okay, Ily. Costen understands it isn't because you don't want him. He's been there the whole time on this journey. I'm sure he knows it has been a harrowing adventure and that you haven't been purposely putting it off." The words are punctuated by the door slamming open and a grumpy, scarred Alpha struts in, followed by Costen.

"What are you doing with my mate?" Hagon grumbles at me, but there isn't any heat in the words, just playful ribbing.

Hmm... So he's accepting my presence now. This is a fortunate turn of events because we are not leaving this room without my claim on Ilaris. The pretty striped male behind him hesitantly steps towards the steaming bath where I stand with Ily. My mouth waters just watching him move. I can't wait to get that male under me.

"Where's Eram?" Stupidly, that's the first thing out of my mouth.

"He's pacing by the door. His anxiety over Dani's absence is giving me a headache, but he's fine," Hagon replies with a sour pinch to his lips. "He doesn't want anyone except Dani anyway, so he does not need to be here for this."

A curious hum is my response. He is highly attached to Dani, but because he is still part of the pack, we should include him in our bonding. It's funny how quickly my mind changes, but I'm growing fond of this pack thing.

Pushing Eram from my mind, I refocus on my pretty boy. Ilaris is slender and short, but it fits his body perfectly. All that gorgeous tanned skin on display before me is a buffet of delights. Those smoky grey eyes watch me with desire burning in their depths.

Even though he is slim, he still has the usual Omega padding. An Omega can never possess the same muscle mass as an Alpha, or even a Beta, but still, he's fit and mouthwatering. I'm sure Hagon has spent time training him, especially after his time in a cage. My pretty Omega needs to know he can fight, that he can protect himself if none of his Alphas are around.

At least having Costen around, I know my pretty Omega hasn't been all work and no play. The pale Alpha isn't much for fighting, but he has been wonderful at setting both Omegas at ease.

With a playful swat, I usher Ily towards the tub. Hagon and Costen relax against the vanity, intending to watch. I'm sure it won't take much for Pooki to join, but at least he's allowing me some time with Ily. And Costen will obey my will, whatever it is. He's such a good boy. A purr rumbles in my chest, and Ily's shoulders slowly relax.

My tail strokes over my Omega's round, biteable ass as he climbs over the edge of the tub, earning me an adorable squeak. I'm quick to join him in the warm water, not giving him any time to overthink.

Smoothing my hands over his shoulder, down his arms, over his chest and lower, I thrill at the chance to touch him as I've desired since the moment I scented Ily.

His hands land on my hips, less hesitant now that his mate is here. With a salacious grin, I urge him up to my breasts. They ache with the need to have his mouth nibble and lick over my pink skin and dusky nipples.

"Don't be shy, Sweet Boy. I plan to have your touch all over me before we're done here," I croon to him, my face nuzzles into his hair with a moan as Ily's scent strengthens with his arousal.

Using my tail, I grab the bar of soap and lather him up. My hands massage and press the soap over every inch of skin. Ilaris releases sweet little sounds as I dig into tense muscles. Slowly, he relaxes bit by bit until I have a puddle of sweet Omega, ready to play.

It will be better if we head to the giant pack bed, so I toss a look at Hagon and urge him to help by drying off our Sweet Boy. For once, the scarred Alpha doesn't complain, just does as I ask.

Hagon lifts Ily into his arms and carries him out to the bed. I follow close behind, with Costen trailing us. The big grump surprises me by placing Ily in the center and shuffling towards the headboard, leaving the panting Omega for me.

My grin turns feral as arousal floods my body. The need to have my Omega has reached a fever pitch, and if I don't have him under me in the next minute, I may turn as rut-brained as the King.

Costen settles near the foot of the bed, his arousal standing tall and dribbling pre-cum. The pretty male has already disrobed and sits patiently, watching Ily and me with fiery lust in his gaze.

Ily sits up, eyes wide as I climb over him, positioning my cunt over his long, pretty cock. He can't hide his moans from any of us, and I don't want him to either. Leaning in, I take his mouth in a messy, licking kiss. The need to have his taste on my tongue drives me to dominate this pretty male.

Rocking my hips over him, letting my wetness cover his length before I use my tail to lift him to my core. I hold him there, just the tip slipping in, letting him feel my heat. The tease is perfect, and Ily groans, fingers tightening over my hips. His forehead rests against my breast, lips nibbling when he's not distracted.

"Please, Lia?" His sweet voice is full of need. "Please, Alpha, I need you! Goddess, you're so hot and wet, I can't wait to feel your lock. I think I'll go mad waiting." His head rocks against me as he pleads and begs so prettily.

"Oh, Sweet Boy, you'll get my lock," I purr, "my claim, and my bite. We are not leaving this bed until I have your bond. Maybe we'll invite poor Costen to join us? Hmm? He's been waiting even longer than I have to make his mark on your pretty skin."

"Yes! Yes, please, I want that," Ily trills, excitement and desire have him shivering with need.

"But first," I start, and then let my weight slide down his length with a long drawn-out moan.

I've never locked anyone before, and I'm not totally sure of what I'm doing, but I know I'll hold back until I have Ilaris writhing beneath me. I'm determined to make sure he's well taken care of but out of his mind with lust and allows his Omega free rein.

This sweet boy will be mine.

CH. 16

Ilaris

Oh Goddess! My eyes roll back at the way Lia's cunt clutches me. The sensations are clouding my mind, and all I feel is a consuming lust. I need her to move, to ride me, to do something!

"Please! Lia, Alpha, please! I need more." My voice is high and whiny, but I can't help it. She's not moving! Why is she teasing me so much? I'm going to lose my fucking mind.

"Hmm, yes, that's what you want? What about this?" Her words are sultry, and I don't understand what she means until something strokes over my ass.

I forgot about her tail. The flexible tip feels soft as she smooths it between my cheeks.

It's covered in oil or something as it slips over my skin and brushes against my twitching hole. Oh, Goddess, yes! I need her. I need whatever my Alpha will give me.

The tip breaches me, and I release a long, low moan. My eyes slip shut, and I throw my head back as that flexible appendage pushes deeper into my body, searching for my O-spot. Between her hot, tight cunt and the tail, I'm in heaven. My desire for this female mirrors my need for Dani.

But, I don't let my worries about Dani tarnish this time with Lia. My Alpha deserves my full attention. Especially when she does *that*.

Her tail wriggles inside me, and the tip brushes over my O-spot, earning a shouted '*fuck!*' as my eyes roll back again. A devilish grin, showcasing bright teeth against rosy skin, sparks a burning desire within me, and my longing for her grows.

Finally, she rises over my stiffness too slowly. At the same time, her tail pumps in and out of my ass, sending my body writhing. Her hands grab my wrists and pin them down beside my head, trapping me under her blissful body.

The glide of her hot cunt over my cock is mind bending and I can no longer see or hear anything except my Alpha. Lia rides me faster and fucks my ass, matching her pace. My neck muscles strain as I cum for the first time. I'm an Omega. I can keep cumming until I'm too exhausted to move.

"Yes, that's a good boy. Give me all your sweet cherry cum. I want to be filthy with your spend by the time I lock you," Lia purrs, leaning forward to kiss me.

The new angle sends my legs twitching as her hips roll, forcing another orgasm out of me. My Alpha devours my groans, and her rich dowan scent pours down my throat, adding to my pleasure. She's irresistible, and I can't wait for the moment she allows me to eat her cunt. I bet her cum tastes as addictive as her scent.

After she forces three more orgasms out of me, our bodies meet in a slippery mess of cum and slick. She rolls us, so I'm on top. Her tail slips out of my ass, and I release an embarrassing cry of need. Why would she take that away from me?

That thought is fleeting as a new set of hands lands on my hips, caressing over my skin.

"Oh, Ily, you're so gorgeous. I can't wait to be knotted in this tight ass," Costen's sweet voice murmurs in my ear.

His cool, snowy scent reaches me through the thick pheromones of Lia and my sticky cum. It brings a bit of clarity to my hazy mind, and I remember Lia telling Costen to take my ass so they can lock and knot me together. Claiming me, marking me and making sure their mating bites will be deep and clear on my skin.

Lia already warmed up my ass for Costen, so he lines up with my puckered entrance and slowly pushes inside. There's always a pinch of pain, but it only adds flavor to the pleasure coursing through me.

As he breaches my body, my eyes roll back at the way Lia clenches over my hardness. Fuck. I won't survive this. But what a hell of a way to go.

My thoughts are fuzzy and full of sass, almost like I can hear Dani in my head. Smirking at me as she mutters dirty words in my mind.

Costen slides his thick cock into my ass right up to the knot, and I cry out at the fullness. He's perfect. Now if only he would move.

"Oh fuck, Ily, you're so tight. You feel so fucking good. Oh, Goddess, I'm not going to last. Lia why did you put on such a show before I could get inside our mate?" Costen rambles, voice thick with desire.

"Buck up, kitty cat. You're going to ride our Omega until he cums again and then we're going to lock and knot him together. You have your spot picked out?" Lia is speaking words, but they don't fully penetrate me through the fog of lust. What spot?

"Yes. Now hold on tight, Ily," Costen replies before pulling his hips back.

He wastes no more time and fucks me hard, riding me the way Lia told him to. The glide of his cock in my ass, the tight wrap of Lia's cunt, the way she kisses and nips my neck all have me crying out, an Omega whine slipping past my lips, begging them to give me what I need and sink their teeth into my skin. The desire to feel them inside my heart, the way I sense Hagon and Dani, is all-encompassing. I want my entire pack tied to me so I can wrap their love and care around me anytime I want.

Soon, my muscles clench, and my core tightens. More and more until it snaps and I'm thrown into euphoria. It doubles when Costen's knot breaches my ass and settles inside me, pressing on my O-spot nonstop. It only gets better when Lia forces my hips down, tight against her body, and then something amazing happens.

The muscles inside her cunt contract over my cock and then clench tighter and tighter until I swear my soul leaves my body. I don't know how much time passes as I revel in pure bliss. I've left the earth, floated up into the clouds and am somewhere beyond the earthly realms. It's so overwhelming that I only know she's claimed me because I can sense the connection forming inside me.

I come back to my body slowly, my muscles twitching and body writhing between my mates. Lia's licking at her mark over the front of my neck. My teeth are already deep in Lia's pink skin, right over her breast. Pulling back, I lick over the mark with satisfaction before turning to look for any part of Costen that I can reach.

He pushes his wrist in between mine and Lia's body and instinct takes over, sinking my bite into his arm before I have even thought to move. Costen bites the back of my neck, a pinch of pain accompanying the snowy white that lights up inside me. Their bonds flood my body, sending ecstasy through me until I cum again, and again.

Finally, my body lies limp between my two new mates. They readjust us until we're lying side-by-side, and I have one last thought before sleep takes me.

'I'm surprised that Hagon let them near me for so long without grumbling.'

My eyes blink open sleepily. I'm exhausted, but the little pops of emotion I'm getting from my new bonds send thrills of pure joy through me. Soft moonlight and the fading glow of the fireplace illuminate the dark room where Lia and Costen sleep peacefully. But... I don't see

Hagon or Eram anywhere.

My bond with Hagon, a feeling as familiar as my heartbeat, confirms his absence. My mate isn't too far away, but where the hell did those two go? I thought Ward placed guards at our doors to make sure we didn't go searching for Dani?

Panicked thoughts send me spiraling. Did they knock out the castle guards? Did they cause trouble and are now sitting in the dungeons? Have they barged in on the fucking King? I have a bad feeling that Hagon wouldn't hesitate to punch Seren in the face.

I figured Eram was more sophisticated than that, however... He only completed his bond with Dani yesterday, and not being with her must be difficult. Yeah, I bet he's let his Alpha take full rein, and Hagon would only encourage it.

Strong pink arms wrap around my shoulders, pale striped ones join Lia's. My new bonded mates must have felt my anxiety and woken up.

"Shit, I'm sorry. I didn't mean to wake you guys." The night's silence absorbs my whispered words. My shoulders hunch and my head drops, staring down at my naked lap.

"Easy, Sweet Boy. You did nothing wrong. It's understandable that you'd be missing Dani. I haven't even had much time to get to know her, and I miss her too," Lia purrs in my ear, hugging me tight.

"Yeah. It's okay, Ily, we've got you. And I'm sure as soon as the King's rut breaks we'll hear Dani before we see her," Costen adds, his own purr mixing with Lia's, creating a symphony of comfort that washes over me, soothing my tense muscles.

"Right, thank you both. But while I am missing my Omega, I'm more worried about where Hagon and Eram have disappeared to. Didn't you think it was too quiet in here? No Hagon grumbling away, or a pacing and muttering Eram?" I ask in a hushed tone.

My body may be relaxed now, but my mind has not stopped swirling. Those two have definitely gone and done something stupid. I just know it.

"Fuck." Lia sighs, head swiveling as she scans the room for either Alpha.

"Wait, what? I thought... Nope, you're right. They are both gone. I doubt they're taking a bath together either," Costen adds, staring down the short hall towards the bathing room.

The image he described sinks into my mind, and a snort of laughter explodes into the room as I imagine the two grumpy Alphas in the bath together. I could see them snapping and snarling, barely saying one word to each other as they washed.

Lia's rich, sultry laugh joins mine shortly before Costen's. Soon, the three of us cackle with laughter at that notion. I must remember to tell Dani when I see her again.

"Thank you for that, Pretty Kitty. We all needed a good laugh. Now," Lia sits up, "let's go find our missing pack and hope they haven't done anything stupid yet."

CH. 17

Eram

Watching and listening to my pack fool around was getting on my nerves. How can they relax and play while our little Omega is being hoarded away like a dragon? Fuck! I need to find her.

My fresh bond with Dani itches with the need to go to her. Fuck this. I'm going to find my mate. Those four can mess around all they want, but I'm not sitting around waiting for the King's rut to finish before I get to see Dani. I'm her mate! My scent is on her, in her, and he shouldn't see me as a threat. We're technically pack, so I *should* be able to join them.

Yeah, that's what I'm going to do. I can't wait anymore. My feet are already moving towards the enormous doors leading to the hall. I can follow our bond and it will lead me straight to her.

A big scarred palm lands on my shoulder stopping me. I turn towards Hagon with a muted snarl but he just smirks at my attempt at dominance.

"Yeah, yeah, I know you're stronger than me, but fuck off. I can't stay here while Dani is off with the King; I should be with her!" I whisper-shout at Hagon, not wanting to disturb the trio on the bed.

"Easy, Eram. I'm not stopping you. I want to help. Dani should be with us. Even the fucking King, since technically he's pack now," Hagon mutters, with a sour pinch to his lips.

We all felt it when their bond snapped into place. When Seren sank his teeth into our mate. He'll have to join our pack bond once they're done for us to feel him properly. Right now he's faint, through Dani's connection to us.

My lips form a grim line as we both pull the doors open. I know Ward set guards on our doors, but maybe I can talk my way around them? Instead, the hallway is dark and silent. Not even the tiniest critter stirs.

Hagon meets my eyes with a shrug, then we close the doors to our room and set out down the hall, following the pulsing, lust-drenched mate bond we have with Dani. I know Seren is in rut and we'll find Dani in a sort of mock heat. But the thought of that strange Alpha's hands on my mate has my instincts snarling. We only just completed our bond yesterday, and a fresh bond requires that we stay near each other. Skin-to-skin is even better, but I was robbed of my time with her.

It doesn't take us long to find the King's quarters. Ward was kind enough to keep us close, knowing our Alphas would revolt if he truly tried to stop us or push us away from our Pixie. But here is where we finally see life in this stone mausoleum. I'd think in a place this size, there'd be maids and cleaners and other workers all over, but I guess they get the night off like the rest of the world. Perhaps Ward was trying to protect Seren by limiting how many beings might anger him, considering the King's current state.

While in rut, he's going to be overprotective of his 'den' and his mate. Hopefully, since Dani has our scent on her, he will accept us in his space.

I meet Hagon's eyes as we come to a stop around the corner to the King's quarters. "There are guards. Do we just... walk through like we belong? Or do we fight them for the right to approach our mate?" The question, though whispered, reverberates through the ancient marble and stone, its sound amplified to a shout.

"Yep. If they don't let us through," Hagon shrugs, but there's a gleam of violence in his eyes, "I will make them."

A snort of laughter escapes me, and I grin at my grumpy Lead Alpha. I was wary of Hagon for a long time after we first met, but I'm starting to appreciate his gruff nature.

Straightening my shoulders, we march towards the richly lit hall. I'm careful not to make eye contact. I have a feeling they would take that as a reason to speak to me, and I really don't want to waste more time. My mate is waiting for me.

We do not make it far before both guards step forward, spears crossed and blocking our path.

"Halt! This is the King's quarters, what right do you have to approach?" One male bellows at us. He's young, untried and nervous.

"Our mate is here, and you will not stop us from joining her." Hagon's voice comes out in a growl, low and rumbling. He is not an Alpha anyone would want to cross right now.

"Sir, I-I can't let you in. I have orders," the young one stutters out, eyes flicking to his companion, as if seeking help.

But the other guard appears bored and uncaring, not giving the young male any support. I roll my eyes. Why would the King employ such incompetent protection? That seems like a poor choice and poor training. I feel like Ward should know better.

"The *King*," Hagon snarls the word with fury, "has bitten and bonded our mate. And do you know what that means?" The question hangs in the air as the young male frowns and tries to figure out what Hagon is hinting at.

"It *means* he's part of our pack now." I'm too impatient to wait for the male to understand. "Now, get out of our way so we can join our Omega and pack-mate." I may not be as grumpy as my Lead Alpha, but I'm far past my limit, and I need to get in there and lay eyes on my Pixie.

The young Alpha swallows hard, eyes searching both Hagon and me before he tosses one more angry look at the other guard. His shoulders slump, and he steps back.

"Yeah, okay. Just... if Ward or the King asks, we tried. I... I don't want to lose my job. But, pack and Omega... That's sacred and I won't stand in the way."

Hmm... This young male may be better than I expected. It's the other guard now that has my scrutiny. He should not be here. His lazy, uncaring demeanor means my new pack-mate and Pixie could be in danger. This male would not have stopped us if the young one hadn't stepped forward.

I make a note to discuss it with Ward when the King comes out of rut.

Marching past the guards, Hagon and I head straight for the ornate doors, lined with a shimmery gold around the edges. My bond with Dani pulses, pulling me towards that room.

Breathe, I remind myself, and regret it instantly. Now I understand why the guards are so far from these doors. The scent of Alpha musk, arousal and heat cloud my mind with that deep inhale.

Oh fuck. Is this going to throw us into a rut too? I shake off the question and push the doors open. I need to be in there.

The cloud of scents puffs around us as we close the doors again. Seren's room is set up like ours, but it is much bigger and more ostentatious. He is a king though, so it makes sense.

A bone-chilling snarl echoes through the room, drawing my gaze to the gauzy canopy around the circular bed, past the luxurious couches and fireplace.

I don't bother taking in the rest of the chamber; my cock is hard and my mind is set on seeing my Omega.

"Don't you snarl at my mates." A slap and Dani's beautiful voice scolds the King. "Now, are you going to behave? I'll make you if I have to, don't test me!"

Hagon is grinning as big as I am. That's our precious Omega. Even in a mock heat, she's fierce and commanding. Goddess, I love her so much.

"Now, you two, stop standing there staring like a couple of lumps, and get naked! This may not be a true heat, but I fucking need you both. Get in here and don't mind the growly Fae." Dani takes control and before she's finished talking both Hagon and I are nude, striding towards the bed.

"I missed you, mate," I growl as I throw back the gauzy curtain and climb into the nest-like bed.

"I need you!" she cries, turning and presenting her dripping slit to me.

All the blood in my body goes straight to my cock, and I don't even acknowledge the snarling Winter Fae by Dani's head. He's all bark after being scolded by his mate.

A delighted sigh gusts from me as I slide deep inside my Pixie. She's so slick and covered in cum that I plow into her with no resistance right to my knot. Her wild moans only cloud my head further.

Fuck. I needed this. *Needed her*.

"Hagon, feed me your cock and cum. Now!" Dani demands, turning her flushed face towards our scarred Wolf.

For the first time, Hagon has nothing to say. He just grins and presents his cock to her pouty lips.

Seren snarls again but makes no move towards either of us. That might have something to do with Dani's hand clutching his manhood, though. She's multitasking like a pro, and I'm so proud of her.

"Fuck, Dani, my beauty. Fuck, you feel so good. Slick and hot, ready for my knot." The words tumble from my mouth, and I can't stop it.

The faster my hips move, slapping into her pretty pink ass, the more filth spews from my lips. But my devious little Pixie loves it. Her cunt clenches beautifully every time I speak.

"My gorgeous mate, taking all of her Alphas so perfectly. What a good girl," I coo sweetly, even as I wreck her with harsh thrusts. "You're going to take my knot, let me plug you and fill you past full. Breed your sweet pussy. My Goddess."

Yielding to my desire, I push my knot into her swiftly, catching her by surprise. Enjoying the muffled moans as she screams her pleasure into Hagon's cock. Clearly, I caught him by surprise too.

The Wolf groans as he unloads in her tight throat, feeding her precisely what she desires. As soon as Hagon is done, she shoves off him and swallows down Seren's length. After how long she has been working him, the Alpha cums instantly. Feeding our mate potent Alpha seed.

I don't think Dani has had a proper heat yet, and this mock one may push her closer to the edge. Especially if we continually give her our cum. It should bring on her true heat fairly quickly.

My knot settles inside her after my mind practically melts out my ears from how hard I cum. Turning us onto our sides carefully, I settle us down to rest. Seren curls up against her front, and Hagon lays his head on her belly.

This is much better. There's no way I could have slept the night away from my Pixie. Nuzzling my face into her short messy hair, I heave a delighted sigh and close my eyes.

CH. 18

Dani

A little squeak escapes me as I wake to Eram's knot releasing. The gush of fluid always feels a little strange, but this hazy mock heat has me thinking it's the best scent in the world. My hands are shoving Eram's seed back into me before I know I'm moving.

Hagon rumbles, not opening his eyes, as I jostle him. Forgetting that he'd wrapped himself around my legs after I fell asleep last night.

Once I am free of the knot, Seren yanks me from Eram's embrace, ignoring the low sleepy growl from both my Alphas. My King is a greedy male, which shouldn't surprise me, but he's going to have to learn how to share. I will not give him more attention than the rest of my pack.

"Seren! Quit hogging me!" I whisper loudly at my newest mate as he covers me with his enormous body. The way he wraps himself around me is protective and dominant, and I won't lie and say I hate it. Because I really, *really* love it. But I'll make sure Seren earns that truth.

"Mine," Seren purrs in my ear, his chest vibrating against me. The sound sinks into my entire body, turning me into a melty puddle of Omega. It's so unfair that all my Alphas can turn me into such a weak female with one sound.

"King. You need to behave! Those are my mates too," I try again, my voice soft. Stroking my hands over his back muscles, I work to soothe my newest Alpha.

It's a challenge though, because the mock heat is fogging my mind again, urging me to sink into his embrace. To relish what he's offering me. I nuzzle my face against his neck, over my fresh claim on his skin.

Seren purrs in response and scent marks my hair, face and anywhere else he can reach. I am *much* shorter than he is, so it isn't much. A snort of laughter bursts from me when he bodily drags me up the bed and begins nuzzling, nipping and kissing my chest, stomach and legs.

My mad cackling wakes the other two Alphas, and they surround us, adding their happy purrs to the mix. Even while I'm laughing my head off because it tickles, I'm also melting into a puddle of delighted Omega.

When Seren switches from playful to sensual, my giggles trail off into moans as his lips and tongue play over my pussy. One taste of my fragrant slick and he growls ravenously, diving into my cunt as deeply as he can, not caring one bit that my other Alphas seed is still leaking from me.

Hagon takes advantage of the King's distraction and leans in to nip and bite at my peaked nipples. Eram's hand grabs my chin, turning me towards his lips. I sink into the dominant kiss and let my Alphas pleasure me beyond anything I've ever known. The only things missing are my Omega and my other two Alphas.

With that, I reach for my bonds with Ily and Costen, finding them sleeping. Pleasant dreams must have a hold of them because their end of the bond is soft and full of joy. I can faintly feel Lia through Ily, and a burst of joy flows through me. I need Lia's mark on my skin too.

Our pack is almost complete; I can feel it. I don't know how I know that, but it's merely a slight tickle within my mind. Something in my gut is pushing me towards Ward, too. I don't know if he's just supposed to be a friend or if he's meant for us, but that's something to figure out later.

I tug on my bonds and send a wave of urgency, of need, to my mates, hoping they get the hint and join us. Seren's rut may last a few days, and I refuse to go that long without my whole pack. They belong here too.

Now I can return my focus to my males. I let myself soften into their embrace and just feel. The sensations fill my body and mind. Their hands caress me; their mouths a flurry of kisses and nips, tongues teasing and thrilling, and the heady mix of male scents is almost overwhelming.

They blend together, creating a mouthwatering dreamy haze, and I let my mind sink into the mock heat. I rock my hips, urging Seren to stop licking and start fucking me. But these males are determined to force me to take only what they give.

Seren's hands clamp down on my hips, and he increases his efforts to make me cum. Hagon pinches and tugs on my nipples, the bite of pain adding to the growing coil of bliss in my stomach.

Tingles spread through my body, the tightness in my gut ready to snap at any second, but it's only when Eram pulls back from devouring my lips and whispers in my ear,

"Let go, sweet Pixie. Let us revel in your pleasure. Give us your slick and scream your release to the heavens, telling everyone in this castle you are ours."

I had no idea that Eram had it in him to murmur sweet, filthy words to me. But it's exactly what I needed, and my orgasm hits me like a runaway horse. My mouth opens in a soundless scream as pleasure washes over me. Maybe it isn't soundless; I just can't hear anything. My eyes roll back in my head, and I swear I see the Goddess as tremors wrack my frame.

Never in my life did I think it was possible to cum that hard, but I guess it makes sense. The Goddess made fated mates to fit together perfectly, and this seems like a reward for finding each other.

As sound slowly comes back to me, I open my eyes, not realizing I had closed them. Ily's face comes into view, looking down on me with heat burning in his gaze.

"That was the most beautiful thing I've ever seen, mate." His voice is a sweet song to my ears, and his face brightens me more than any sunshine ever could.

"Ily! You're here! Are Costen and Lia with you?" Excitement laces my voice, but the words are a little shaky as I come down from that life-changing orgasm.

"Here, Pix! As soon as I felt you through our bond, I was up and moving. If my mate needs me, I'll always be there." Costen's cheerful words draw my attention towards the far side of the bed. My Sweet Snow stands nearly nude beside a robe-clad Lia.

As soon as my eyes land on the Succubus, she sheds the robe, standing tall and nude, pink skin glistening in the low light.

"Oh, don't worry your pretty little head, I wouldn't miss this for the world, Omega." Her voice is a sultry rolling purr, and it instantly melts me into the hands of my Alphas surrounding me.

Hagon grins at Ily and Costen. Eram barely acknowledges them, his gaze planted firmly on me, and Seren snarls at the newcomers, but there isn't much heat to it. My newest Alpha is coming to terms with his new pack life.

"Mine." The King is still deep in his rut, but at least he can acknowledge the scent of pack. If anyone else entered this room, there's a high chance that he would tear them apart.

"Yes, big guy. I am yours. But, I'm also theirs. You have to share a little more, okay?" I reach down and smooth a hand over Seren's messy hair. His blown out, dark eyes focus on my face. As soon as I touch him, he releases a deep purr and nuzzles into my touch.

"Okay, so Seren will be staying with me, but everyone, into the nest. Lia, get over here and touch me. I need your mark on my skin, please." I turn my question towards the statuesque beauty waiting patiently for instruction.

"Yes, ma'am." She grins, her sharp little fangs winking at me. I can't wait to feel this sarcastic, protective Alpha alongside the rest of my mates.

The bed grows crowded, but I wouldn't have it any other way. The King clings to my legs, staring down the others as if he thinks they will displace him. It's only Ilaris that Seren softens for. But he doesn't seem interested in mating my Omega, only giving him the deference that he deserves as one of the rarest designations.

That move is so endearing to me that I throw myself at the Alpha, knowing he will catch me. Seren's arms wrap around my slick skin, and purrs vibrate through my body as he kisses and nips any part of me that he can reach.

A soft, yet muscular body molds to my back, nuzzling into my neck. The strong scent of dowan reaches me through the medley of our pack and my arousal. Lia's breasts press into me, and the sensation sends a thrill shooting through me to my core.

The feeling of her against me is exciting in a way I'm growing to love. My chest rumbles with a sweet Omega purr that soothes all the Alphas around me. Seren doesn't even snap at Lia. He gives her a bit of side-eye but ultimately returns his attention to my pink skin.

Lia's pink complements my own, a slightly different shade against me. My head grows fuzzier as the scents of my whole pack send my mind spinning into the mock heat. I try to keep my focus because I want to be present when Lia marks me.

"Lia, Alpha, please! I'm growing hazy, and I want to remember your claim on my skin," I plead with her and Seren to fuck me. I need my mates, all of them. My core is empty and twitching, aching for a thick knot.

"Anything for you, sweet Pixie," Lia purrs in my ear.

I jump as something slender slicks up my side and around to my clit. When I peer down, I remember that Lia has a tail. Oh, fuck. I can't wait to feel it inside me!

"Now, King, sit our mate on that thick cock and let me play with her ass." The Succubus directs the rut-brained Seren, and, surprisingly, he complies. I did not expect him to accede so easily.

It isn't long before I'm stuffed full of Seren while Lia's tail plays with my clit a little longer, gathering slick before she moves down to my ass. Her fingers run over my skin, and she takes two handfuls of my breasts before focusing her touch on my peaked nipples.

I'm so distracted by her motions that I barely notice when her tail breaches my ass and slips inside far too easily. My moans echo loudly through the room, matched by Ily's as Costen and Hagon fuck him. Eram sits against the headboard watching me with heated eyes as he strokes his cock.

"Don't worry about me, pretty mate. Focus on your Alphas. I am enjoying the show." Eram smirks at me, and I see the truth in his deep brown eyes. He truly likes to watch.

Lia's tail strikes something phenomenal in my ass and Seren fucks up into me hard, rattling my brain, ripping my attention back to the two playing with my body.

"Oh, fuck!" I shout to the roof, leaning my head back against Lia.

The Alpha is careful of my delicate wings, even though I've told them they're stronger than they look. But she nibbles on my neck, her fangs scraping over my skin, sending shivers down my spine.

"Yes! Bite, bite please, Alpha!" The words tumble from my mouth.

Lia isn't one to make me wait, and as her tail fucks into me harder and Seren's knot slowly sinks into my cunt, her teeth punch through my pink skin and her bond slides into place alongside the rest of my pack. She presses her wrist against my mouth, and I sink my claim into her skin.

CH. 19

Costen

Joy flows through our bonds as Lia grows stronger in our metaphysical link. Dani is fuck-drunk, but delight weaves through the arousal and lust she continually pushes through our bonds.

Our family is growing, and I didn't know I could be this happy. I love my Pixie, but I'm growing to love Ily, Hagon, Lia and even prickly Eram. I don't know Seren very well yet, but as soon as his rut passes I'm sure he'll fit in as he's supposed to.

Snuggling tighter against Ily's back, I settle in for a nap knowing Seren's rut will keep Dani in a state of mock heat until it naturally passes. Ily will likely sink into the same state.

The Alpha's powerful rut pheromones will compel an Omega to participate in the rut; it's a biological imperative. The relationship between Alphas and Omegas is one of perfect harmony, a delicate dance of give and take where they constantly circle and react to each other's subtle shifts in mood and behavior.

I am stunned that I remember all of that. I read those words in a book once. A cluster member had violently hurled it at me. He'd screamed I needed relationship instructions, and they've seared themselves into my memory. I reread that book countless times, the worn pages a testament to my longing for a partner who would cherish me.

The Goddess must have heard my prayers because she sent me to Dani, my gorgeous Pix. Running into her was fate pushing me towards the life I desired. Now, I couldn't imagine living without my Pix.

The King's rut lasts four days. Four exhausting yet thrilling days where our entire pack stayed in the King's quarters, tending to each other and bonding deeper than I thought possible. Although Seren and Eram kept their focus on our pretty Pixie, the rest of us played with each other. The touch of many hands, lips and teeth was thrilling, a symphony of sensations.

Lia and I solidified our growing relationship even more while she rode my cock and called me a good kitty.

Those words will forever send a shudder of delight through my body, arrowing down to my core and plumping my cock. I was captivated by the beauty of the Alpha female's dominance as she fucked me with her flexible tail.

Throughout this time she played with the possibility of taking a knot. But she didn't force it, concentrating more on the Omegas. Which is fine; that lock of hers had me losing my Goddess-damned mind. Especially when she used her tail to squeeze my knot.

On day four, I rouse to pale sunlight filtering in through the balcony windows. My pack slumbering, scattered around me. Exhausted and covered with bodily fluids, we look a mess. But I've never seen a more beautiful group of beings.

Dani lies on her stomach, half over Seren and half over Eram. Ily's hand clutches Dani's ankle, Lia wraps her tail around Dani's wrist, and the rest of my Alpha female nestles between Hagon and Ily.

I'm cuddling Seren, with an arm thrown over his big pale body so I could touch Dani as well. The King doesn't seem to mind being my little spoon; it's nice. But, I'm awake now, and I have a feeling that my Omegas will want to wash after four days of fucking constantly.

Strolling through the King's quarters, I peek behind closed doors until I find the bathing room. The tub is massive, pack-sized, and chiseled from pretty, sparkling marble. The Elves use the same system. I wonder if that's the first thing the Elves have traded. That would be popular with everyone.

The tub fills with steamy hot water, and I rifle through the baskets along the edge. I open each container and take a sniff, looking for the right scent for my Pixie and Wolf. Once I've pulled out a couple, I set them aside and search for bath sheets to dry my mates after they are clean.

I'm just setting those aside on the countertop when the half-open door swings the rest of the way.

"Sweet Snow, what'r you doing?" Dani mumbles, rubbing her eyes as she shuffles into my arms.

My Pixie isn't awake yet, but she sensed my absence and came to find me. That sends a burst of love exploding throughout me. Dani's eyes widen when she feels it slam into her through our bond. She stares up at me, her bright green beauties meeting mine.

"Oh, Costen. I love you." Her voice is breathy and full of emotion as she thumps into my body, arms wrapping around me.

"I love you more than the sun and moon. More than snowy mountains and sunny forests. More than I thought one being could love another. There was none before you, and there will be none after. You are my everything, Dani." I don't mean to unload all that onto her, but she isn't offended. If anything, she clutches me tighter, her face nuzzling into my bare skin.

"You're perfect, Costen. My Sweet Snow. You always take care of me exactly the way I need. I don't know how I got along before you, and I know nothing would ever be the same if you were gone," she says, each word thick with emotion, "don't leave me, please." Whispering the last, almost inaudible, but my cat lends me his excellent hearing so I can catch everything my Pixie says and does.

"You two are so sappy. I love it!" Ily's cheerful voice cuts through our moment, pulling both Dani and me out of our embrace. "Sorry... But, I really would like to clean off days of crusted cum and slick... Soooo... is there room in that bath for me?" Ily's cheeks burn red, and he grows hesitant.

"Of course, Ilaris. You are just as important to me as Dani! I prepared the bath with both of you in mind. You deserve every luxury, just the same." I grin and open my arms to my male Omega.

He came in so bright and brave, but the demons haunting him sank their talons into his mind, and he hunched in on himself. But I will not have that.

Ilaris slams into my chest, his breath hitching. Dani brackets his back and we both clutch his slouched form, pushing our care and affection through the bond, inundating Ily with love and happiness.

His shoulders straighten, and he rises tall once again. Before pulling away, he rubs his cheeks against my chest, his scent joining Dani's on my skin. I don't want to wash it away, but all of us are disgusting.

"Come on, my sweet Omegas. Into the bath. Let me wash both of you, tend to your aches and care for your bodies and minds." I urge them both into the steaming water.

"You're joining us in the water, right?" Ily asks shyly.

"Of course!"

None of us bothered to dress for the walk from the bedroom to the tub, so we all slip into the bath. Both Omegas sigh in unison. They share a brief gaze, then giggles burst free.

There's the happiness that's been a constant background in our mate bond. Both of them are sweet and bubbly. Their scents intensify in the bathing room as they wash the layers of Alpha cum from their skin.

Armed with a washrag, I soap it up and tend to both Omegas, one at a time lapping up their praise and sighs of delight. While also ensuring each mate knows they are perfect the way they are.

Our pack meanders into the bathing room, interrupting our peaceful moment in the tub. The King leading the way, brows furrowed and a slight pout on his lips. I think he's piecing together everything that landed us all in this position.

I feel on edge just sharing a room with King Seren, the ruler of Saforia. My hands shake a little, but I turn my full focus onto my mates so I can finish cleaning them.

"Well done, Costen!" Hagon's booming voice is loud following the soft conversation between the Omegas and me. "I'm sure those two desperately needed to be clean after four days of rutting and mock heat." A bright-eyed grin accompanies his laughter as he finishes.

Hagon's approval has warmth flush my cheeks and a shy grin tug my lips up. I don't know why I get flustered whenever he praises me. But it means so much to me. I enjoy pleasing my Lead Alpha.

That thought has me pausing, eyes wide and staring between Hagon and the King. Is Hagon still our Lead? The King has more dominance... doesn't he? I mean... he's the leader of our entire land.

I spin back to my Omegas and try to stop the shock from seeping through the bond. I don't want Hagon to know; he's so happy with me right now.

"The rest of you better get in here. Everyone that was in that nest seriously needs to be clean." Dani's bright voice cuts through my worried thoughts.

"Yes, my Queen," Seren's deep silken voice replies.

As soon as the Q word comes out of his mouth, I have a feeling that my sweet Pixie would revolt. It brings a grin to my lips, and I hide it in Ily's hair. My lips curl into a smile as I envision the hilarious chaos about to unfold. My Dani will not want to acknowledge that she's technically the Queen of Saforia now.

"EXCUSE ME?" Her shriek is painful as it echoes off the tile and stone. Her eyes are wider than I've ever seen them, almost popping out of her head. Those iridescent wings flutter madly, splashing water everywhere before she moves to stand out of the bath.

Yeah, I don't think Dani will accept that title readily.

CH. 20

Dani

What the actual fuck is this male on about? Queen? Me? HA! He just doesn't know me yet. If he did, Seren would never call me Queen. I'm about to rip this male a new one. We still haven't had a chance to fully explain to him how badly he's already fucked up in my eyes.

I can't be Queen. This land is falling into darkness and despair. The number of horror stories I've heard about Omega abuse is chilling, and the King has done nothing about it. Plus, he has to be aware of the bullshit God that wants to steal mine and my sister's powers.

On that note, why the hell haven't my powers revealed yet? I've mated Eram and now my newest male. Bassanai said my magic was already breaking through, but I have seen nothing yet, and we've been in some pretty dire fights since I left Pekayan.

All I've felt is my normal amount of excitement for bloodshed and a deep bubbling pit of rage inside me. But that's always been there. I feel an urgent need to avenge all those too weak to protect themselves. That and a serious devotion to my growing pack. I need them more than I need air to breathe. They are my everything, and I will fucking destroy anything that threatens my family.

I still need to get Jerrik back for murdering my parents. That slimy fuck doesn't seem to want to stay dead. It shouldn't surprise me that he's teamed up with Nyurel to capture me and attempt to steal Luella. If that mess of a Beta thinks he can handle my sister, take her from those Elites and live… well… I always knew he was a fucking idiot.

It takes a moment to realize I've been lost in my head and the entire bathing room is silent except for the light splash of water as Costen continues to dote on Ily. Right, I shrieked in a pitch so high it hurt even my ears.

"Yeah… I'm no fucking Queen." I focus on Seren's icy blue eyes. "Just because we're mated doesn't make me a Queen! I mean… in that case,

Lia could be Queen!" I don't mean to put my female Alpha on the spot, but I should have known that she'd play it up.

"Oh. Yes. I could definitely be a Queen. My horns would hold a crown perfectly! I think a shiny gold headpiece would look amazing against my purple hair and pink skin, don't you?" she drawls, her voice sultry and warm as she turns to me.

"Hmm… Yeah, I could see gold looking quite fetching against your pretty colors," I return with a smirk.

"No! I am not even mated to the Succubus!" Seren protests, throwing his hands in the air. "Not that you wouldn't make a successful Queen, but Dani is mine. She's the perfect Queen. Sweet and strong, fierce and deadly. It's the perfect combination to help rule our people." His words are actually quite lovely, but he doesn't even *know* me.

How can he know that I'm everything he thinks? I mean, I am, but how does he know that? We've barely had a single conversation before his rut took him. We must now find a way to get along, and we still have some crucial discussions ahead. *Not* about me being a Queen though.

"Yes, you have a point, Frosty." Lia cocks her head as she watches my frustration bubble up.

"Frosty? Excuse me?" Seren yelps as he whips his head to the smirking Succubus.

My Alpha Female is so good at getting under a male's skin. I love the way she taunts Hagon, and now Seren will join my grumpy Wolf in glaring at the female every time she opens her mouth.

"Yeah, Frosty! Since you're a Winter Fae and all. Plus, we're pack, I will not call you King." Lia curls her lip at the word 'King' as if she can't stand the fact that he's our leader.

"I think it has a nice ring to it," I pipe in, feeling a desperate need to draw focus away from the whole 'Queen' thing.

"Not you too! My sweet Pixie? Why would you join this female in taunting me?" Seren attempts a playful pout, but it doesn't suit his strict visage. I can tell he has had little reason to laugh or smile in many years.

Well, my pack of misfits will change that! If we have to live in this castle, then I'm going to make sure I have fun. This whole place is a little cold and lacking, but we're here to fix that. The King will learn to laugh freely again.

"Well," I clap my hands, the sharp sound cutting through Seren's glare, "I think I'm clean enough—where can we find some food around here?"

My question has Ily and Costen joining me at the edge of the tub. The rest of our Alphas need to clean themselves before they join us. That's fine; it'll give me a chance to go out and explore this vast stone monstrosity. Plus, maybe we'll run into Ward and I can hassle the male out of his stoic stare.

Costen and Ily trail behind, bath sheets haphazardly wrapped around them, a stark contrast to my joyous, uninhibited nakedness as I stride through the room. My wings flutter and dance, a light and cheerful rhythm matching my cheerful mood. It could be from the almost weeklong fuck-fest. I feel especially mischievous today.

Throwing open the closet, I rifle through Seren's clothing, looking for something I can toss on that won't interfere with my wings. I do not know where my clothes got to, and I know I left the rest of my stuff at Luella's, so I'll have to make something for the short-term. Finding the seamstress in this place is essential. Hopefully, she'll allow me to use her space so I can sew something pretty out of Lia's gift.

A long tunic with ties that go all the way to the waist catches my eye, and I figure it will work if worn backward. Not the most stylish item, but we can undo the ties to fit my wings through before re-stringing the top so it doesn't fall off my chest.

While I'm digging, I snag a few things for my mates and toss them at Ily and Costen, who are just standing there watching me in silence. My eyes roll at their helpfulness, but I just find it amusing. They're still treating Seren like the King and not like a fellow pack-mate.

"C'mon, get dressed! I'm hungry, and I'm going to venture through this dizzying place in search of food whether you join me or not." My words have them hurrying to slip the clothing on.

The trousers fit Costen well, while they're much too big on Ily. Hmm… I stare at the problem with a critical eye before nodding to myself.

"Wait there, Ily, I've got an idea!" I shout as I flutter around the room searching for something I can use. Finally, I settle on one of the drape ties. This will make a fancy little belt for my Omega, at least until we can get him some proper clothing, too.

With quick work, I have his trousers cinched tight. All the while, both mates watch me with a curious tilt to their heads, but they don't interrupt. It brings a grin to my face. My adorable mates already know that once I've set my mind to something, I'm doing it. Nothing is going to stop me.

"Perfect! Okay, put your shirt on and let's go!" I chirp. The idea of wandering through this place has me bouncing with excitement. I wonder if there's secret doors, tunnels and hidden rooms! It's a castle… isn't there a rule or something that castles *have* to have secrets? Oooo, I hope this place has a dungeon. I'm so curious to know what an actual dungeon looks like! I don't count Jerrik's prison. Although it was pretty dank, dark and creepy. But I don't remember seeing anything like in the stories. No torture racks, rusty and stained with age, nor other strange devices were visible.

Shaking off my odd thoughts, I grab each male by the hand and drag them towards the big doors leading out to the hall. Ily chuckles as I release them both to put my full weight behind the heavy oak. Footsteps sound from the bathing room, and urgency pushes me to yank it the rest of the way and slip out. My responsible Alphas will most definitely stop me from exploring. I know they'll want to talk about our changing lives, but right now I'm just not in the mood to sit and chat. So out I slip, Ily and Costen close behind me.

Since I'm peering back at Costen as he closes the door, I slam into a large muscular wall.

"Oof! Whoa! What?" I ramble out as thick hands steady me.

My gaze trails up from feet to head. Lingering over the bulge in his pants and the vein pulsing in Ward's forehead.

"Where do you think you're going?" Ward's deep voice rumbles through his hold on me, sending a pleasant shiver up my spine.

"We're going to find the kitchens. I'm hungry," I state as I attempt to wiggle out of his grip on my shoulders.

"Uh huh... Why didn't the King just summon breakfast? There's really no need for the three of you to go wandering. You're more likely to get lost than find the kitchens. Plus, Cook really would shoo you out with a wooden spoon. She's fiercely protective of her domain," the big guard replies, skepticism heavy in his every word.

It makes me want to throttle the male for ruining my fun. If I don't get past him, the rest of my pack will soon catch up to us. My mind races, flying through suggestions until I pause on one with a quiet snicker.

This feels like a very naughty thing to do, and the thrill of being able to mess with Ward has me giddy. Letting my shoulder go loose and my wings relax, I drop suddenly, letting his hold keep the loose shirt I'm wearing slip over my arms and wings.

I pop back up a few feet in front of him, now nude and cackling like a madwoman. My wings flutter wildly, and I let them pick me up off my feet to hover in front of Ward with a mischievous grin.

"Dani! What are you doing?" The exclamation doesn't come from the male slowly turning beet red before me. Seren's voice sounds from the doorway we'd attempted to escape.

"Oh, nothing really. Just playing with your guard and trying to find some breakfast," I reply casually, as if I'm not flying naked in the castle hall.

A weary sigh falls from Hagon's lips while Lia laughs as madly as I'd been just a few moments ago. I'm so glad she's part of my pack; she fully supports my impish behavior. I just know I'll be able to get her to help me plan some fun jokes on our mates.

CH. 21

Seren

What is happening right now? Why is my mate flying naked in the castle halls? What is Ward doing with her clothing? Why was she only wearing one of my shirts? My inner Alpha purrs loudly at that last thought. My mate was wearing our clothing, our scent.

"Dani, mate, pretty Pixie, will you please come back to our room? I will have someone bring some appropriate clothing for you." My voice sounds as tired as I feel.

My rut persisted for four days, and the arrival of my new pack unleashed feral carnality. I'm very pleased that I didn't snap at any of them... At least I don't think I did. All of us emerged from this rut unscathed.

I would love to sleep for at least a few more hours, but that won't happen unless my new mate is in my arms. Watching her now, I doubt she's tired. Pixies are famously energetic; however, seeing it so vividly is something else entirely.

"I could use some clothing, but I don't think I want to go back in the room. I'm positive that if I do, I may not get the chance to wander the halls for some time," Dani muses, a slow smirk spreading across her face, her eyes crinkling at the corners. "Although... Ugh, fine. We all need to have some serious conversations. But you'd better have food brought up or I may go feral."

The loud rumble that punctuates her statement has a grin pulling my lips up. My fierce little mate looks as though she might stab someone for a loaf of bread.

"Of course, sweet Omega," I agree readily. "Someone will be up shortly. Now, would you please stop giving Ward a show? The poor male may pass out if any more blood rushes to his cheeks."

I can't help ribbing Ward about his embarrassment. He's seen naked females before, but I know how much he respects me and the bond between Alpha and Omega. His family is very traditional; they believe Omegas need a solid pack to keep them happy. And as one of his fathers is fond of saying, '*Happy mate, happy state.*'

"Ugh, fine!" Dani sighs dramatically and slowly flutters back to the polished stone floor.

Regardless of how much I want to show my mate respect, I cannot keep my eyes off her beautiful, lush body. Dani has curves in all the right places, and muscles that show my Omega doesn't sit around eating sweets and demanding things from her mates. Actually, this little Pixie may be petite, but she's toned.

I have nothing against the Omegas who wish to relax and allow their mates to pamper them, but I'm proud to say this fiery female is *mine*. She will make a wonderful Queen. Her actions and words make it clear that she will not just be a figurehead. Dani will step into the role with grace and ferocity. She cares for more than just herself, and I'm ecstatic that she wandered into my home and set off my instincts so fiercely that I *had* to have her.

Head held high, the little pixie strides past, her iridescent wings catching the lights. Despite her nudity, she possesses an almost regal bearing, her posture suggesting power and grace.

Fuck. My cock is hard again. I fear that as long as Dani is near me, I will never be soft again. The thought has a muted chuckle vibrating in my chest as I follow her back into our rooms. The rest of my new pack falling in behind us.

Dani throws herself onto one of the plush couches in the sitting room, the male Omega joining her and snuggling in close. Eram, the Elemental, steals the spot next to her. She sighs with contentment, unabashed in her continued nudity.

My sitting room slowly fills with my pack, their murmurs and rustling filling the space, and I take a moment to let it sink in. *I have a pack.* A new family. I wish my parents were still around to see this. My mother would have been thrilled for me. She always wanted a big pack for me. And this odd group of beings will make for an amazing family. I just need to get to know them better.

After a short silence while everyone finds their place, a knock sounds. Tugging it open, I use my body to block the rest of the room from any servants that have brought up my requested items. But it's only Ward with a tray of food piled high and garments hanging over his arm.

For some reason, I do not mind that Ward has seen my mate nude. Hmm... Does that mean he will be pack too? Perhaps, though Dani and the male Omega will decide.

"Thank you, Ward. Please come in and set that down on the table. You should probably be in on these discussions too." I step aside and usher my guard into the room.

The big Bear Shifter slowly turns red again but does as I bid. After placing the tray of food down, he presents the pretty dress my seamstress has fashioned for my little Pixie. Ward uses the fabric to block his view of Dani's continued nudity.

"Here, Omega. Please take this and dress?" Ward mumbles the words and asks her softly to save him from his embarrassment.

"Oh, fine!" Dani sighs dramatically, but jumps up and snatches the dress from his hands. "I will put this on, but only because this fabric is incredible! Where did you get this? Who made it? Can I see them? I have questions and maybe a few pointers. I'd also love a chance to work on my own patterns. Lia bought me this gorgeous fabric in the market, and I've been itching to create something with it." Her questions tumble out one after the other so quickly it's difficult to follow, and I know Ward hasn't heard a word.

He's too busy trying to look away from the amusing Omega as she pulls the dress on right in front of him.

"Can you tie this, please?" Dani chirps and spins around, giving the Bear her back.

"Uhh... Y-yes, sure." Ward stumbles over his response and stares down at the iridescent wings slowly opening and closing.

Dani flutters constantly, as if she can't contain her restless energy. She's too full of life to remain still for very long. When Ward finishes tying her dress, she shuffles around him and starts piling a plate with all the goodies my cook sent up.

My eyes watch her every move. I can't help it. That feisty little female is my everything. The instincts that I've buried for years have come roaring back with a vengeance, and my inner Alpha is all but drooling after her.

Dani returns to her seat and starts munching on the fruit with a pleased hum. She's so short her feet don't touch the floor, and they sway and kick with her delight. It's the most adorable sight, and I don't know if I'll be able to stop watching her long enough to gather my own plate.

The grumpy one stands, blocking my view, and finally I can focus on what I was doing. Settling down on the opposite side from Dani, I grab something to eat and a cup of tea. As the rest of my new pack settles into their seats, munching on snacks, I decide the time is right to begin our talk.

"As you all know, I am Seren, Winter Fae and King of Saforia." My gaze trails over each being, and I straighten my shoulders. "Please introduce yourselves. I remember little from before my rut set in. The whole thing is a bit of a blur now." A light chuckle tips my lips up.

"Hagon. Wolf and Alpha of this pack," the grumpy one snarls out, daring me to challenge him.

Oh, I plan to challenge this male for Lead Alpha. I am far more dominant and am better suited to leading our pack. I already have the experience necessary.

"Hmm... The two of you will be quite entertaining. Let me know when the challenge is going to happen because I plan on grabbing snacks to watch," the tall female purrs, staring at me with her startling pink eyes. "Right, I'm Lianis, Succubus and Alpha."

"Costen! I'm a Snow-Cat, and it's wonderful to meet you, sir, uh, or Your Majesty?" The pretty pale Alpha starts off brightly but grows hesitant as he tries to figure out how to address me.

A grin stretches across my face. It's hard to keep a serious facade when he speaks; Costen is quite adorable for an Alpha.

"Just call me Seren. I am your pack-mate. When it's just us, I hope we can all be casual," I reply gently. Something in me urges me to be soft with this male. He needs a little coddling, and

I'm perfectly happy to do that.

"Okay, Seren. Thank you." Costen smiles brightly.

"It's nice to meet you properly, Seren. I am Eram, Earth Elemental and Alpha," the dark brown Elemental says stiffly. His arm slips around Dani's shoulders and tugs her a little tighter to his side.

Interesting. I make him nervous. That's reasonable, however, I hope he can relax in my presence; we are family now.

"Hi, Seren. I'm Ilaris, but you can call me Ily. Everyone does," the male Omega says, interrupting my thoughts and drawing my gaze towards him.

He's got an arm wrapped around Dani's waist and shares nibbles off her plate. The two of them make a beautiful picture. Her soft pink skin against his tan. The way she fits against his side. And the gentle affection they have for one another. I don't think they even realize all the little ways they touch. A brush against her shoulder, lips pressing into any skin available, and hands always reaching for the other. It's the sweetest picture, and I'm glad my little mate has someone as soft as him. They clearly belong together.

"Hmm?" Dani peers up from her plate when all conversation ceases as we all turn to her. She's like the sun —bright, warm and alluring. I just need to be near her to feel lighter.

"Oh, uh, right, introductions are happening. Well, I think we're pretty well acquainted by now, but okay. I'm Dani, Pixie and, ugh, Omega." She rolls her eyes and huffs when she states her designation, and I know there must be an interesting story there.

"Now, that's all out of the way. Let me just blurt it all out, 'kay?" Dani passes her plate to Ily and hops off the couch. "We came here because we have a few things to say to you, mister!" She paces around the table, slowly making her way closer to me, and my smile widens. My mate wants to be closer to me!

Instead of jumping into my arms and letting me cuddle her, Dani jabs a finger into my chest and begins an angry rant.

"Listen good, *King*," she sneers my title, "why the *hell* have you just left Omegas out there to suffer after you announced your law that *'all Omegas are to be brought to the castle'*. You state this and then don't check the villages and cities for Omegas that are hiding or being *forced* to bond so they don't venture to Varough? *What the fuck?* In my journey to get here, I met *two* Omegas who have suffered greatly. What are you doing about this? Why don't you have teams of guards traveling from village to village to collect newly revealed Omegas? *Fix this!*" Dani is shouting by the time she's done, and I am still with shock.

What is she talking about? Abused and suffering Omegas? That... *Oh, fuck.* That's definitely a possibility. Why *haven't* I enforced this law? I've been suppressing my Alpha so deeply that my mind has grown fuzzy, and I haven't been thinking clearly for years.

Now that I am free, I realize she has every right to be furious with me.

CH. 22

Dani

Seren sits there, a shocked look taking over as I hurl my angry words at him. The thought of Ily and Allista suffering because my newest mate has done nothing to ensure their safety infuriates me beyond anything I've ever felt.

"Well," I snap, "what do you have to say for yourself?"

"Shit." Seren scrubs a hand through his hair, wide-eyed and pale. He shakily meets my eyes, searching for something. The truth, maybe? "I… What? No… Alphas are supposed to be better than that! Parents should immediately rush their newly revealed Omegas to Varough… Why would beings all over Saforia be devolving into this despicable depravity?"

The poor male is so lost and confused, stuttering out his weak explanations. My jaw clenches; a vein in my forehead throbs as I silently vowed not to give in to his sad puppy eyes.

"Ily, Eram, do you want to tell him your experiences or should I? I can do it; you don't have to be here and relive it again." My tone softens as I nuzzle each mate and offer to explain in detail how much the King has failed.

"Thank you, Dani, but I'll be okay. You can tell him for me," Ily replies, his eyes shuttering as if he's built a wall to hide behind while I put words to his pain.

"When you are done, I will tell Seren about my sister's history. It is only right after I failed her so." Eram grimaces, but straightens his shoulders. He's strong in the face of his perceived failures. It only makes me love him more.

"What is so bad that you have to clear it with them first? You're an Omega too. Did you not have a similar story?" Seren asks softly, afraid I will say yes.

"No." I spare Ily another glance before focusing on Seren. "No, I was a Beta until I met my Alphas. My story is a bit more detailed than that, but we can get into it later. This is more important." My lips press together tightly, a harsh glare leveled at my King.

I explain in excruciating detail what Ily suffered before Hagon saved him. With each sentence, Seren shrinks deeper and deeper into himself. Flinching at the angry words and awful pain my sweet boy has been through.

When I am finished, Seren stares at Hagon with awe and humility. My grumpy Wolf meets his eyes with a coldness I've never seen before. I didn't know ice could be purple.

Eram picks up after I've finished, and Allista's history is just as bad but in a different way. By the time Eram is done, Seren's eyes are closed and he's grown even paler than before. A greyish pallor, a stark contrast to the pristine white of his usual form, hinted at the Winter Fae's nausea. He looks like a snow-covered statue tinged with the color of illness.

"Oh, Goddess... How have I failed so badly?" Seren whispers, staring down at the rug. "Why didn't I anticipate this? Was I so far gone that my brain had ceased functioning? This is something I should have foreseen! Ward? Did you think any of this was a possibility?" He spins, looking for his head guard.

When Ward meets his eyes and nods, Seren cries out in pain, clutching his stomach with one hand and his heart with the other.

"Why didn't you say anything? Why Ward? I would have listened to you!"

"I did, sir. You brushed me off and said you'd address it later..." The big guard's voice is loud in the silence.

None of my pack makes a sound as we watch the King's heart break and his spirit crumble. Huh... Maybe I shouldn't have been so hard on him?

"How could I do this?" Seren's words are forlorn and whispered softly.

"You can still fix it," I pipe up, ready to help. It's why we came here anyway. We all want better lives, especially for the softest designation. Well, most Omegas are soft. I think with a small smirk.

"How?" Seren whips his head towards me. "I can't turn back time and stop it from happening. How can I fix it? Please, my Queen, I am but your humble servant. Tell me and I will do as you ask." He drops from his chair to the floor, his knees hitting with a painful thud.

The title is starting to sound better. Especially when the fucking King prostrates himself before me.

"First, there's nothing you need to do for Ily now; his life improved the moment he met Hagon... and me," a chuff sounds from behind me as I flutter towards Seren, "but, Allista stayed with the Elves in Banell and I know they can handle her unwanted mates but it might be nice to send a small group of well-trained warriors to aid them when her pack finds her."

"Done." Seren just angles a look at Ward, and the guard steps into the hall for a moment. Muted murmurs reach us, but I can't hear what they're saying.

"What else?" my newest mate asks, honesty and determination shine back at me.

"Second, you need to put together an Omega task-force. Their job will be to travel to every village and city in Saforia to check on any newly revealed Omegas. Next, not every family will want to allow their teenage children to leave without them. Make sure there is housing here for families as well as dorms for lone Omegas, that way they will be less inclined to hide and put their young at risk," I continue, feeling pride and strength bolster me as I tell the Goddess-damned King how to run his Kingdom.

"Now, this task-force should be composed of mated males; it will put Omegas and families more at ease knowing the warriors will not descend into a rut the moment they smell slick." That comment is aimed at Seren in particular. Although he didn't fall into his rut until he scented my blood, it still counts.

"Yes, my Queen." Seren bows his head to me, and I feel powerful with this male on his knees before me.

My hand reaches out to brush hair away from his face. I let one finger graze over his long, pointed ears and revel in the groan he lets out. Seren stays still and allows me to leisurely stroke my hands over him.

Perhaps being Queen won't be so awful.

The morning passes quickly after that. Our pack spends a little more time getting to know Seren while we eat breakfast. It's difficult for me not to include Ward. The big guard stands silent by the doors, protecting us from… other guards? I am unsure why he feels it's necessary, but my eyes keep straying to his tall form.

The male doesn't appear as tall as he really is because of his stocky form. Ward has a thick build, and he is almost as tall as Hagon. The guard is very hairy though, hairier than any other male I've ever met. Although Hagon sports a furry chest, it's not too thick.

I assume Ward keeps his hair cut short because it's far easier to manage in a fight, although he keeps his beard longer than I would. I snort at the mental image of me sporting a thick beard of light pink hair.

"What's so funny, Sweet Pixie?" Seren's voice pulls me from my silly thoughts.

"I was just imagining myself with a pink beard," I reply without thinking, my gaze still trained on Ward.

There's just something about the furry male that piques my interest. I haven't even scented him properly. I'm sure I caught his scent when we first got here, but that feels like so long ago.

"What? Why?" Seren questions, but my feet are already carrying me over to the guard.

"She's our Pixie," Lianis responds. I swear I can hear the shrug in her tone, as well as laughter, but I'm far too focused on my prey to pay much attention.

Stopping in front of Ward, I meet his curious gaze as he peers down at me. I lean in, not breaking our stare, and inhale deeply. Making it bluntly obvious that I'm scenting him.

A loud moan passes over my lips, and my eyes shut at the decadent smell. Bright aromatic spice with green, citrusy notes and a slightly sweet undertone mixes well with a deep, smoky and earthy leather. It adds an almost dark, primal quality. Together, Ward smells exotic, seductive and a little dangerous. The awakened Omega in me salivates and urges me to climb the thick male.

He's *mine,* a little voice in my head shouts, and I'm agreeing with that voice more and more. Moments pass where I'm lost inside my mind, talking and raised voices sound around me but none of it matters. Only this primal, spicy male matters.

When I rise above the powerful instincts, I find my face pressed deeply into Ward's neck, his thick beard tickling my cheek as I lick and suck on his throat. His flavor explodes across my taste buds, and light Omega whines and moans pepper the air.

Ward's large hands cup my bottom, keeping me held tight to his body since my legs can't reach all the way around his body. When he speaks, his voice rumbles pleasantly against my lips, arrowing down to my pussy.

I don't know how I could want more sex after Seren's rut, but dear Goddess, I desire this male as much as I lust for the rest of my pack.

"I can't put her down, sir. I just can't. There's no way I can explain the instincts screaming at me right now, but if I try to put her down, my Bear will rampage. She's mine," Ward murmurs to someone behind me.

A loud snarl, growls and a scuffle echo off the stone walls as my mates fight behind me. I want to say something, to tell them to stop, but my mouth is busy marking up this male as mine. My teeth ache to sink into his skin, leaving a pretty silvery scar announcing my claim.

"Boys!" Lia shouts angrily. Thuds sound and then all fighting halts. "That's better. Now we all know Omegas make the pack, so how about you three shut the fuck up and let our pretty Pixie make her choice?" The Succubus' voice is hard and full of anger, but she softens when she continues, "Ilaris, why don't you go get a whiff of the big Bear too? I have a strong feeling that you'll enjoy his scent as much as our little Pixie does."

"Umm... Okay?" My sweet boy sounds so unsure, and that gets me to relinquish my hold on Ward's neck.

"Come here, Baby." I turn and coo at my Omega, extending a hand towards Ily.

Ward makes no move to put me down or to stop Ilaris from approaching. I take that as a sign that he's interested in my sweet male, too.

As soon as Ilaris reaches me, the heat of his body sinks into my back, and I listen for him to inhale. My lips tip up into a smirk. I anticipate his response will be similar to mine. I hope Ward can hold both of us.

"Oh, Goddess!" Ily moans out.

CH. 23

Ilaris

The moan that escapes me is loud and full of want. I rush to join Dani in Ward's arms and bury my face in his neck on the opposite side of her.

The big male groans as we both lick and suck on his skin, claiming him with little bruises and rubbing our scent on him. He's ours now. This big Beta will be our mate. There's no arguing that.

When Dani first climbed him, Hagon, Seren and Eram all snarled, but I was just confused. Isn't our pack big enough? But I get it now. He belongs to us. He belongs to me.

"You boys are fucking stupid, ya know that?" Lia's voice growls behind us, but I can't truly focus on her scolding our Alphas right now.

Ward is far more important. My Omega instincts are urging me to take him to our nest and claim him. From my bond with Dani, I know she feels the same. This isn't something we can ignore, and I don't want to stop to deal with my Alphas being all possessive and growly.

"Nest, please?" I chirp, leaning back to look at Ward's face.

The tall Beta stands dazed, but at my words, he focuses his glassy eyes. Between Dani and me, our pheromones must be driving him crazy. The thick cloud of our sweet arousal fills the surrounding air. Dani's sugary scent mixing and dancing with my tart cherries.

"Must protect. Can't leave my post," Ward mutters, attempting to focus harder on what's happening around him.

"Ward, take them to my bed. I'll have Dralton assume this post." Seren's deep voice cuts through the haze in Ward's eyes. "We all know Omegas choose, and they have definitely made their choice. You belong in our pack, and while I'm overly possessive of my mate, I know better. Our Omegas will always be safe with your protection."

His words make it through the fog of lust around me, but I don't grasp them entirely. What

I know is that we're going to claim this big Bear. He's *mine. Ours.*

The room rushes past me as Ward heads for the large messy bed that smells like home, like everyone that I love, and my teeth and cock are aching for him.

Though the chaotic sounds and movements near the entrance nearly steal my focus from the rough nest, more important tasks demand my attention. Our Beta pauses at the bedside, unsure of himself now, but Dani and I know what to do.

Together we scramble out of his hold and onto the bed, working to reshape the nest into something more comfortable. Shifting clothing and pillows, patting things into place to form a proper wall, I sit back and grin at the nest. But, something is missing. I turn to my Pixie, our eyes meet and as one, we crawl over the bedding towards the dazed Beta.

Ward's gaze flickers between us, and a sultry grin creeps over my face. A quiet purr of excitement rushes through my veins. It's almost like we didn't spend days fucking in this very bed.

Dani reaches for his tunic and tugs on it with a cute little snarl. Ward's brows furrow for a moment before his eyes widen and he rushes to undo the ties to his leather armor so we can take his clothing for the nest. That's what is missing. We need his scent in this mix. His spicy cardamom and leather fits perfectly with the rest of our pack. Together, our scents make me feel as if I'm in a mountain forest, with a roaring fire warming my skin from the chilly winds and a sweet treat melting on my tongue as my mates wrap themselves around me, protecting me from all harm. It's safety, companionship, and warmth. It's Home.

That's what our pack smells like mixed together.

Home.

Once Ward's tunic comes off, Dani snatches it and hurries to pat it into place. My Bear quickly pulls his trousers off, handing them to me gently with a grin peeking out of his thick beard.

I follow Dani's lead and find the perfect spot for his scent to sink into our nest, and when we're both finished, we turn and stare at the Shifter with mischievous smiles. Dani's playfulness is rubbing off on me, and all I want to do is jump on Ward and drag him down into the center of our creation.

"Omega's, you honor me." Ward's rumbly voice sinks into my skin, sending shivers of excitement down my spine. "May I enter your nest?"

"Yes," Dani and I answer together, tossing matching grins at each other as the word rings out into the now silent room.

The quiet is almost enough to pull my focus off my future mate, but he moves, placing a knee over our carefully constructed wall and climbs into the nest. As he moves, I am drawn to his thick, long cock.

For a Beta, Ward has an impressive member. It is certainly as big as Hagon's thickness, and I need it rearranging my insides. A small whine escapes my throat at the thought, drawing both Dani and Ward to my side.

"What's wrong, Sweet Boy? Do you need some tending? Do you want his mouth on your perfect cock? Or do you need that monster to sink inside you?" Dani speaks sweetly in my ear, her breath brushing over my skin, sending needy pulses to my length.

All I can do is whine again in response. Yes, to all of that. I want everything as long as it ends with my teeth somewhere in Ward's skin. My Omega gently presses on my shoulders until my back hits the fluffy nest and I lay open for both of them to stroke and touch me.

"Beta, come here," Dani purrs, one finger inviting the Bear closer. "Touch him, map his skin and learn our pretty Omega. Give him everything he wants."

"Yes, Pretty Pixie. Anything for both of you," Ward rumbles, eyes switching from her to my prone form.

Calloused hands run up my legs. The touch, like lightning streaking from his fingertips to my hard cock. Anticipating those big hands on me, a rush of excitement tenses my muscles, and my body responds with slick precum. Ignoring my length, he gently traces his fingers across my tight stomach, pausing at my peaked nipples, evoking a moan of delight from me.

Dani's tiny hands run through my hair, nails scraping over my scalp, sending goosebumps rippling over my skin. Together, these two will surely drive me mad before I get that massive cock inside me.

Ward's lips come down on mine, gentle at first. Nipping lightly, licking up the sting, testing me. Testing to see if I want him. Silly male. How could he think otherwise?

I lurch up, my lips crashing into his, hands clutching at his shoulders, nails digging in. He can't escape me. He needs my claim before I'll allow him to go anywhere. Ward needs *our* marks, or he won't be leaving this bed.

"Easy, Pup, I'm not going anywhere," Ward's deep voice rumbles in my ear as he pulls back from our kiss. "I'd be a fool to leave you and our Queen alone in this nest."

Dani scoffs at her new title, but I grin brightly at her, earning myself a glare. There's no heat in it though; she's coming around to the idea.

"You can't leave us here without our claims," Dani proclaims, her tiny body prowling closer to where Ward's hands have been toying with my hip. "You're ours, Big Boy, and the only way you're getting out of this bed is after we've fucked you silly." My Pixie's grin is mischievous and sultry all at once.

"C'mere, Tiny, I'll show you silly." Ward chuckles as he sits back and reaches for Dani.

Their mouths clash in a riotous kiss. Dani is always trying to dominate even though she's the Omega. It's one thing I love about her. I'll always bend to her strong will, but even our new Beta can make her submit, and I don't think she minds at all.

As one they turn back to me, laying in the nest watching my pretty mates. Dani's hands land on my hips and rove over my taut stomach, her lips following. Ward's thick fingers wrap around my dick, and the touch makes my eyes roll back. Oh, Goddess, I need more!

"More, please! Bear, Pixie? Please?" I babble out pretty words, begging for them to make me cum.

Each touch coils pleasure tighter in my stomach. Ward's hot breath warms my cock-head a moment before his mouth envelopes me and my hips jerk with need. He sucks me down and pins my hips so he can play with me. Force me to take only what he gives. I love it so much I have to stop my hands from pressing his head down harder. Instead, I reach for my Pixie.

Dani's little hands land on my shoulders, pressing me into the soft bedding. Her lips take my mouth, and she swallows down my moans. *Fuck*. These two are going to kill me, and I will go willingly to the realm of the Goddess as long as it's my mates overloading me with pleasure.

Ward pulls off my tip a second before I cum for the first time. He gathers the sticky release and uses it to prep my ass for his thickness. One finger, two, and three he uses to stretch and ready me for his use. I want to tell him he doesn't need to bother, but I doubt he'd listen. All my mates are careful with me. Always making sure I'm ready for them. It's sweet.

"Fuck, Pup, you're going to strangle my cock. You're so tight. I don't know if I'll fit," Ward mutters as his fingers pump in and out of me.

"No!" I gasp, pulling away from Dani's plush lips. "Do not stop! You'll fit. If I can take a knot, I can definitely take you, Bear."

My assurance must soothe his concerns because he pulls his digits out and replaces them with his cock.

With a slow glide, he pushes into my body. There's only slight resistance before the head pops in past my rim, and the way he fills me has my eyes rolling back again. It doesn't help that Dani's mouth nips my neck and chest. The sensations send my body into another orgasm. Cum splashes against my stomach and against Bear. He doesn't seem to mind or care as he pushes deeper into my body.

"Good Boy." Ward's deep voice rumbles through my body.

Zings of pleasure shudder through my muscles. Goddess, I don't know if I'll be able to walk when these two are done with me.

His cock feels thicker the deeper he presses into me. Until his hips meet my ass. I swear I can feel him up in my throat. How is a Beta's cock bigger than my Alpha's? My Bear amazes me, and we're only just getting to know each other.

"Hold on tight, Pup, I'm going to fuck you hard enough that walking will be impossible," Ward warns a second before he truly fucks me.

CH. 24

Ward

Holy fuck. I can't believe I'm inside my Omega. With my pretty female watching, and touching Ily as I fuck my thickness into his warm, wanting hole. Goddess, he's so tight and snug, caressing my cock with each heavy thrust.

Never have I felt this fulfilled. I never expected to be chosen for a pack. Despite my unwavering dedication to duty, refusing these two is not an option. That would be foolish, and I certainly possess more sense than that.

The moment Seren gave his blessing, I forgot all about duty and the rest of the beings in this room. The two adorable Omegas determined to mark me captivate my attention.

Their lips and teeth on my neck had my cock hard enough to drill a hole through stone. That and their scents. Oh Goddess, the way these two smell together is enough to fog even a Beta's mind.

Sweet, fluffy sugar and tart cherries. An airy cloud of spun sugar delicately resting atop my favorite cherry clafoutis; the tart cherries and sweet syrup create a symphony of flavor. A wave of intense desire washes over me; the aroma alone is enough to make my mouth water, and I long to bite into them. A possessive roar, a rumbling in my mind — my Bear is eager to claim these two Omegas, to make them undeniably and eternally ours.

Now that I'm inside Ily, my sweet Pup, nothing could tear me away. The castle could fall down around us and I wouldn't notice. Only Dani can divert my attention from Ily. And the sweet female crawls over our pup and sits her dripping cunt on his gasping mouth.

My motion pauses, curious to see what he'll do, but I shouldn't have concerned myself. Ily's hands snap around her hips, fingers digging into pink flesh as he groans and devours her slick. The sight has my cock straining with the need to release inside my mate, but I hold back, to make sure he cums again first.

Resuming my fierce pace, I pound into the

pup, eyes trained on the two Omegas. My hips slapping against Ily's tight ass. Pleasure throbs in my veins, and I know I can't hold out any longer, so I whisper Dani's name, urging her to give me a helping hand, or mouth.

Her eyes snap up to mine, glazed with lust. She grins when she notes my strain, veins popping out in my forearms, and my face is likely red with the effort.

"Don't worry, Big Bear, I've got you." Her voice ignites a fire in my veins, urging my hips to move even faster, eliciting muffled cries from Ily.

The surprisingly dominant Pixie leans forward, careful of my thrusts, and sucks Ily's cock down into her throat in one swallow. My pup tightens around me, causing my hips to stutter, his moans loud into her delicate flesh.

The way his ass contracts around my thickness urges me to fuck him harder. A fleeting worry, a whisper of doubt, crosses my mind, but the firm, reassuring pressure of his weight against me silences any fear that I might be too rough.

Pounding into him, until his muscles flex over me, dragging my orgasm out so quickly all my blood rushes away from my head and I grow dizzy as I cum so hard the world blanks out for a moment. Ily's cries of bliss, free from Dani's flesh, echo around me, and my Bear takes over.

Teeth plunge into Ily's ankle, claiming this Omega as mine. He bites back, tugging my arm away from his hip, and clamping his little mouth down on the space between my finger and thumb. A flicker of pain, and then it's as if the sun parts the clouds and shines down on us.

Ily makes a space for himself, nestled in my heart, where I can always sense the warmth of his love and the subtle shifts of his moods. He's pure light, joy and laughter. I just want to bask in his warmth forever. Although there's a small part of him that contains dark misery and I have the urge to do anything in my power to erase that. To make certain that the bone-deep chill of that bleakness would never touch him again.

Hopefully, to him, I feel as safe and comforting as any of his Alphas. I want him to come to me if he ever needs anything. My Bear will shelter him and use our body to keep him warm and safe.

"Goddess, you two are adorable." Dani's voice interrupts my moment of basking in the new bond with my pup.

It reminds me I have another Omega to claim. My Bear rumbles at her, eager to feel her inside him the same as Ilaris. I need to clean myself, but I do not want to leave my pup just yet.

"Give me a moment, Omega. I need to cuddle and tend to our pup." My words are low and relaxed, hoping she will not push me just yet.

"Easy, Big Bear, I'm more than happy to snuggle into our nest with you and Ily. The rest can wait." Her smile is soft, and her eyes gentle as she wiggles her way to Ily's back and shoves her face into his neck.

My pup giggles tiredly, reaching a hand back to her with a quiet murmur of nonsense, his eyes already closing. I forgot they've just come out from my King's rut and are likely beyond exhausted. What was I thinking, pushing them into a bond right now? Fuck, I'm dense.

"Quit it and lay yourself down so Ily can cuddle into your soft, fuzzy chest." The Pixie's words, no longer sweet, cut through my self re-criminations and my eyes focus down on the soft pup.

"Right, sorry, my Queen," I add in her new title knowing she's resistant to it, just so I can see more of her fire.

"Shut it and get down here. Your mates need Big Bear to cover them and keep them safe," she snarks, knowing those words will get me moving.

My hips pull back, and my now soft cock slips out with a rush of cum. Damn, I didn't realize how long it's been since I found pleasure. With anyone or alone. I snag a shirt from the edge of the nest and wipe down my male. The need to tend to him over-coming any worries I'd had.

As soon as my arms wrap around Ily and Dani, both of them snuggle into my soft belly and thickly furred chest with the most incredible sound. Sweet Omega purrs. Fuck. It is the most *stunning noise* that has ever graced my ears. It sinks into my very being and relaxes every muscle in my body. How have I lived a hundred years without ever hearing this?

"My Omegas are spectacular. Thank you," I quietly murmur to them, earning sweet, sleepy smiles from them both.

"Rest now, Big Bear."

It's the last thing I hear as their purrs pull me under with them. My Bear is happy to stay in this nest and let the rest of our pack protect us. I can feel my new pack vaguely through Ily and I know they are giving us space to settle into the new bond.

My hips rock as tight suction tugs on every nerve in my cock. The dream seems incredibly realistic. Except this time it isn't a nameless, faceless being pleasuring me. No, it's my pretty Pixie and sweet Pup. Their hands roam over my thick middle, toying with my balls and stroking over my furry chest.

Their touch lights a fire in my veins, and the throbbing of my blood finally forces my eyes open to realize this isn't a dream.

My new mate rests his head against my chest, fingers dancing in my chest hair as Dani, the vixen, devours my cock, seeming to swallow it whole.

"Goddess, you little minx! How in the world do you do that?" The question pops out as she does this thing with her tongue and swallows around me.

With my eyes rolling back, I attempt to sit up, but Ily turns to me with a smirk and pushes my shoulders down.

"Just lay back and take what she gives you, Bear." The way he says my nickname is alluring, and I can't resist my Omega's wants.

I stop fighting the urge to get up and take control, doing as my Pup asks and relaxing into the suction this little Pixie has on my cock. After a torturous few minutes, Dani relents and sits back proudly.

"Now, I'm going to ride that monster like there's no tomorrow, and you are going to take what I give you," the cheeky minx states, heat burning in her gaze as she stares me down.

If she thinks I'm going to let her control

this entire claim, she's got a surprise coming. But I allow her to toss her leg over my lap. I can't help but let out a tiny, almost silent chuckle, watching her comedic struggle. I'm big for a Beta. Nowhere near the same body type as the rest of her pack.

My middle is soft and thick with a fluffy layer of padding, but powerful muscles lie beneath. Being a Bear Shifter means I'm heavier and covered in a thick coat of fuzz, unlike most other beings.

But I work hard to maintain the skills required as head guard. I may be thick, but that's deceiving. Just the way I like it. Many opponents have underestimated me because of it.

This sets me apart from most other Betas and Alphas. But, I am not ashamed that I do not have a flat washboard stomach or bulging biceps. I am exactly the shape I want to be, and so far neither of my new Omegas seem to care all that much about the extra padding.

Once Dani has finally centered herself on my lap, she stares down at my thickness with pure lust dripping from her eyes and slick from her cunt. The little minx tries to kneel up high enough to place my crown at her greedy opening, but she's having difficulty balancing her knees on my thighs.

With a snort of amusement and a pleased grin, I scoop her tiny body up with ease and flip us over. My enormous body surrounds her little one, and her arousal surges. She releases such a deep moan it rumbles through my chest, and I know I'm a goner for her.

With controlled, assured movements, I align myself with her wetness, entering her as if it were my natural place. This pretty minx is my fucking mate, and I'm going to claim her as deeply as I claimed Ily. My little cubs. Beautiful slight things though they are. They are mine.

When my hips meet hers in a light press, she lets out a faint whine before begging for more.

"Beta, Bear, mate, please!" Dani pleads, her gaze trained on mine. Adoration and need painted across her face in the shadows I cast over her.

Leaning in, I kiss her. She attempts to take charge, but I'm not having it. Little Minx is my tiny mate, and she surrenders, allowing me to devour her moans and whimpers as my hips move in and out of her core.

Slick, filthy sounds fill the air, and my mouth trails down from her lips to her puffy rose nipples. The moment my teeth nibble on those pretty peaks, her cunt slams down around me, trying to suck me in deep, and it's damn near impossible to hold back my release, but with a herculean effort I do. She needs to cum first. Always.

Fingers trail from her hip to that sweet little button peeking out at me. It only takes a few swipes over her swollen clit before she screams her release into the air, deafening me. But I follow her over that cliff, pressing my cock as deep as she'll take me. It's difficult with how hard she's contracting over me, but my need to force my seed as deep as possible has my hips pressing through the hold.

My teeth have a mind of their own and sink into her right breast, over her heart. Making a permanent claim on this tiny Pixie. She returns the bite, matching Ily's mark on my opposite hand. My Bear rumbles a pleased sound that my Omegas want their marks so visible.

CH. 25

Seren

Pacing back and forth in the sitting area of my suite is getting old. I want to go to my Pixie but the Succubus is determined to give those three their moment together.

Fuck.

Need pulses under my skin, my Alpha roaring loudly in my head making it ache. The bond with my Queen is fresh, and I have to be close to her. To touch her skin and inhale her delectable scent.

Fuck.

"Quit your whining, Frosty!" the female Alpha drawls, her tone always containing a sliver of lust because of what she is.

"I'm not whining, and I'm not Frosty!" I snap back at her, "I am your fucking King! How dare you mock me?" I stop in front of the tall female, and my scowl is fierce, the very air vibrating with my fury. Tiny ice crystals materialize with every breath, a testament to my powers.

"Oh relax. We're pack now, so you're going to have to stop thinking of yourself as *my* King. We're family, so we don't hold to all that stuffy shit." She waves off my ire before continuing, "and all those frost crystals you keep making beg to differ, *Frosty*."

She doesn't have to point out my lack of control. I huff at her and then continue pacing. I do not need to respond to her taunts. Lianis is family now, and I know she does not need to treat me like a king but my inner Alpha is too furious at the distance between me and my Omega to think clearly.

Also, that's my fucking head guard in there! How dare he be a scent match to *my mate*. Fuck. Even in my thoughts, I'm being an alphahole. Goddesses damned Succubus. She's not allowed to be right.

The bond with Dani lights up with pleasure, and then Ward is there in our mate bond. Their emotions stop me dead. I close my eyes and just feel. Dani is so happy and sated; my pretty Pixie is okay. Ward is ecstatic, showing more emotion through the bond than I've ever seen on his face in the years that we've been together.

My anxiety calms a bit, and I can finally take a full breath. Pack. *Family.* I've been longing for this very thing for centuries, and now that it's here my chest expands fully and I feel as though I'm actually breathing for the first time in years.

A sense of completion washed over me as Dani bit Ward, like a circle had nearly closed, and my feelings calmed. Even with the missing piece, this sensation provides a feeling of stability.

Dani tugs on my bond, and my feet are moving before my brain has caught up. My Queen needs me, and nothing can stop me from going to her. The Succubus steps aside with no argument. That female always seems to be one step ahead of me, and it's going to drive me mad for the rest of our long lives.

I reach the edge of the nest, the air thick with the scent of sex, Dani, Ily and Ward. He adds a spicy hint to the Omega's sugary aroma, and I'll never admit it to him, but it's quite nice.

"Come to me, Alpha." Dani's sweet words soften any lingering anxiety, and I crawl to my pretty Queen, ignoring the big Bear wrapped around her side. My focus is all on the Omegas. I snuggle up behind Ily as he plasters himself to Dani's other side. Ward and I press the two tiny Omegas together between us, and my entire body relaxes.

Ily's scent is calming, especially mixed with Dani's. Even though I'm not romantically attracted to him, he's still my Omega, and I will protect them both with all my strength.

"Mmm... My pretty Omegas. So sleepy and soft after the Bear has worked them over, hmm?" I tease lightly, earning drowsy chuckles from all three of my pack mates. "Sleep now, your Alphas will protect you."

None of them argue, even Ward, and they all drift off into a light slumber. Now that they're asleep, the rest of our pack slowly meanders their way into the nest and surrounds us. We're in the most secure wing of the castle, but none of us would feel as relaxed as we do without us Alphas to protect our precious mates.

There's nothing like a mated Alpha in defence of their Omega. Even the best-trained warriors cannot stand up to a raging, protective mate. Even Omegas have been known to sink into a protective rage when their mates are threatened.

This has me thinking of Tawson's pack and his Demi-Goddess of a mate. The story they'd told me of the battle against Nyurel is the perfect example of an Omega protecting their mates. I mean, yeah, Luella has the blood of our Goddess in her veins, so it's different, but it gets the point across.

Obviously, my Dani knows Pack Foreastra since Tawson's the one who brought her here. I wonder what their relationship is...

"So, Frosty, how's this whole thing going to work?" Lia's drawling, sultry tone sounds from behind me.

My entire body tenses up, only to relax when Ily whimpers. Fuck. Damn Succubus, startling me. Why must she choose the spot behind me? Couldn't she have gone to the other side and cuddled Ward?

"What do you mean? We're pack; we just find where we all fit together and live." I shrug, not taking her question seriously.

"No," she replies, her words growing serious. "No, how is this going to work? Are we going to live in the castle? Do we get a big pack suite, or does each pack-member get their own room? Since you're King and Dani is Queen, what does that make the rest of us? Consorts? Are we going to join your Council? I know each of us has something we can add to help run this land better than it has been. Stop!" she barks when a growl rumbles to life in my chest. "You've been in a suppressed fog for how many decades? Things can definitely be improved."

Each word has me flinching, I know I've

been out of it for a very long time and I have greatly failed the beings of Saforia, especially the Omegas, but does she have to spell it out so plainly? I see at least one of my fellow Alphas is going to make sure I don't fuck up again. But now that I'm mated, I can already feel my strength and clarity returning.

Lia and Dani are both going to take no shit from me, and though I'll never admit it, I secretly appreciate their blunt honesty. I can sense Hagon's dark cloud of grumpiness at my back and know that he will also put me in my place, but he will wait until we're in the sparring ring.

"Right. We will convert my suite into a proper pack bedroom. There are enough spaces in here to ensure we all have our own separate areas to get away from each other. This bed isn't quite big enough for all of us, so I will have my head of staff work on having a proper one built." My eyes glaze and I stare off as I muse about the changes to come now that I've claimed my fated Omega and she came with a bonus pack.

"Tomorrow, I'll resume my Kingly duties but I will sort it out to have my pack-brothers, and sister," I flick my eyes towards Lia, "find a place on my Council or wherever each of you would prefer to contribute. Hmm... We should invite your families to the castle. We're going to have to throw a bonding party. It *is* what's expected of me, and I apologise now for the chaos."

My words are wry, and I can't stop my smirk. Dani seems like she might hate and love a ball.

"Oh, this should be fun!" Lia snorts quietly. "I'm not sure how we're going to get Hagon and Eram into proper finery, but if anyone can do it, it'll be Dani. I'm not even sure Ily is going to want to be in the spotlight. It will be nice to see my family, even though that many Succubi and Incubi will be a strain on this place and our guests."

"I don't mind. It will be amusing to see some of those stuffy Lords and Elders brought down by their cocks!" My laughter wants to boom out of my chest at the imagery of Yan's scowling face when one of those sexual beings turns their powers on him, but I withhold my amusement, not wanting to wake my sleepy pack. It's barely evening now, but I doubt the Omegas will be awake before morning.

My rut took a lot out of all of us and I think one more evening of rest together and my pack will be ready to face whatever challenges come from joining my royal house.

CH. 26

Costen

My eyes blink open into the faint sunlight shining through the large windows in front of the balcony. Slowly, I stretch my arms and legs out, gently avoiding smacking my pack-mates. Everyone else still seems to be fast asleep. My gaze slips over each form in the nest with a soft smile.

This family means everything to me. It's all I've ever dreamed of and never thought I would have. I'm the luckiest Snow-Cat ever to descend from the mountains.

With light, slow movements, I creep out of the nest and make my way to the bathroom. The peaceful morning is full of soft light and the scents of my pack. Each inhale brings a sigh of happiness as I dress for the day.

Seren stated that he must return to his duties as king, and would secure a place on the Council for each of us. It seems unlikely that he'll have something for me, but I'm happy to tag along with any of my pack-mates. Or I can stay with our Omegas. That seems like the perfect place for me to spend my time.

Dani will likely find herself in the training ring taking down all the King's soldiers as she practices. I'm not sure if that's the best place for me, although she has been eager to give me more training.

My clumsy hands still have great difficulty with sword work. There must be a better weapon for me... Maybe our newest pack-mate will have some suggestions. Ward looks as though he's well versed in many arms. I'll have to ask him when everyone is awake.

As I make my way down the short hall back into the main sleeping area, the sound of bare feet against the marble floor pricks my ears. My steps speed up at the thought of one of my pack also being awake at such an early hour.

Lia's sleepy pink eyes meet mine, a slow grin spreading across her face, showing off dainty little fangs, as she walks toward me with a swaying gait. Her adorable spade-tipped tail peeks in and out behind her as she makes her way down the hall.

"Morning, Pretty Kitty," she breathes, the words heavy with sleep but laced with a sultry undertone that sends a shiver down my spine.

“Morning, Lia,” I reply, my eyes wide and trained on her bare form.

She and Dani are both shameless in their nudity. I’m in awe of their confidence and beauty, and I pinch myself just to make sure this whole thing hasn’t been a dream.

“Looks like it’s just the two of us this morning. Shall we go out and explore our new home?” Lia asks, stopping an inch away from me. The heat of her body seeping into mine, sending arousal through my chest and down to my cock.

All the blood heads right for my thickness, plumping it to prepare for whatever she wants to do with me. I swear I would mindlessly follow both Lia and Dani wherever they led. My females are mesmerizing in their beauty.

“Sure,” I say breathlessly, leaning into her.

Even though I know it’s just the voices of my old cluster in my head, I tense as if she will withdraw from my attention. But I should know by now that none of my pack will refuse my touch.

Lia wraps her arms around me and draws me into her chest. I lean into her soft breasts, marveling at the dichotomy. She's packed with muscle, yet still has a marked softness to her that is inescapable. Not that I want to move.

The hug is all-encompassing and full of warm affection. A sigh gusts from my lips, and I melt into her hold.

"Hmmm... Just one more second and I will go dress," Lia murmurs as she presses a kiss into my hair, inhaling my scent. "You feel so good in my arms, Pretty Kitty."

The embrace is over too fast, but as soon as she's dressed we slip out into the hall. The tall ceilings and shiny ebony stone walls echo loudly with each step we take. Regardless of the early hour, we find guards stationed throughout the twisting halls.

"Do you think we can find the kitchen?" I ask Lia, my voice muted in the silence of the surrounding stone.

"We can surely try! I am feeling a little famished myself." She does not soften her tone. The sultry rasp reverberates over our path, and if I hadn't been watching, I would have missed the guard ahead of us twitching at the noise.

Her hand, warm and soft in mine, sends a wave of calm through me; a comforting pressure against my palm. I'm not sure I'd be so brave on my own. There's a high possibility that I would have just sat out on the balcony alone until the rest of my pack woke up.

I'm pleased to have this time alone with my female Alpha. I haven't had the opportunity to spend time alone with her, nor with Eram and Hagon. As we settle into our new life, I hope we can steal away moments together within these castle walls.

Lia tugs on my hand, yanking me from my thoughts, and as soon as I focus, the rich smell of yeast baking and meat roasting has my mouth watering for a nibble.

"Oh, Goddess, that smells so good!" I moan; the words are full of hunger and need.

"I think if we follow our noses, we'll find the kitchens," Lia replies, a gentle laugh lighting up her pretty pink eyes and a grin flashing her dainty little fangs at me.

My desire for food shifts towards lust as her sensual voice sinks under my skin. I'm still starving, but I could postpone that need to slake another.

A rumbling purr starts up in my chest at the thought of this gorgeous Succubus taking control of me. Taking what she wants from my willing body and claiming me like I desperately crave. Either my inner Alpha or inner cat demands that this female claim us as she claimed

Hagon, Ily, and Dani.

Lia's hold on my hand tightens a second before she pulls me into an open doorway on our left. In a flash, she spins and slams the door shut, pinning me against it. Her eyes blaze with fiery lust, and I sink willingly into her hold.

One hand lands on my stomach and slides up under my shirt, raising to my head. With gentle urging, I lift my arms so she can remove the fabric blocking her from my pale, striped skin.

The same hand encircles my neck, forcing my head against the wooden door. A happy sigh, bubbling up from deep within, morphs into a soft, joyful whimper. I yield to her dominance, relishing the freedom of letting her lead me in any way she sees fit.

It's Lia's turn for a delighted purr to rumble to life in her chest as her eyes soften with adoration.

"Oh, what a sweet boy you are, Costen," She breathes and leans in to scent-mark each cheek. "You've been neglected, haven't you? My Schatje." The term of endearment is unfamiliar to me, but the emotion behind it softens me into her hold even more.

"Please, Lia, Alpha, please. I-I need you." My voice trembles as I beg her for more.

More touch, more claiming, more pleasure.

"Patience, my sweet Schatje. I will take good care of you," Lia purrs. Her other hand roams over my chest, paying attention to my peaked nipples, earning light whimpers before trailing lower.

My stomach flexes as her touch reaches my waistband. I press into the hold on my neck, driven by an unrelenting need for more. The pressure has an embarrassing whine slipping out, but all she does is grin and slide her fingers into the knot keeping my trousers up.

The clothing loosens and tumbles to the floor, leaving me bare for her hungry gaze to devour. Lia lets out a low moan that sinks into me, urging me to bare my neck for her. It's easy to submit to her. I trust this Alpha to take full control the same as I trust Dani. They do not want to hurt me.

Anticipation thrums, a sweet ache of delight at the exquisite pleasure to come. Lia does not disappoint.

"What a sweet Schatje for me. Already submissive and pliant. What shall I do first?" Her sultry words are the only sounds to reach my ears.

"Anything, Alpha," I breathe. My body is loose, knowing she will take care of me.

"Good boy."

Those two words have a soft moan echoing between us. My cock flexes and drips precum, desire pulsing through my veins.

"Let me trace each of your pretty stripes, Schatje, before I sink down onto your thickness and claim you as *mine*," Lia says, with a purr rumbling continuously from her chest.

As she speaks, her hands roam over my chest a moment before her tongue lands on the stripe under my ear. Stroking along the pattern over my body, Lia follows one stripe after another and moves down to my waist. When she's face to face with my leaking cock, my breath catches in anticipation of her touch on my sensitive, needy length, but she doesn't touch me.

Her breath ghosts over my need before she moves down one leg, still tracing the pattern on my skin with her tongue and hands.

A whine vibrates in my chest as she moves back up my body, paying no attention to my length. My hands itch to grab her horns and direct her, but I press them into the wooden door behind me, resisting the urge. I know she will touch my cock when she's ready.

Lia will not leave me wanting.

CH. 27

Lianis

Costen is such a good boy for me. I can feel the tension building in his muscles as I play with him. Laving my tongue over every inch of skin I can reach. His cock leaks and flexes with each touch, calling to me.

He's long and thick with that bulbous knot that I ache to sit on. I didn't bother with Hagon the first time; I was more focused on getting him to submit, and I knew it would take more work to fit a knot inside my lock. It might even hurt, but I badly want to try.

When I've got Costen weak and whimpering, trembling for more. I grin up at my Schatje. He truly is my Little Treasure. I didn't know submissive Alphas existed until I met him. But Costen is a unique soul, and I'm fortunate this pack accepted me so readily.

Not only do Ily and Dani call to my Alpha, but Costen does too. From the moment I laid eyes on his sweaty, pale form, I knew he needed me just as badly as those sweet Omegas.

"Come, Schatje, lay down on the rug for me." The moment the order hits his ears, Costen scrambles to comply.

"Yes, Alpha."

Those two words are music to my ears, and my purr thrums louder. I didn't realize that a purr could affect an Alpha, but the way Costen melts into the floor as the sound reaches him tells me otherwise.

I can't wait any longer. My feet follow him down until I'm kneeling over his dripping length. Costen's eyes follow my every move, and pretty little whines slip from his plush lips as he holds himself still for me.

My cunt engulfs his tip, and the feel of him inside me has me gritting my teeth against the urge to force myself to drop over the rest of him, but I hold back that desire and take a deep breath.

His crisp snowy scent, extra sweet with lust, fogs my mind, and I can play this game no longer. Sinking him deeper inside my warmth, I luxuriate in his moans and restraint.

"Touch me, Schatje," I demand, my voice breathy and full of desire. "Run those big hands over my pink skin. Pluck at my nipples and play with my clit."

With each order, Costen's cock kicks inside me. A warm flush spreads across his face with each command. This pretty kitty finds comfort in being told what to do. I think he will feel more settled outside our intimate moments if we all remember to command him, as well.

That thought is important, but it flutters away as his thickness reaches every nerve inside me. A purring groan rumbles from my chest as pleasure lights up my veins. Costen fits inside me perfectly.

"Yes, fuck! Good boy. You feel so fucking good," I praise him, enjoying the way his eyes light up at the compliment.

The way he responds to each word, the stutter in his hips as he restrains himself from fucking up into me only encourages the fire in my blood.

My hips rock and grind over him as my lips rest on his thick knot. Each moan and whimper from my pretty kitty only encourages me to fuck him harder. The way I drip over Costen surprises me, but I spent too much time teasing him before I finally slid him inside me. I've been more than ready for this male to be mine, and my body is in full agreement.

"Do you want me to lock you, Schatje? Do you think I can squeeze your knot inside my tight Alpha cunt?" I murmur the words, watching his glassy, lust-filled eyes focus on my face.

"Please, Alpha! Yes. I want to feel you... clamp down over me... and hold me tight... inside you." Between each few words, Costen breathes heavily, as if he has to force his thoughts out from the depths of the pleasure that completely consumes him.

"Good boy," I purr, "now brace yourself, this might hurt. But it will hurt *so good.*"

Costen's fingers dig into my hips, hanging on to me as his anchor. It sends a thrill of joy through me that he looks to me as his port in the storm.

My hips grind down against his knot, wetness leaking from my cunt at the way he fills me. And the anticipation of seating that thickness inside me and letting my lock clench around it. Slowly, bit by bit, I work his knot into my tight pussy. There's pain, yes, but it is divine having that intimate connection to my Schatje.

Finally, my pussy stretches far over him, and I settle with my hips pressed tightly against his. The knot settles inside me, and I glance up at Costen's face.

His mouth is open in a silent cry, eyes glassy with pure bliss and a pretty red blush over his cheeks and down his chest as he lets the pleasure roll over him. He looks wrecked in the best way, as if he's touched divinity and lived.

I'm not that far behind him as my lock snaps down around his bulbous knot inside me and I shout my pleasure to the room and beyond. It's unbelievable how good this feels, and I wonder briefly why I haven't done this before.

My orgasm washes over me in a tidal wave of bliss, and my inner muscles clench and pulse over him rhythmically, forcing him to cum.

With very little space inside me, as my lock keeps his knot from moving, his thickness kicks and pulses, filling me with his hot spend. The sensation of his cum, his knot, my lock, all of it sends me higher. I wrap my tail around his thigh and hang on tightly. My hands claw at his chest and shoulders, needing an outlet for all this pleasure, and my fangs ache with the need to claim him.

Dragging him up to me shifts his knot and sends my mind spinning again, but I don't let go. I need him. He's *mine*.

Teeth aching, fangs dripping, I sink into

his shoulder, shivering at the cool, sweet taste of Costen's blood as I mark him. This male is my mate, and I will never let him go.

"Bite me, Schatje, claim me back. You belong to me, Costen." I release my mark long enough to encourage him and then return to tending my bite.

Costen nuzzles my chest, breathing a sigh of satisfaction and relief before he marks the outside of my breast, near my heart. There's a tiny pinch of pain before I feel him settle inside my chest. His bright, snowy cord lights up with joy and arousal.

"Mine," Costen says, the word full of happiness and belonging.

We tend our bite marks as we wait for both my lock and his knot to release. I know it'll be some time before we eventually find the breakfast we'd been searching for. But I regret nothing. This male is my Little Treasure, and I couldn't be happier about finally claiming him.

As we dress, and my brain is no longer stuck on fucking this sweet kitty, I peer around the room I shoved us into. It's fairly large, but looks to be mainly a storage space. Boxes line the back wall, a couple of couches rest butted up against each other and crammed into the corner, and a few rugs lie rolled up and piled atop one another.

With a relieved laugh, I realized how lucky I was to have found an empty room. They would have gotten quite a show. I'm a little surprised with myself for being so focused on sex that I hadn't let my Alpha senses check for anyone. But this castle is supposed to be a safe place, especially now that the King is part of our pack.

"C'mon Schatje, let's go find the kitchen. Now I'm quite famished," I say with a laugh.

Costen's bright chuckle joins mine. "Yes, I think I could eat an entire cow by myself. What does Schatje mean?" he adds curiously.

"It means my Little Treasure. Because that's what you are to me, to all of us. A sweet, priceless treasure to our pack," I reply, nuzzling my cheek against his.

Holding my hand out for his, I tug him towards me and lead us out into the hall. My feet freeze at the guards standing around the doorway, weapons drawn and pointed at us.

"Halt!" one of them barks. "How dare you impose on the King's castle, after he invited you to stay in good faith?"

My brows furrow, and irritation blooms. Did the King not relay what happened between us to his guards? I thought Ward had spoken to them before he was dragged into our messy pack.

"Okay, first, put your damn weapons away. That's fucking rude. Second, barking at me is only pissing me off. And third, didn't you hear? The King is part of our pack, so I would back the fuck off if I were you." My seductive power threads through my voice. I'm fully topped up after my romp with Costen, so it's harder to restrain the sultry influence.

The guards standing closest all waver in place, eyes beginning to glaze over, a flush reddening their faces. They drop their swords with a clatter, and the guards a little further away peer at their comrades in confusion even as their hands lower the pointed tips to the floor.

"Wh-what? N-no, I... What's happening?" The male standing the furthest away speaks through the seduction clouding his mind.

He's lucky I didn't intend to use my magic or he'd be a zombie just like the ones closest to me. I watch dispassionately as the rest of the guards bumble into each other and sweat dews on their brows.

"Lia?" Costen bumps his shoulder into mine. "Maybe we shouldn't magic Seren's guards. He might not like it. Let's just go back to the room?" His words are hesitant and soft, as if he's worried about the consequences of messing with these fools.

"Seren will be fine. I said we'd find some breakfast, and that's what we'll do. Come, Schatje, let's leave them to figure out what just happened and follow our noses towards that heavenly smell of freshly baked bread." I gentle my tone for my Little Treasure and wrap my arm around him, pulling him along as we skirt the group of confused and aroused guards.

The magic will fade, and the only thing remaining will be a confusing jumble of what had occurred.

CH. 28

Dani

When morning comes, I wake relaxed and happy. I got to sleep in as long as I desired, and my body feels well used in the best way. My stretch bumps into Hagon and Eram, who're wrapped around my body like clingy beasts.

A grin stretches over my face. I don't mind their clinginess. I love these males so much. Having found my family, everything in me feels settled and at peace. I still have a mischievous streak a mile wide, but I don't have this driving urge to get up and wander. I found exactly what I set out to do.

Now that I'm awake, my stomach rumbles. The sound of laughter erupts, echoing through the room, and I sit up quickly to find my mates.

Seren and Ward stand near the doors discussing something quietly enough that I can't hear without using some of my magic. Ily is sprawled out beside Hagon, still snoring. Lia and Costen are missing, and that brings a frown to my face.

Looking inside, I check my bonds with my missing mates, finding them happy but a little farther away than I'd like. Although, I pause, taking a deep breath and stilling my body to focus. They're growing closer. Good, that means they're on their way back from wherever they'd wandered off to.

Hagon and Eram watch me with soft adoration in their eyes and amusement on their lips. I stretch with a groan, my hands 'accidentally' bumping into Hagon's face and my legs pushing against Eram's lanky bulk.

"Quit laughing at me! You worked my body hard for the last week, I'm starving!" I grouse, rolling to the edge of the nest.

"Hmm. Yes, I am quite famished. I wonder if our missing Alphas have gone to scrounge up some food for us?" Eram hums thoughtfully. His face turning towards the towering door to the hall.

"I'm pretty sure they meant to go for food, but I know they got distracted along the way," Hagon grumps, crossing his arms and moving to stand. His nudity momentarily distracts me from my hunt for clean clothing.

That thick, scarred body is mouthwatering, especially that cock. Even limp, it's got girth, and when he moves it slaps against his thighs. My eyes stray towards the place where his knot inflates and heat trickles through my veins, but I shake my head and push it down. I've had my fill of sex for the past few days. I shouldn't still be so ravenous for dick!

I shuffle to the closet and dig through Seren's clothing, finding myself another large shirt that hangs off of me like a dress. I'm going to have to figure out where Lia put the cloth she bought me. The soft, dreamy fabric ignites a desire in me to make more dresses. It feels like a caress against my skin.

But first, breakfast!

The door to our room opens behind me, and I spin towards the sound with excitement. My Alphas!

"Did you bring food?" I ask excitedly, completely forgoing any greeting.

"Is my Sweet Thing hungry?" Lia replies with a laugh.

"Sorry Pix! I didn't realize how long we'd been gone," Costen adds, eyes wide and hair mussed. "We brought food though!"

Sweet Snow, always so gentle. I love that male more than anything. I'm also quite pleased to see that Lia is taking care of him. He deserves all the love and affection our entire pack can give him.

"Oh! Yes! I'm starving. Thank you, Alphas!" I chirp and clap my hands as I march towards the basket Lia carries.

Our entire pack gathers around the small table to eat. I gaze around at each of them, a sigh of pure happiness slips out.

My pack is whole.

While we eat, Seren outlines the events planned for the day. Most of my Alphas will be with him, observing and Counselling on Saforia affairs. Ward is taking Costen and Ily down to the practice sands. I plan to join them after I've spent some time in the seamstress's wing.

There's an entire wing of the castle dedicated to the royal seamstress, and I'm eager to get my hands on some needles and thread. Lia gave me the bolt of fabric she bought me in the market, and I'm going to work my magic on it to make a gorgeous outfit.

Afterwards, I will join my mates in the practice arena and reacquaint myself with some physical work. Blood thrums in my veins. Fighting is my favorite thing to work on, and it's been far too long since I've had proper exercise that wasn't in a nest.

A slight tremor runs through Ily, and he looks pale at the thought of swinging a sword, but this will be good for him. I know I will feel so much better if he at least knows the basics to defend himself.

Costen is brimming with as much enthusiasm as I am. He's been getting better as Hagon and myself have worked with him along the road, but this will be a little more intense since we're not on edge in the safety of the castle wards.

I also need to work on the powers Bassanai said will break free once I've claimed my entire pack. There's an extra something brimming in my core, but it still feels as if there's a blockage. But… My pack is complete! According to the Goddess, that should break the barrier holding me back from my Demi-Goddess powers…

When I concentrate, I swear I can sense more magic than my regular illusions and air, but when I grasp at it, the power stays just out of reach. It's frustrating, but I know these things take time to master. I've had plenty of experience in working on my skills.

It strikes me that I haven't practiced magic at all since I left Pekayan. A frown creases my brow, and my nose wrinkles as I curse myself for relying only on my steel. I know better. Bernon taught me better than that.

Looks like I'll be spending this time exercising my innate magic instead of playing with sharp things. Maybe with some dedicated work I'll be able to access the power that dances just beyond my metaphorical fingers.

With a sigh, I split off from my mates and head down a set of stairs in the direction Seren explained. I'll worry about my powers and swords after I've made my new dress.

As I roam through the halls towards the seamstress, I let my mind wander through old designs and possible new ones. I have an idea for this soft fabric, but I won't know for sure until I can feel it and see how it drapes on the table.

"Oh! Hi! You must be Dani. I'm so excited to work with you! The King says you're a seamstress too. Oh, Goddess, look at that cashmere! We can make something beautiful with that." A bright, cheerfully enthusiastic voice drags me out of my thoughts, and I meet a pair of pretty brown eyes.

"Hi, yep, that's me. What's your name? I can't wait to get my hands on a needle and change this fabric into something functional! It's called cashmere? I love it. I don't know if I ever want any other fabric against my skin." My response to her is rushed and enthusiastic. Her energy matches mine when something excites me. I love it! We're going to be fast friends.

"Heh, right, I'm Sherrah the royal seamstress. It's amazing to meet the new Queen." The sweet female replies with a light blush. She's almost as pale as Seren. I bet she's also a Winter Fae of some kind.

"Oh Goddess, don't call me Queen. I'm just Dani, please." I roll my eyes skyward and sigh. "Let's get sewing! Where can we spread this out? I need to visualize potential patterns before I decide on something."

Sherrah waves me to follow her and leads me through the door to her workroom. A good portion of the room is occupied by a massive table. Bolts of vibrant fabric adorn the walls, while a few mannequins stand frozen in place with unfinished designs and an entire section brimming with a seamstress's essential tools.

I grip the edge of the fabric, rolling it out and unfolding it so I can see every inch. It only takes a few moments before I've got an idea and I turn to Sherrah, vibrating with excitement. My wings buzz and flutter, lifting me off the ground in little hops. We chatter and work around each other with ease, as if we've been doing this for years. Before long, I have a few injuries from jabbing myself with needles and the most gorgeous dress that I rush to put on.

With a tight hug, I squeeze Sherrah and tell her to expect me back soon. I'm going to make all the things I've ever wanted but my mother wouldn't let me. Happily skipping towards the training area, I allow those thoughts to dance through my mind.

The sandy arena is massive, butting up against the ebony stone surrounding the castle grounds. On the right, fabric-and-straw dummies await blade practice. Targets on the far left for archery and a space just in front of us with a rack of weapons ranging from daggers to broadswords, and spears to quarterstaves. All the shiny metal I could ever dream of.

My mouth drops open in awe, and I swear hearts are visible in my eyes as they grow wide. I really want to play with the stabby things, but I know where my focus needs to be today.

Tomorrow, I promise myself. Tomorrow I will play with the shiny steel. Today is for the magic swirling inside my core.

My feet carry me towards the weapons rack, watching as Ward gives instructions to my males. He meets my eyes with a wide grin and motions at the weapons.

"Sorry, Big Bear, today I need to work on my magic. Is there a space for me to do that without getting in anyone's way?" My voice is pouty, but I'm determined to expand my repertoire for fighting and defense.

Plus, Bassanai said that I will need that power in order to protect myself and my pack from Nyurel... and Jerrik the Jerk.

"Sure, Tiny," he says with a smirk. "You can't see it from here, but near the wall behind the dummies there's a space for Users to practice. The brick wall separating the practice area hides the space and adds a protective layer between the fighters and any rogue powers. But, please wait until I can have a guard watch you."

"Great." I bristle at the nickname, even though I secretly love that he's already got a term of endearment for me. "I don't need a guard," I mutter.

Ward may be new to our pack and our intimate bond, but he feels like he's always been here. That, along with his calming Beta scent, soothes my always-turbulent energy.

As soon as my Beta is preoccupied with Ily, I quietly sneak away leaving Ward to teach my mates proper sword work. I slip behind the dummies into a small, circular fenced ring. There's a very faint humming that signifies a protective barrier built into the fence-line. I'm assuming it's there to stop rogue magic from harming those in the fighting arena.

My feet carry me to the center, and I close my eyes, searching inside myself for each strand of power. The illusions and air come to me, wrapping around my body like old friends, but there's three other colors that elude my grasp.

Fine, I'll start with my regular magic and then work on those stubborn strands. I send a whirlwind of air around the edge of the circle, stirring up sand and debris. My chest expands on a deep, soothing inhale as my magical muscles work. It feels so good I have to wonder why I didn't use this when fighting the hordes of beasts that attacked us.

But I push those frustrations away, centering myself on the feel of the ground beneath my feet and the calming rhythm of my breath. Throwing my arms wide, I call my wind to whip around my body, thrilling in the feel of the innate power to tug on my clothing and send my hair in a frenzy around me.

The wind is easier to control than I remember... I have a feeling that's because of my new mate-bonds and completing my pack.

Letting my wind settle, I call up my illusions and flick through one scene after another, pushing myself and working those metaphysical muscles.

Forest, desert, grassland, mountain, ocean — each illusion is merely a drop in my magical core. It was never so simple. I look back on my time in Jerrik's dungeon and curse him once again. Had my power been easier to control then, we would've escaped within days.

Letting those images fade away, I close my eyes and focus on my magical core and the three elusive strands of magic. Maroon, forest green and a happy sky blue. They dance out of reach each time I stretch for them, staying just at my fingertips.

Instead of letting my frustrations get to me, I center my breathing and sit in the middle of the circular ring. Maybe a little meditation will help.

With slow, deep breaths, I let sight and sound fade away, leaving me with just my magic swirling inside me and clearing my mind of every thought.

Because of this, I don't hear footsteps approaching. I miss the sinister sensation that raises the hair on the back of my neck. And the goosebumps that prickle over my arms.

Pain erupts in my head, and then everything goes black.

CH. 29

Ilaris

Ward stands tight to my back, hands placed over mine as he shows me the proper way to hold a longsword. This weapon is wrong for me. Honestly, it's awkward to hold.

"I… I don't like this one, Bear. Can I please try these little daggers? Or maybe a bow and arrow? I think I'd be more comfortable with a bow," I plead, my tone carrying a light whine.

Weapons are not my idea of a good time. That's Dani's specialty, and I'm more than happy to leave it to her. But I think archery might be kind of fun.

"Yeah, this sword does not suit you, Pup," Ward sighs in reply, gently taking the longsword out of my grip and placing it back on the rack. “Let me get Costen set up, and I’ll take you over to the Archery Clearing.”

My eyes track his heavy steps as he makes his way over to Costen. My pale Alpha frowns over some short swords, confusion clear in his creased brow and down-turned lips.

Pain explodes throughout my body, and I gasp, hands clawing at my chest. What the fuck is happening? The searing agony hits me like a white-hot brand, intense and sudden, then vanishing as swiftly as it arrived. But with its parting, there’s now a blank void inside my chest.

"Dani..." I choke out, my heart pounding against my ribs as I frantically scramble towards her hidden practice space.

Footsteps pound against the sand in my wake, Costen and Ward overtaking my panicky movement. Goddess, I just know that something bad has happened to Dani. We’re supposed to be safe here! The fucking Goddess even told Dani she would be safe!

No... Wait! She told Dani she’d be safe at her friend's home!

Fuck!

We should have stayed there. Visiting the King wasn't necessary; I didn't need to berate him for letting me down. I’m fine now. It’s all in the past...

My own thoughts are distant and frail, whispers faintly audible above the rising panic. The crushing weight of my self-loathing presses down, but a flicker of hope remains, a fragile spark I cling to with determination. Maybe something went wrong as she practiced her magic. Maybe the new powers rebounded or something.

But... there's a heavy foreboding inside me. I know she's gone. Taken by that stitched-together monster that's been hounding us. Brought to the God that plans to steal my mate's essence and power.

Our entire pack has claimed her, branding her with our mark. She should be too strong for that monster to steal her magic. I have to hold on to that thin strand of hope. She'll break free of whatever restraints they place on her and we'll find her.

The space inside me, where her bond lies, is muted and dark. Dani is unconscious, but I just know, as soon as she wakes, there will be a burning fire of rage and retribution. She will not be pleased with this turn of events.

I will see my mate again.

"FUCK!" Ward's swear draws me out of my inner turmoil, and what I see makes my blood run cold.

Footsteps in the sand. There's black and purple gobs of something in each imprint. Bright red spilled over the space Dani once occupied. No signs of a struggle, so that beast snuck up on her and BAM! Just like that, she's gone.

Simple.

Terrifying.

Heartbreaking.

"How could this have happened?" Costen asks, tears thick in his voice. He hugs himself as he stands at the edge of the circular ring.

"Fuck!" Ward swears again, pacing around the ring. "There are heavy wards over the castle and some along the walls, but we never thought-"

His explanation cuts off as an echoing roar shakes the very ground. As one, our heads swing towards the ebony castle, glinting in the sunlight that seems too bright for how I feel. Although the longer I stare at the castle, the darker the sky grows. A frigid winter breeze blows over the training arena, and tiny snowflakes fall.

"Oh, fuck." Ward's face turns a shade of white, matching Costen, as he whispers.

Just as I open my mouth to ask, four enraged Alphas fly around the walls, blocking our view of the castle.

"Oh, shit!" I curse as my eyes land on the rest of my pack.

Each Alpha seems bigger, muscles straining, eyes burning with fury and snarls so loud it's deafening.

How the fuck are we going to explain this? Will we be able to contain these furious beasts?

"Where. Is. My. *Omega*?" Seren grits out the words between clenched teeth, his gaze swinging between the three of us.

Tiny ice crystals, like shimmering dust, dance off his skin in a swirl of frost and snow. It reminds me that our King is a Winter Fae. That his rage is affecting the weather terrifies me. Has he ever revealed how much magic he contains?

Ward shuffles forward, and I'm secretly pleased that I won't be the one to deliver this unsettling news.

Hagon, my beautiful scarred Wolf, is taller, muscles straining against the tunic. As my eyes stray over him, the arms of his shirt tear. Just slightly, but it's enough that I shuffle back a step.

I'm not afraid of my Alpha, but the last time I saw him like this, he was tearing through the Wolf pack that caged and abused me. I do not want to get in his way. He will eviscerate anyone who attempts to stand in his path.

Flicking my gaze to the other two, Eram appears to have grown in height, and branches reach upward like antlers growing from his head. Colorful leaves and sharp points decorate the regal spires.

That brilliantly colored foliage is likely poisonous. I've seen similar things in the forests, and they are never a good idea to touch. Rashes, boils and instant infections can bubble up from a single graze.

Lianis, my adoring Succubus Alpha, is gone, and in her place is a monstrous female. Her twisted ebony horns have doubled in size and now point forward, ready to maim and injure. Her muscles have bulked up, and her tail thrashes wildly from side to side.

Plus, there's an aura of golden sensuality dripping from her body. Anyone who draws too near will instantly succumb to her allure. Too dazed to defend themselves, they will be simple for her to dispatch.

My Alphas are deadly when provoked, and with Dani missing and only blood staining the ground, it's a surefire way to unleash their fury.

I fear for our kingdom.

The encroaching cold mirrors the bleakness in their hearts, a silent promise of oblivion if the King remains enraged.

"Y-your Majesty, S-seren, we... Dani had come here to practice her magic and try to unlock the hidden powers the Goddess told her about," Ward starts off with a stutter, fear thick in his voice, "she was alone. I... I thought she was safe! The wards should have protected her, but... W-we don't have any over the courtyard or the training arena. I should have-."

Seren interrupts my Bear's nervous ramble with a snarled, *"FUCK!"*

That single, shouted word reverberates off the stone walls around the castle, the snow falling faster and thicker. Soon, a thick layer of frigid powder will cover our entire kingdom.

"Come," Seren demands after a deep inhale. He turns and marches back towards the castle. "We will consult my Users."

None of us questions it. If my King, and Alpha, has a plan, I will follow.

Hagon pauses long enough for me to catch up and wraps a furred arm around my shoulders, tugging me into his body. Even enraged, my Alpha knows I need him.

The moment his heat sinks into me, I break. Heavy, gut-wrenching sobs pour from my mouth, and my legs collapse beneath the weight of my guilt and fear. Hagon doesn't miss a beat and scoops me into his furred chest.

My Omega was supposed to be *safe*. Why wasn't I with her? Why did I blindly trust that this place was safe? How are we going to find her? Dani could be anywhere!

There's no scent trail to follow. It's as if she disappeared in a puff of foul, tainted smoke. An icy dread grips me; I know *who* has her, but the whereabouts of Nyurel and that monstrous Jerrik feel like a gaping black hole swallowing my hope.

Please,

Dear Goddess, if you're listening, protect my mate.

Protect your daughter and keep her safe until we can find her.

CH. 30

Dani

Drip.

Drip.

Drip.

Each tiny droplet sounds like a hammer blow against my brain, drumming a rhythm of pain in my head.

Why does it hurt so badly? Lifting my hand, I'm met with double the usual weight and the unmistakable sound of chains. Also, something prevents my arm from reaching me.

Fuck.

The struggle to lift my eyelids is too much, so I let my body relax... into hard-packed earth and little stones digging into my side. Okay, that's not any better. Why can't I just pass out again? Maybe I'll wake up and this pain will all be a horrible dream.

"Fuuuuuuuck," I swear, letting the word drag out, a slow, drawn-out sigh matching the misery permeating my entire body.

"Quiet!" A sharp, angry whisper cuts through my internal whining, and my eyes snap open.

Not that it helps me see anything. Wherever I am, it's pitch black. Not even a candle to light the area.

"Hello?" I whisper, hoping the sound won't irritate whoever is in here with me.

"Do you have a wish to invite those fiends back here faster?" he hisses back.

The voice is definitely male. Deep and gravelly, as if he hasn't spoken aloud in a long time.

"No? I… I don't know what's happening. The last thing I remember is practicing my magic in the sandy arena. And now everything hurts," I murmur back, trying to keep my voice low but also hoping he can help me put together what the fuck is going on.

He heaves a deep, exasperated sigh before I hear shuffling steps and then warmth lands on my shoulder. Not just warmth… A tiny zap stings my skin, and his sharp inhale is thunderous in the darkness. I know what this means... Does he?

"Mate."

For fuck's sake! Don't I have enough mates? What the fuck, Bassanai? I do *not* need as many mates as my sister. She needs the protection, not me. I am quite skilled, fuck-you-very-much.

"No!" I hiss at him vehemently, "I can't be your mate! I have seven other mates already!"

"Too bad. I am your mate, and I will do all I can to keep those foul beasts from touching you again," he replies, confidence and promise thick in his voice.

"Oh, so now that you know I'm your mate, you'll protect lil' ol' me? Whatever happened to chivalry? Were you going to let me fend for myself if I were just some random female? How rude." My sass is in full force, the pain in my head only encouraging me to snap.

Another weary sigh, and his hand on my shoulder soothes down my arm. The rhythmic pressure and heat soften my ire.

"No, I'm sorry. I would have helped any female, but... My Alpha is screaming at me to care for you louder than any other thought in my mind. I yearn to hold you close, but these cold, unforgiving bars cruelly obstruct my longing," his reply softens my annoyance and caresses my Omega instincts to be near an Alpha fated to be mine.

Regardless of my anger at my mother, the fucking Goddess, I can't deny the relief at knowing I have someone here with me.

"Where are we?" I breeze past his pretty words of longing and try to get my head on straight.

"We are on an island off the coast of Varough. I've only ever heard them call it Monster Island. Not very original, but they aren't the most intelligent beings I've ever met." Each time he speaks, combined with his soothing strokes over my skin, has the pain in my head easing.

I've always known of the special magic between mates, but to feel it actively healing the wound on my head—the pulsing warmth and gentle thrum—is truly extraordinary. It's the same as when Jerrik tried to rip my throat out and Ily helped clean and bandage it. Within hours, the torn skin had completely healed, so by the time we reached the next village, I felt as good as new.

"An island? Fuck." An amused silence follows my declaration. "I've never even seen the sea and now I'm on a fucking island. How are my mates going to find me? How are we going to get back to the mainland? Who the fuck has us?"

I rapidly spit questions into the darkness as my thoughts churn.

With the injury healing, my ability to reason is returning, and I'm already working through different scenarios, but it would help if I knew who the fuck has me. Although I suspect that it's Nyurel. Others warned me about him enough times.

How the fuck did they even take me? Weren't there wards over the castle? I'd think the fucking King would have better wards than Luella's pack.

"I don't know, Mate. But I will help any-way that I can," the male replies, bleak worry thick in his words.

"Okay, I need your name. You can't stay a faceless voice, especially since you're another damn mate. I'm Dani, Pixie extraordinaire," I add a bit of amusement to lighten the mood.

"Heh, right, I'm Tev, Wildling. It's… I never thought I'd find you. I'm very glad to meet you, Dani," Tev chuckles.

"A Wildling? I've never heard of them… Is it rude to ask what exactly that means?" I reply, confusion furrowing my brow. Not that he can see me in this blackness.

His thumb caresses between my brows, smoothing out the wrinkles. Ooookay, I guess that means I'm the only blind one here.

"Not you, Mate. You can ask me anything, and I will gladly answer," his response is thick with emotion as he moves to stroke my cheek, "a Wilding has two forms, similar to a Shifter, although we only get our Wildling form once we hit puberty unlike a Shifter who is born already able to switch between the two. I even look a little similar to the midpoint shift of a Wolf, but I stay in that form. I'm beastly. Being tied to a Wildling brings shame, I know, but I'll protect you as best I can, Mate."

A thrill runs through me at his description. I'm sure it doesn't do him justice, and I can't wait to see what he truly looks like in beast form.

"Listen, Tev, since I've never even heard of a Wildling, how can it bring me shame to be mated to one?" I question, but continue before he can answer. "Regardless, I don't care what you look like; you're fated to be mine, and the Goddess wouldn't have done that unless she knew we were perfect for one another. So get that self-pity shit out of your head and understand *you are mine* and that means I don't care what other people think." My words are firm, and I hope he can see the determination on my face.

"Okay, Dani," his reply is soft, and his hand caresses my jaw, turning me towards him. "I am yours. Wholly."

"Now, I need to figur-" I say, but a flash of light erupts, forcing me to squeeze my eyes shut and recoil.

"Ah, my sweet. You're awake; how pleasant." The voice sends an icy shiver up my spine. That isn't Jerrik, but it sounds like the voice that took over his patchwork body a few times.

Fuck.

"Who the fuck are you?" I say, resorting to my usual angry taunting.

"Now that's no way to speak to a God," he replies, and something lashes out, cutting across my cheek.

A cry rips from my throat, and I bring my hands up to the injury. I can finally see more than just the blinding light spots, and a blurry robed figure takes shape in a doorway.

The urge to peer around the prison I find myself in, and to look at Tev, is strong, but I fight it, and keep my eyes on the threat.

"What the fuck? How did you do that?" I snarl at the figure.

"Just one of my many Godly powers," his response is casual, and he waves a robed hand. "Soon I will have more in my arsenal. You, sweet little Pixie, will give me all the power I need to continue my work. *Yesssssss.* My pets will take over Saforia, and we will all live in my dark utopia."

The more he speaks, the less I understand. There's definitely a screw loose under that hood. But I get the gist. He's going to steal my powers and make more of the deformed monsters I fought in the forest.

Great.

"Jerrik will be in shortly to restrain you. This is going to be *fun*!" The demented male claps his hands with a laugh and then leaves as quickly as he arrived.

As darkness covers my vision once again, I turn towards Tev. Urgency presses down on me to *do* something. My mother's words come back to me: '*You need to accept all the mates I've chosen for you, then you will release the block on your true powers.*'

"Tev, you need to bite me, and I need to claim you in return," I say, with a seriousness in my voice that isn't usually there, "it's vital that we mate. We don't have time to discuss it; just do it, please."

Thankfully, Tev isn't one of my males that feels the need to talk in circles before doing as I ask. He grabs my hand and pulls it through the bars. The next moment, his sharp teeth sink into my hand, and a faint blue strand glows between us. It's so pretty, shimmering in the darkness.

My momentary distraction is now my biggest regret because the door slams open again and Jerrik rushes inside with a screech.

"Stop that right now, you beasts!" As he yells, purple and black smoke shoots from his hands and winds around my limbs, tearing me away from Tev.

"NO!" Tev and I both shout as his teeth tear my skin, marring my newest mark. Anger burns in my gut at the half-claim. I can sense my Demi-Goddess powers lashing out at the block but unable to fully manifest.

Fuck.

CH. 31

Dani

The door to my cell clangs open, and the shackles around my wrists drop away as I'm carted out of the prison and away from Tev.

A ground-shaking roar follows me as the door closes on Tev's devastated face. It's a look of pure horror, intertwined with heartache, that greets me as I finally see my new mate. Although I caught black eyes, like pools of obsidian and dark green skin covered in fur.

Hair had sprouted over his body, but I don't get to see anymore as I'm taken away from him down roughly dug tunnels.

I struggle, trying to escape the bonds that hold me aloft, but it's no use; the smoky power follows wherever I try to move. No, think smarter, Dani!

My body settles in the hold, and I inhale, attempting to center myself. Let's try to interrupt Jerrik's forward march. I don't think I'll like what's at the end of the path.

With calm focus, I spin an illusion and send it out to surround both Jerrik and myself. It's an image of Naargeestig Forest, with thick old growth blocking the sun from the forest floor. Massive trees with trunks bigger than anything I've ever seen before and prickly bushes that make travel near impossible.

Jerrik curses and stops abruptly; the smokey bonds containing me halt with him. I've tried to make sure the illusion is blocking me from his view so I can attempt to wiggle out of these impossible manacles.

"What the fuck is this? Fuck! *He* will not be happy if I'm late. This is your doing, you sneaky little bitch. I'm going to make it hurt before *He* even gets his bony claws into you," Jerrik's threat, sharp and edged with a palpable intensity, scares me more than I ever thought possible from that Beta.

Trying not to let the fear overwhelm me, I settle down and breathe deeply again. I'll try my wind magic this time. Slowly, I let the wind build and direct it to surround my right hand, slipping underneath the black magic containing my limb.

The wind expands slightly, giving me room to pull my hand out of the black and purple smoke. Finally, the damn bonds don't follow; they stay around the wind tunnel I created, and I heave a muted sigh of relief.

But even with my powers boosted by all the mates I have claimed, it's still not enough, and my illusion flickers as my concentration focuses on the wind.

Fuck.

"There you are! I'm going to enjoy this," Jerrik sneers at me and marches through my waning illusion.

I've only got one hand free, and that's not enough to fend him off. His off-color hand, stitched to his body, grabs my free wrist in a bruising grip. I swear I can hear my bones grind together, and he snarls at me.

"How the fuck did you get this loose? You know what? I don't care. Maybe if you're in pain, you won't have the concentration to fuck with me anymore." The air grows cold as Jerrik's words echo, each one a phantom touch sending shivers down my spine.

The crushing force of his hand around my wrist grows tighter and tighter until I hear, and feel, a snap. My scream of pain is piercing, and it echoes down the dirt-strewn tunnel. Tears leak from my eyes, and I'm blind to the world around me as the sharp pain radiates down my arm.

A deafening roar answers my scream, and it has Jerrik pausing enough that he's no longer grinding my broken bones together. The agony is still there, sharp and aching, but it's not overwhelming my mind anymore.

"I must get you to the altar," Jerrik mutters, releasing me only for his black magic to return to my limb and circle my broken wrist.

Before he continues down the path, he levels a hateful glare at me and reaches for my other hand.

"Another little reminder not to fuck with me." His mouth pulls into an ugly smirk as he grabs my pointer finger and quickly snaps it backwards.

I release another scream, which is soon joined by a heaving sob as he snaps my middle finger too. A wave of nausea washes over me at the sickening crunch of my breaking bones and the searing pain that rips through my body. I heave twice, a sour taste filling my mouth, but nothing comes up. At the very least, it deters Jerrik. The hateful male backs away and resumes his march towards my doom, but not without another slur.

"Disgusting Pixie. At least you'll be dead soon." Jerrik's words are barely audible above my pain, but I hear them. "You know what? This isn't enough. You constantly got in my way of wooing Luella, an irritant that would never shut up! You deserve much worse."

The smokey bonds lift me higher until Jerrik is level with my wings. A shot of terror rushes through me, reawakening my struggle. Panic has me thrashing, my broken bones sending waves of agony through me, but I can't stop.

"This will teach you not to get in *my* way ever again," Jerrik sneers over my cries.

His thick, ungainly fingers grasp my left wing at the base, the other hand braced against my back. The moment he pulls, horrified screams leave my throat raw, but there's nothing I can do to stop him. Jerrik only puts more power behind his hold, and my wing tears from the base with a sickening sound.

A sharp, high-pitched snap sounds a moment before wet papery crinkles echo alongside my shriek of pain. A faint hum vibrates my back as my other wing and muscles twitch at the loss. The anguish of losing a huge part of who I am, layered with the physical agony, has my screams reaching such a high note that it's almost inaudible.

Jerrik doesn't wait; he reaches for my

other wing and yanks even harder until that one pulls free of my body too. The snap makes me scream again, followed by the wet, metallic smell of blood as it pours from the new wounds.

A choked cry claws at my throat, echoing in the long passage, and my stomach twists in the face of utter despair. A hollow echo reverberates in my chest, a desperate plea lost in a world now devoid of hope.

"There. Now if you could stop that annoying wailing, this would be perfect," Jerrik says, tossing my torn wings carelessly into the tunnel wall. "Let's get moving. Your fate awaits!" His tone grows cheerful, loud in the silence of my loss.

A wave of hopelessness washes over me, and I hang suspended in the air by the black magic bonds. I'm never going to see my pack again. I won't get to hug my sister one more time. Oh, Goddess, my Ily and Costen. They're going to be so heartbroken when our mate-bond snaps. Shit, I hope Hagon and my other mates are prepared to carry them through the pain.

The tunnel thunders with loud roars, showering dirt onto my prone body. I swear it sounds closer. But it's likely the ache of my shattered bones and bloody back messing with my mind.

My head hangs backwards and I watch the

ceiling go by in a daze, not even bothering to turn my face as dirt sprinkles over me. Nothing matters. Tears blur my vision as I realize how close I was to ending their reign of terror, the weight of my failure crushing my soul.

When Nyurel sucks the magic from my body, I imagine I'll end up a shriveled husk and he'll cover Saforia in nightmares. Calling up monstrous beings and enslaving thousands.

I'm sorry, Mother. I'm sorry I didn't listen better, and I did not know that I had another mate waiting for me. How could I have known that our pack wasn't complete? I've ruined everything.

My thoughts only grow bleaker as Jerrik drags me closer to my end. A deranged cackle draws me out of my black depression, and a flickering light ahead signifies my doom.

"Good. *He's* ready for you. I can't wait to watch him suck the life from your veins and drain your powers dry. It's everything you deserve for helping keep pretty Luella from me. Did you know that once *He's* strong enough, he will gift that winged bitch to me? I'll finally have her chained to my bed. Servicing me whenever I desire," Jerrik's taunt reaches deep into my black mind.

The thought of him abusing my sweet sister like that rekindles my ever-present rage, and I find my desire to fight again. Even through the pain of my brokenness, I feel life returning to me.

A deep breath catches in my throat; the fetid air of the underground, thick with Jerrik's sickening stench, assaults my senses, a grim reminder of my inescapable prison. The damp chill of the earth clings to my skin.

More tremors wreak havoc on the tunnels. The thunderous howls resume, gaining on our position. A spark of hope ignites. Maybe Tev got free. I could see his Alpha and Wildling, revolting at his Omega being taken from him the moment he started a bond.

Alphas are fiercely possessive of their mates, and the intensity of a new bond can send them into a frenzy of protective instincts. I can't imagine the destruction a Wildling could wreak; I barely know what one looks like.

But, hope is a dangerous thing because it niggles at my mind, urging me to hang on. He's coming for me. They're all coming for me.

CH. 32

Eram

Rage burns inside me. The Elemental magic bubbling in my veins pushes against me and forces strange changes to my body. I've never shifted shape before, and the branch-like antlers and poisonous leaves are new. If I hadn't been battling the Alpha fury, I would have marvelled at my new defences.

However, someone stole my mate, and my Alpha only wants to break things and rampage through Saforia until I can get my hands on my Little Beauty again. Instead, we're all standing around in some tower, watching the King's User cast a locator spell.

This inaction is driving me mad. I'd rather be out there following my bond to Dani. At least then I'd be doing something instead of watching this strange, short male. The User's eyes are locked on a bowl of water as he mumbles incantations in a language I don't know, the rhythm of his words strangely captivating. A thick haze of incense hangs heavy in the air of the small room, stinging my eyes and clouding my mind with its potent scent.

"Aha!" the short male shouts, startling every single one of my pack, including myself.

"Did you find her?" Seren snarls, the Winter Fae freezing the surrounding air.

Our entire pack has to give him a wide berth; otherwise, we'll need thick winter cloaks, mittens and scarves. Dani's disappearance has rattled the King beyond civility. I can now see why he's King. Seren's power is potent and extraordinary, but he usually keeps a tight hold on it. I'm sure most beings have never seen him release his chilling winter magic in such a wild show before.

When we all felt Dani's bond shift from happily humming to pain, and then the silence of unconsciousness, each one of us lost our minds a little. With a surge of primal power, our inner Alphas propelled us forward, unleashing a torrent of magic that exploded from our chests. The room he'd been showing us, once pristine, is now a chaotic mess of splintered wood and shattered glass, and I'm not sure how he'll repair the extensive damage. Even the obsidian stone walls sustained some damage.

Seren's power, though… It was stunning and beautiful but deadly. Once we'd emerged from the castle, he transformed the weather from a pleasant fall day to a raging snowstorm. If he weren't a pack-mate, I might be afraid of him.

"Well, you see…" the small male starts, shrinking away from Seren's frigid aura, "T-there's black magic blocking the spell from properly locating your mate-"

Before the male finishes his sentence, Seren roars, and ice pellets swirl throughout the room. Stinging against my arms and face, I heave a sigh at his impatience, although I understand it; we should let the User tell us everything he knows. I doubt Seren would have him on staff if he weren't a master at his work.

"Seren. King? *Your Fucking Majesty!*" Hagon's first attempt at gaining our pack-brother's attention fails until he roars through the icy haze.

"WHAT?" Seren snarls back.

"Let the tiny male finish. And can you at least put a lid on it until we get outside? Not all of us are made for winter," Hagon snarks back, with no fear of the enraged Fae.

"Fine." The pout in Seren's tone has a hysterical laugh attempting to flee my lips, but I press them tightly together. Just as I hold myself intact and lock down my magic from exploding throughout the castle.

The full extent of my powers would raze this entire gleaming castle. Nature will always reclaim the land if we let it.

"Continue," Seren demands of the small male.

"R-right, s-so the spell cannot penetrate the bubble of magic hiding her precise location. I know the general area she's in a-and you c-can follow your mate-bond to find her once you're there." The stuttering, slow speech irritates me, but I count my inhales to refrain from shouting at the male too.

"Great, so where is she?" I speak up before Seren can shout some more.

"M-monster's Isle." The User pales as he speaks the name, but I'm already turning towards the door, marching out of the tower room and down the stairs. "Seren, I assume you've got ships?"

"Yes," my pack-brother states sharply, following me down to the main floor. With the rest of my pack trailing behind, leaking magic wherever we go.

Costen and the Wolf are bigger, taller and their muscles bulked up as they withhold their shifts. Lia is another pack-mate that we need to give a wide berth too, as her seductive powers form an aura of sensuality around her and place anyone who comes into contact with it into an immediate lusty trance.

Through our bonds with Dani and Ily, we aren't as affected by it, but I'd still rather not be loading up on weapons with a hard cock. It would make fighting very difficult.

Ward may be a Beta, but his Bear is furious that someone stole our mate right from under his nose. He feels responsible, and I blame him for not watching her closer. I know it's unfair, but he's head of the King's guard, dammit! Although he is a master of every single weapon in that arena, someone bloodied her right fucking there!

The irritation flowing through me has my sharp branch-antlers growing even bigger. I only try to slow it down a little because I have a feeling that I will change fully into a new, unknown, form before the end of all this, and I am expecting the usefulness of whatever my powers want to give me.

Our pack makes a quick stop in the royal armoury, and even though I am not well versed in fighting, I grab a few sheaths of short blades and strap them to my hips. Seren reaches for an ornate longsword that shimmers with cold magic.

Lia and Hagon each grab a sword that they test out before sheathing them, and Ilaris even snags a bow and quiver full of deadly looking arrows. Does he know how to use that thing? I'm actually surprised that Hagon is not insisting that the male Omega stay here. But blinded by rage, his thoughts are likely muddled and focused on only one thing.

Costen, our nervous, simple Alpha, stands in front of the rack of weapons unsure of what to do. I pity the male right now. He thrives when Dani is around, but at the moment he just appears lost and miserable.

"Which of these weapons have you touched before?" I move next to him and ask quietly.

"Huh?" Costen jumps and stares at me with dull shimmering eyes.

Is he going to cry? Fuck, I can't deal with that. Please don't cry, please don't cry. I repeat over and over in my mind as I watch the Alpha.

"I... I've never really handled any of these," Costen replies after a moment, "b-but I think I'll just shift and allow my Snow-Cat to rip and tear until we can touch Dani again."

"Yes, that's a good plan. You do not need any of these weapons; you *are* a weapon. Especially in defence of our mate," I respond with confidence, patting his shoulder.

For everyone's sake, he's much better off just relying on his Shifter. I've already heard of how he's acted in defence of our Omega before they met me. He'll do much better with that, rather than a steel weapon. Plus, I think I'd worry for the rest of us if he started swinging a sword he does not know how to use.

My encouragement, though small, has Costen straightening from his curled in, hunched position, and strength radiates from him now. Yes, he may be a 'soft' Alpha, but with the right words and motivation, he can be deadly to our enemies.

I scan the room, observing my pack, and my eyes snag on Ward. The Bear Shifter is far bigger than any Beta I've ever met, especially with anger fueling his inner beast to push forward. He's as tall as Hagon now, and his muscles bulge, tearing the sleeve of his shirt, and his pants have long rips throughout. Before long he'll be too big for his clothing and end up fighting nude. His indifference is clear; finding Dani is his sole priority, and everything else is secondary.

With weapons loaded down, my pack looks ready to fight an entire army to get our mate back.

"We ready?" I ask, aiming the question at Seren. "Where's the dock?"

"Come," Seren replies, marching past me.

None of us feels the need to converse; our entire focus is on the direction our mate-bond is pulling us towards.

'We're coming, Dani. Please hold on. Fight with everything you've got, my brilliant mate.' I attempt to direct this thought down the cord connecting me with my pretty Pixie. But I run up against a wall of impenetrable darkness, silencing the connection between us. A palpable sense of dread hangs heavy, the darkness pulsating with a sinister energy; this must be the shroud of black magic the User was talking about. It troubles me deeply to see how this is impacting the connection we share.

Seren leads us towards the back of the castle, through a heavy stone doorway that trails through the grounds and down a steep zigzagging staircase to the base of the cliff. Normally, being so high off the ground would send my mind spinning with nausea, but I'm far too angry to let something so small stop me from getting to my Omega.

It feels as if it takes hours to reach the base, but when we do, a large ship takes over the horizon, bobbing gently on the waves washing past it. A slew of small boats rests on the rocky shoreline, and I assume we're going to have to row our way over to the large vessel.

Before we reach the rowboats, a group of familiar males waits in our path. Seren hardly notices them as he marches past to one boat. I huff and roll my eyes. That male is going to leave us all behind if we let him.

"Tawson, Brenth, Brynd, and… Rake? Rav? I'm sorry, I don't recall your name at the moment."

I try to greet the males of Dani's sister, but I can barely focus on names at the moment.

"Rafe! And I don't blame you," the ochre male responds brightly. "Our son had a vision, and we're here to help. We've tangled with Nyurel before." His tone grows dark with anger.

"Good. Let's go." Is all I say as I head towards Seren's rowboat.

We're getting our Omega back if it's the last thing we ever do.

CH. 33

Tev

Howls of fury rip through my throat. The pain is inconsequential compared to my mate being ripped from beneath my fangs. My Wilding is beyond anger, and I don't want to stop the shift.

Fur grows rapidly over my body, and I tear out of the rags I'd been wearing as my body gains height and muscle mass. Enraged far past anything logical, I give my Wildling free rein. Each howl is so powerful I feel the earth shake beneath my paws and dirt rains down over me.

My feet carry me to the bars, and I wrap my long, serrated, dagger-like claws around them and pull. The metal bends beneath my strength, and it gives me hope I can force my way out of here.

Muscles bulging, snarls echoing and feet digging into the dirt floor, I strain to move this obstacle keeping me from my mate. My fur grows matted with sweat, and my claws dig long furrows into the ground before I catch a slight creak.

Putting on a burst of effort, I heave the bars out to the sides and one snaps near the top. Perfect. I can use this. It takes less strength to push the now-broken bar down to the ground. With one foot in the gap, I push it against the next bar while putting all my weight into the other bent one, making a big enough gap for my bulky body to fit through.

Free at last, I yank the door open and lean down on all fours. I'm much faster like this. My paws thunder over the tunnel floor, howls echoing down the passage, as I barrel towards my mate.

Our bond may only be one-sided for now, and it's faint, but I can still follow it to my Pixie. Those fuckers who captured me and my mate will die for this.

When I'd first been ripped out of my solitary life in Naargeestig forest, I'd put up a hell of a fight, but they used some strange black magic that froze my body and allowed them to cart me away on swirling smoke. The patchwork male sneered and spewed slurs at my rigid form. He is only brave when he knows I cannot fight him. The weak piemel.

The other male, though. He frightens me. Cloaked in thick fabric and surrounded by a sinister aura. His taunts carried some weight. He'd threatened to pry my body apart piece by piece and use the best limbs to create a new nightmare to unleash on Saforia.

Luckily, something happened, and they'd tossed me in that prison and forgot about me. I haven't eaten in weeks. I should be weaker than I am, but my Wildling form is hardy and made to survive even the harshest conditions. Though I'm not at full strength, I must try to rescue my mate.

Dani's heartrending screams reverberate down the passage and infuriate my inner Alpha even more. What are they doing to her? Why do those cries injure my heart so badly? It sounds as though they're torturing her.

Fuck.

My paws beat against the dirt floor, kicking up dust and debris as I put on more speed. The scent of Dani and blood grows thick in the air, and something shimmery and opalescent catches my eye.

Skidding to a stop, I stare down at… at her wings? Oh Goddess, I'm going to be sick. They plucked her like a fucking bird and threw something so precious against the filthy ground without care. How could they be so heartless?

I want to grab them, bring them to my mate, but… there isn't time. They could be killing her right now. At that, I resume my mad dash towards her and the miasma of darkness infecting the air ahead.

Dani might never recover from this kind of torment. With a heart full of desperation, I vow to the Goddess, *'If you help me get her out of here alive, I will use every ounce of my strength to support her through her indescribable grief.'* I can't even imagine the devastation of losing such a significant part of herself; it's a wound that will bleed into every aspect of her being.

The glow of candlelight flickers ahead, and with a burst of speed, I crash into a large open room. My eyes take in everything in seconds.

Dani, tied down to an altar, her blood trailing rivulets of red over the dark stone.

The patchwork monster, leaning casually against the wall, watching her with glee.

A robed figure, leaking purple and black smoke, pulling open an aged, dusty tome.

Since I cannot speak in this form, I unleash a bone-chilling snarl and charge the closest being to me.

My body crashes into the robed figure, taking us into the far wall with my speed. An eerie shriek pierces my ears, and I swear blood drips from them onto my fur. But I ignore that slight pain and let my fang-filled maw rip and tear at the male beneath me.

When only chunks remain, I turn my furious gaze to the patchwork piemel and snarl. Saliva and blood drips from my exposed fangs, and the male shrinks back with a satisfying scream.

There's no waiting; instinct takes over, and my body reacts before my mind can process the need to move. I bite down, and the crude stitching holding this male together gives way. His blackened innards spill out. In what feels like mere seconds, he's reduced to small pieces scattered across the dirt floor; the air thick with the smell of gore and black magic.

My dark gaze finally falls on my injured mate. Heavy manacles clamp onto her wrists, chains anchoring her spread-eagle on the cold, damp stone. Each sob is a shard of ice in my heart, punctuated by the fresh scent of blood welling from the gashes across her back, the salty tang of her tears mixing with the coppery metallic taste of her wounds.

Damp with sweat and coated in viscera, I don’t want to touch my sweet female with the stains from those males, but I need to get her out of here. My claws are gentle as I stroke her cheek.

"No! Please, no more!" Dani flinches away with a cry.

I can't speak in this form, so I rumble a purr, hoping it will get her attention. The sound soaks into her body. I can pinpoint the exact moment it hits her because her entire body relaxes and her pretty green eyes finally open.

She forces a wan smile, but her eyes flick past me, and a look of sheer terror washes over her features. I spin around to face what fresh horror has come to fight me but I have no time to understand what's happening before black and purple smoke snaps tight around my arms and legs and I'm being dragged across the dirt leaving long furrows from my claws.

"You actually thought you could kill a God?" The cackle that leaves the horrific skeletal male sends fear streaking down my spine.

How the fuck is he alive? What the fuck is he? Did he call himself a God? Dear Goddess, I'm in some serious shit.

As my mind attempts to understand what's happening, movement out of the corner of my eye drags my gaze that way, and I watch in horror as the patchwork piemel slowly pieces itself back together.

With a wet squelch, the innards wiggle and squirm across the dirt, leaving trails of glistening slime and gore as they snap back together, the sound echoing unpleasantly. Each chunk of flesh and torn stitch, shivers and moves until the male is whole once again. His face a mask of furious rage.

"Tell me we're going to tear him apart now? He deserves it after that little show," the piemel sneers, stomping over to where the… God has me suspended in his black magic.

"Patience!" the God snaps, red glowing eyes leaving me for a moment to land on his apprentice. "I want my powers from that whimpering mess first."

At his declaration, he swings my body into the chamber wall. The dirt and stone shimmies in place before erupting over my arms and legs, holding me tightly with no room to move.

Fuck.

Both males approach Dani, their movements menacing as she shrieks at the horrifying sight of the exposed deity and the grotesque patchwork male. Her every sound is a torment, fueling my desperate bid for freedom from this new prison. I can't just sit here and watch them torture my mate and steal her powers!

My struggle leads nowhere. The black

magic holding me fast against the wall is stronger than anything I've ever encountered.

How am I going to save my Omega?

CH. 34

Seren

The sway of the ship is soothing to the frosty rage chilling my blood. Although I see nothing calming me until Dani is back in my arms.

How could this happen? How could we all be so fucking stupid? My mate was supposed to be *safe* on castle grounds!

My teeth grind as I try to contain my icy power. If I let it leak out, I may strand us in the middle of the sea. It isn't easy for saltwater to freeze over, but the amount of winter magic that swirls in my core is greater than any Fae of the last few centuries. The only one who could match my ferocity is Tawson, but that male has such a rigidly tight control over his mess of power that I doubt he would even try.

The moment we return to our home, I will set all the castle Users to work laying proper protections over every fucking inch of the grounds, walls and even the Goddess-damned sky. It will be the safest place in all of Saforia.

A soft touch on my elbow drags me out of my furious musings, and I turn to face my other Omega. Ilaris looks rough, a sallow hint to his normally pretty tan skin and hopeless pain in his grey eyes. They match the ever-darkening, gloomy skies as well as my heart.

"A-are you okay?" Ily's voice breaks before he clears his throat trying to get a handle on himself. "I… I know you aren't. None of us are okay. I just… alone, I'm wallowing in everything we could have done better, and I can't imagine you're doing any better than me."

For a moment, I contemplate not responding. I'm too angry, and I refuse to take out this rage on my pack-mate, on my other Omega. He doesn't deserve the vitriol I wish to scream. But the longer I stare at him, the more he seems to sink in on himself and my own shoulders droop. Fuck. As an Omega, he feels everything so much deeper as well as the emotions of those around him. Omegas are well known to be empathic, and I cannot stand seeing Ily so hurt.

I scoop him into my arms and release a

small chuckle at his ‘eeep’ of surprise. Ily seems so small in my hold. When standing beside Dani, Ilaris is quite tall for an Omega. Although that could be just an illusion since Dani is so tiny.

“Thank you, Ily, for your concern.” My amusement falls away as quickly as it arrived. “None of us will be okay until Dani is back. But you are correct. I was glaring at the sea and wallowing in everything that I could have done differently. And working to contain my power so as not to freeze the surrounding water.”

“Wait, you can do that?” Ily stares up at me with wide eyes. “That’s so cool. I wish I had magic. All I can do is shift… But my Wolf is very pretty,” he adds with a haughty lift of his chin.

I know what he’s doing, and it’s working to pull me from my grief. Who knew that having a pack would be so calming to the soul? Ah right, Ward told me repeatedly when I refused every Omega that threw themselves at me.

Speaking of Ward, I think I should stop glaring at the water and rejoin my pack. I can’t be the only one who is beating themselves up over Dani’s disappearance.

Cradling Ilaris, I turn from the salty spray of the water cascading off the ship's edge and meet Tawson's gaze.

“Ah, good. I was just coming over to pull

you out of your rage. But it appears I wasn't needed this time!" My oldest friend quips, a sly grin tugging at the corner of his mouth.

"Oh, fuck off, Taws. I'm fine." I punch him in the arm as I move past him.

Tawson's laugh follows as he joins Ily and me on our stride to find the rest of my pack. If I were angrily pacing, then it only makes sense that everyone else is also either furious or grim.

"Hey! Where'r we going?" Rafe sings as he skips to us. "You guys look like someone stole your candy. I mean... they kinda did, but she's still there, so, y'know, cheer up! We're going to go fuck some shit up, burn out all that Alpha anger and get your Omega!"

My eye twitches at Rafe's annoying presence, and I turn a glare on Tawson for bringing along the worst of his pack. But when I meet Tawson's eyes, they're full of amusement and affection for his Hellhound.

A loud scoff leaves my lips. "Rafe, do you have to do," -I wave my hand at him- "all that near me?"

Before I can berate the annoying hound any more, a slightly hysterical giggle draws my attention down to Ily, leaning against my chest. I sigh. Of course, Rafe is here as comic relief. Well, that and he is handy in a fight.

"I'm sorry!" Ily hides his laughter in my chest. "I'm sorry! It's just so funny how much he annoys you. Dani would love it..." All amusement dies off in a muted sob.

Ily's tears grab Hagon's attention, and the grumpiest male stomps over to us. His purple eyes burning with a familiar rage. Yeah, Hagon understands me more than anyone right now, although Eram is close behind in the anger department.

"What have you done to my mate?" Hagon grits out, his Wolf close to the surface, showing in the sharpened fangs that fill his mouth.

"Easy, Brother. He is upset because our precious mate is fucking gone," I rumble, biting back my own rising fury.

Hagon takes a deep breath, peers over his shoulder at Costen, and turns back calmer.

"Right." He breathes out slowly. "Please give him to me."

It's not a question. My surly Wolven brother does not do 'polite'. Hagon does demands and growls. But, I understand my pack-mate and hand over the teary Omega without a fight. I do not need to be the only one comforting Ilaris. He has an entire pack willing to bend to his will.

Plus, the sweet little Wolf reminded me I'm not the only one struggling right now. My gaze tracks over each of my pack-mates.

Costen, huddled in on himself, tears leaving salty tracks down his pale cheeks as he sniffles and attempts to make himself as small as a big Alpha can.

Eram, with his new impressive antlers made of tree branches, paces along the aft of the ship. He constantly has to stop and untangle himself, and I can visibly see the irritation growing each time he stops. That male is one wrong comment away from exploding, and I do not wish for him to sink our means of retrieving our mate.

Lianis, sitting on a crate by the pacing Elemental working to contain her allure, lest she entrance the entire crew and halt our progress. Even the strong female Alpha sits with a defeated posture, knowing none of us can comfort her without falling to her charms.

And Ward. My longtime head guard, advisor and friend stands alone near the bow, bulked up to almost his Bear's height and muscle mass as he fights with his animal to leave him in charge so he can make well thought-out decisions. Even though we all know he's far past that, anyway.

Starting with the Wolves beside me, I gather my pack so we can sit and make a plan. Talking, being together, will help keep us all from sinking into despair. Plus, we should use the best resource we have against this threat - Tawson and his pack. They've already faced this monster once before. They hold valuable insight that we should take advantage of.

My mind, cluttered with self-deprecation and distress, has made it impossible for me to think clearly, I should have come to this realization sooner.

"Thank you, Ily," I say as I march past him and Hagon. "Come on, let's gather everyone. We have strategies to discuss."

At the sound of my voice, loud over the crash of waves against the ship, everyone startles. Eram spins towards me so fast his antlers tangle once again, and he explodes with curses. Fortunately, Costen pulls himself out of his downward spiral and rushes over to help the Elemental free of the rigging.

Ward stomps towards us, the deck groaning beneath his mass. For a second I fear the planks beneath him will give way and we'll lose another pack-mate, but my guard wrangles control of his form and shrinks to a more manageable size for a ship.

Lianis is the only one who stays seated, far away from us. But I'm not okay with that. She is a part of this pack, and we will control ourselves and help soothe her fears.

"Lia, please join us," I invite, moving into her alluring aura. My cock hardens instantly, and I swallow hard against the urge to demand she strip. "If the rest of us can pull our powers back, so can you. I mean… I haven't frozen the sea yet so maybe you can try not to entice all of us into an orgy while Dani's away. You know she'd be very upset to miss that."

The Succubus watches me, her amusement growing with each word until finally she dips her head in a nod and the need filling my blood settles to something more controllable.

"Very well, Sere." The nickname rolls off her tongue, and I immediately detest it. She knows by the sour pinch of my lips and wrinkle of my nose.

There was no hiding my reaction. But that's exactly what she was looking for if her grin is anything to go by.

"Tawson, grab your pack-brothers and some crates to sit on. We have a plan to strategize and a Pixie to rescue."

CH. 35

Hagon

As soon as our ship's anchor sets down off the shore of 'Monster Island', I'm lowering a rowboat. There's no time to waste. Dani's pain through our bond is overwhelming, and even though she hasn't responded to any of my nudges, I know if I don't get there soon, we're going to lose her.

Waves crash against the ship, rocking the small rowboat against the side with dull thuds. This will not be an easy trip, but my determination is stronger than fucking nature. I leap down into the boat as soon as it touches the water. Eram, Costen and Ily follow.

A second rowboat sets down just behind us, and I know Seren, Ward and the other males are very close behind. Our pack will not leave this haunted isle without Dani. No matter the cost.

An unnatural darkness cloaks the island at midday, a heavy, oppressive blanket that stifles the air and chills the skin. Through the wind and dense fog, mournful howls and terrifying shrieks pierce the air, a haunting symphony of sound.

My bond with Dani pulls harder and harder the closer we get to her. The rocky shore, jagged and grey under the overcast sky, comes into view, and a black smudge against the cold stone draws my gaze. A natural cavern carved into the side of the isle, its entrance partially obscured by hanging vines and dripping water. That's where we'll find our Omega.

I change course, my arms screaming from the effort of fighting the waves and wind, and head straight for that black maw. My pack-mates don't question my choice; they can all feel her too. Time is running out; if we don't get to her soon, our Omega will be gone forever.

Finally, we reach the cave entrance, and the waves push our little rowboat deep into the darkness. There's no light to guide our way, so I let my Wolf come forward enough to lend me his keen night vision. As soon as his presence fills my eyes, our way grows clear, and I put more effort into my rowing so we can reach the small plateau ahead.

A crude tunnel, smelling damp and musty, branches off from the muddy bank where we pull our boats up. My pack scrambles out of the small rowboat, helping me pull it up so the waves don't smash it into the wall or carry it far down the watery cave.

Seren and his group reach shore as we're disembarking, joining us at the entrance to the passage. Without a word, Seren, Eram and I lead our group down the deep, dank path.

Silence encompasses us as we travel, attempting to quiet our footsteps in case beasts await us around each curve. The metallic scent of blood slowly reaches me, and I know without a doubt that Dani is injured.

The smell enrages my Alpha and my Wolf. Seren growls lowly, his aura growing colder by the second, and I have to move away from him before he freezes my limbs. Eram's branch-antlers grow longer, scraping against the tunnel ceiling, dislodging dirt and rocks onto me.

If it were any other moment, I'd snarl at my pack-brothers for letting foolish emotions affect them, but I understand their rage. My Wolf is champing at the bit to release his fury on those who've taken our mate.

The cloying sweetness of Dani's scent

wars with the coppery smell of her blood, a sickening perfume that clogs my nose. *Fuck.* Furious rage boils within me. What could have caused such a brutal injury? Why would they do this? Doesn't this *God* need her alive to steal her magic?

My feet quicken their pace until I'm almost running. Concern and fear for my mate, a beating pulse in my mind telling me I need to hurry. If we don't get there *now*, there won't be anything left to rescue.

We pass a door, blending into the monochrome darkness, and I hesitate, but the pull of our bond tells me she is further down the passage. Urgency pushes me on, and our group thunders down the tunnel, no longer wary of beasts. Anything we encounter, we will demolish. Nothing is going to stand between me and my Omega.

Musty air rushes past my face as I run until the cloying sweetness and metallic tang grow so strong I have to stop. Ily and Costen crash into my back at my abrupt halt. Ily makes a questioning sound, but I focus on the iridescent wings crumpled against the tunnel wall.

"Goddess," I breathe, pain piercing my heart, "what have they *done* to her?" My knees crack as I crouch down, running a finger over the delicate membrane.

"Oh *fuck!* Is that what I think it is?" Ily's question draws my gaze up from the damaged wings.

"They've taken something precious and integral to our Omega. We must end this. *Now,*" Seren replies, his voice as cold as his power, radiating out from his core in frosty waves.

The fury on his face matches my own, burning in my blood. With a quick look at the silent Orc, I motion at the pieces of my mate. We cannot leave them here. Once we rescue her, if she wants them gone, we'll obliterate them without hesitation. But no part of my Omega will be left behind.

The male reverently gathers her crumpled wings and holds them gently, giving me a solemn nod as we rise.

With that taken care of, we resume our headlong rush down the tunnel. The closer we grow to Dani, the more agony inundates our bond with her. She's in so much pain I don't think she can feel us here. She's not unconscious, just… It feels as if she's given up hope.

'No, Dani, please. Don't give up yet! We're here! We're coming for you, Menace. I need you to feel me. Please?' I push this feeling down my bond with her, and pray to the Goddess. I pray she will not lose hope. For her to feel me here. And for her feisty nature to shine bright once again.

A faint light ahead has me putting on a burst of speed, Seren and Eram right next to me as we burst into a large chamber. My eyes take in everything in seconds, but what I'm seeing doesn't sink in right away.

Dani, chained on top of a stone altar, blood seeping from beneath her prone body. A furious, beastly male, stuck against the far wall of the cavern, the rough, cold stone seeming to grip him like a vise. The patchwork male that has haunted our journey and injured my Omega looms over Dani alongside a skeletal male in a tattered robe.

That must be Nyurel, the God that wants to steal my mate's powers. He truly resembles the walking dead, and if we don't stop him, I fear he will unleash nightmares over Saforia.

My Wolf has had enough. He rips through my body and snarls a bloodcurdling sound, gaining the attention of everyone in the room.

"Oh! What a surprise. More critters to play with," the skeletal God says, clapping his hands with excitement.

"Step away from my Omega," Seren growls, a furious roar that sends ice and snow swirling around him in a blizzard of his wrath.

"Now, now, you must be polite! Demands are met with reprisal. Jerrik, take care of them while I get started on this silly little Pixie," Nyurel says with a frown, his skeletal face turning down towards my mate.

The weasily male steps towards our group, but before I lunge, an immense wave of power rushes past me. Electricity crackles in the air, my fur all standing on end, and my Wolf sneezes at the sensation.

"*You!* You will not leave here alive. How *dare* you show your face again? I will tear you apart and bury your pieces across the land so you will never be whole again," Tawson roars as he pushes past my pack.

His nearness sends little zaps of electricity and magic zinging off my skin. I want to shy away from his terrifying rage and overwhelming power; the sheer strength of this Fae is intimidating. But I hold my ground knowing this male is on our side.

With one of our enemies distracted, I turn my focus to the God reaching bony fingers towards my mate.

Costen's Snow-Cat screams, an ear-splitting sound that echoes off the chamber walls, and races past me. His fur brushes against my side, and I let my Wolf take over, joining our pack-brother in stopping Nyurel.

Together we rush the God and slam into

his side, forcing him away from Dani. His skeletal body slams into the wall, near the beastly male trapped in stone. From the corner of my eye, I watch his body shrink and shimmer into that of a human male.

"Free me! Check your pack bonds; I am one of Dani's mates," the male calls out, "I need her to bite me back. She mumbled something about freeing her magic, but she didn't get to complete our mating."

Those words sink in past my anger, and I'm not sure what to do with this information. I can sense him now that I make an effort, but I'm a little busy chewing on a God.

Black and purple smoke explodes from Nyurel's body, tossing Costen and me clear across the cavern.

"HOW DARE YOU ATTACK A GOD!'" Nyurel screams, his smokey power swirling around him in a dizzying whirl. Malformed beasts pour in through a hidden opening on the far wall.

I stagger to my feet, Costen groaning in pain before struggling to get up. With a quick check in our bond, I think he's broken a few ribs. But that will not stop him; he's focused solely on our enemy.

As we move towards Nyurel again, ice and

frost cut off our approach. My gaze tracks Seren as he stands in front of this angry God. Our pack-brother truly resembles his station in this moment. Regal, and wreathed in furious snow, Seren, the King of Saforia, unleashes his wintery magic on the skeletal male. It's clear to me why he's our King.

The snowy power hits Nyurel and pushes him back, clashing with the black smoke that the God controls. The two magics smash into each other, one light, one dark, spewing bits of ice and black ichor as they fight for dominance.

My focus shifts to the right, where I can see Lia and an Orc approaching the male, who is desperately trying to break free from the wall. Ily and Eram carefully make their way toward our prone Omega, the crackling of power echoing around them.

Costen and I will take on the beasts heading towards our pack-mates.

Seren curses loudly, pulling my gaze back to his struggle with Nyurel.

His wintery magic is losing ground.

Fuck.

CH. 36

Costen

Chaos surrounds me as Hagon's Wolf tears into the mass of bodies. My Snow-Cat follows suit, and I roar in the face of the oncoming horde of abominations. I may not be a good fighter with a sword in hand, but after all we've been through on our journey here, my Cat has grown protective and vicious.

A maw of jagged teeth clamps down on my right foreleg. A yowl of pain shrieks forth, and my fangs close over the beast's skull, crushing it in my powerful jaws. The taste of the creature's blood fills my mouth, and my Cat spits out the tainted liquid.

Hagon's Wolf plows into another beast as I pull the dead one off my leg and return to the fight. My razor-sharp claws tear through another's throat, coating my white fur in crimson. Monster after monster tries to get between my pack and Dani, laying broken on the cold slab, but I am far past any fear or reservations I've ever had about fighting and I rip and tear alongside Hagon's black Wolf.

Even though I am a large Shifter, the Wolf beside me is a monster. I swear he's the same size as a horse. Maybe I'll have a saddle made for him in secret so he can be Dani's mount. I know both Dani and Lia would be delighted to see our resident grump in that position.

Claws rake down my side, crushing my amusement, and I release another loud cry at the pain. Turning my own sharp talons ready to rip into my attacker, they glance off the hardened outer shell covering this beast.

What the hell even is this? What kind of creature has an armored exterior? It is slightly rounded, with overlapping plates. With the elongated face of a reptile, a maw full of teeth and long muscular legs, this beast appears impenetrable. How the hell am I supposed to kill it?

It tears open another long, ragged gash in my side, seeming to grin at my yowl of pain. When I retaliate with a harsh swat, it curls up into an armored ball, and my claws grate over it.

As I try to find an opening to damage this

thing, something bites into my flank and locks its jaw. My Cat is furious, and I try to shake it off only to dodge another ferocious attack by the armored beast.

More and more monsters converge on me, and soon I am buried under a pile of snapping jaws and sharp talons. Pain explodes through my body, and even though I don't want to give up, how can I defend myself against so many?

Orange and white flames, screams of agony from the beasts surrounding me and a vicious howl explode above me. Every single beast scrambles off of me, except the one locked onto my flank.

But that one isn't there for long either; a beautiful and deadly Hellhound snaps its jaws around the body of the one trying to take a chunk out of my skin. The determined beast releases its hold on me with a scream of pain as it melts.

This is one of the most disgusting things I've ever seen, and if I could puke in Cat form, I would. The Hound peers up at me, and I startle at the bright orange eyes of Rafe. One of Dani's sister's mates!

Finally, I have some breathing room. Even though every inhale is rough and painful, I'm not done trying to get to Dani.

My Cat inclines our head to the magma-covered Hound and turns back towards the fight. The armored beast watches me from afar, leery of the Hellhound next to me. With an idea in mind, I cautiously nudge Rafe towards that monster and leave it to him. He will be able to melt through anything, including the damnable armor covering that abomination.

Even with as much pain as I'm in, blood covering my body from my own wounds and the viscera of my foes, I dive back into the fight. We're slowly thinning the herd of monsters, and if we want any chance of escaping this place together, we need to eliminate them all.

A group breaks off from the main fight with Hagon, me and Luella's Alphas, and they are heading towards Ily and Eram.

Absolutely *not!* I charge into them with a leap and land on top of two of the beasts. My claws digging in and dragging through flesh and muscle. Their cries of pain pull the attention of the other six. They stop and turn to face me as I rip chunks out of the two under me, leaving them on the ground useless and bleeding out.

Facing off against so many, I stagger, but I hold strong. I can't let them get to Ily. Even though Eram will protect him, there's too many, so I won't risk it.

The beasts circle me, and I don't know if I can survive this, but I will fight to my last breath if it means the rest of my pack can get Dani out of here.

Anything for my chosen family.

They all attack at once, and my two long dagger-like fangs puncture one creature while my claws slash at two more. The other three sink tooth and claw into my already torn skin, and my shriek of agony echoes through the noisy chamber.

A powerful burst of magic sears my wounds as it tosses the attacking beasts off of my hide.

“Ya lookin’ a wee bit scunnered, could ye use a hand?” a tall, fearsome Orc asks. His accent thick and difficult to understand amidst the surrounding mayhem.

Unable to respond in my Cat form, I just pant and gently nudge his leg. It’s my way of saying thank you without words. I think I was about to meet my end before he came along.

“Och, ye’re no lookin yer best, Kitty Cat. Aye, time fer a wee bit o’ healin’ - hold still, this’ll only sting a bit!” the Orc booms before a burst of pain consumes me.

It’s almost worse than getting the damn injuries. As my skin knits itself back together and my broken ribs snap into place, breath fills my lungs - and with it, a fresh wave of gratitude.

My Snow-Cat rumbles an almost inaudible purr as I headbutt the Orc, enjoying his laughter and this quiet moment amidst the fighting.

But the peace ends as quickly as it started, and four monsters charge in our direction. I turn with a snarl and launch myself at the beasts, diving right back into the fray.

All my focus is on slashing, ripping, biting and tearing. Attempts to avoid more injuries are futile, but I've grown numb to the pain. Both my Cat and my inner Alpha agree we need to end every abomination in order to protect our pack and friends.

Everywhere I look, there's chaos and fighting. Magic being flung all over and screams of pain and anger fill the air. We *will* be victorious; there is no other option.

If we don't save Dani, I don't think I could live without her cheery brightness in my life. She was the first to see worth in my worthless soul. The first to love me. The first to show me I can be more. The only one holding me back was me and the voices of those who hated me.

Dani is my everything, and I will not rest until she's back in my arms.

Determination pushes my jaws to bite harder, my claws to rake deeper and my dodges to grow faster. There is nothing else besides this battle.

A wave of seduction and allure washes over the chamber, and even the God pauses for a second before continuing his battle against Seren.

My gaze, like almost everyone else in the cavern, turns towards Lia. Every beast pauses and moves in her direction like puppets pulled by their puppet master.

This is great because it'll be much easier to pick off these creatures if they're not fighting back, but having to fight my arousal in Shifted form is intensely uncomfortable.

I don't think I've ever had to deal with lust in this form, and I don't like it. Thankfully, I'm not alone, and Hagon snarls at our female Alpha. His discomfort loud and obvious.

The Orcs both seem untouched, and a frown drags my brows down until I notice the sheen of magic surrounding them.

Rafe bounds over to the Orcs, using their power to prevent himself from being drawn into Lia's orbit as well.

Tawson is equally unaffected, and I have to wonder how powerful he is to not even seem flushed at the arousal in the air. I've heard stories about that Alpha, and his presence hums with incredible electrifying power.

Ily and Eram lean over Dani, speaking quiet words of reassurance to her. They seem as unaffected as the Orcs, until I look closer and catch the bulges tenting their trousers. I guess we're all lucky that we have some connection to Lia through our Omega's otherwise, we'd be in the same trance as the rest of these beasts.

There's a new male rushing towards Dani, his face flushed and pants tight as he fights through Lia's alluring aura that blankets this entire cavern. To fight against our Succubus like that must mean he already has a connection to our pack; otherwise, he'd be as entranced as the rest of the beasts.

With my part of the fighting done, I make my way towards Dani.

She's my sun, the light I rise for, the warmth I'd chase to the ends of the world.

CH. 37

Dani

The echoing chaos around me is a deafening reminder of my powerlessness, the sharp, piercing agony, a relentless assault. I'm dying. I've lost too much blood, and it continues to seep from my wounds. My mates don't know where I am, and Tev is trapped, unable to allow me to finish our bond.

I've fought so hard to find my family, to find my pack, how is this the end? How will my softer males survive my loss? Will they be okay with Lia, Hagon, Eram and Seren to soothe their agony? Will my stronger mates come out of this okay? I just don't know, and it pains me how badly I want to reassure them it will be alright. I'll be with them, regardless. My love for each mate burns in my chest, and I know that even after I'm dead, I will live on in their memories.

"Dani! Oh Goddess, my strong Omega, please don't give up!"

A searing pain slices through me—Ily's voice, or what sounded like it, rings cruelly in my head. Even his scent — syrupy, sweet cherries, though thoroughly burnt — reaches my nose, and another stab of pain has a small groan slipping past my numb lips.

"Dani! *Fuck.* Ily, can you pick locks? Do you see keys anywhere? Fuck, fuck, *fuck.* We need to get her off this *Goddess damned* alter!" Eram's worried words, a whisper against the silence, briefly pierces my fog of despair, then the fresh, earthy, almost damp scent of him, cool and calming, washes over me.

"Wha?" I attempt to speak, my eyes fluttering open.

The first thing I see is Eram, but... He looks *very* different. He's got... antlers? But they're made of branches, with pretty colourful leaves decorating them.

Oh, I'm hallucinating. *Great.* Nyurel must have trapped me in some mental prison.

"*Dani!* Please, baby, please see me! Oh Goddess, *please,* Dani don't drift away from me," Ily begs, his concerned face pushing Eram aside.

Ilaris appears normal. Maybe I'm not hallucinating? Are my mates actually here? I'm adrift in a sea of confusion; my body is numb and cold, a sensation like floating through a frozen wasteland. The loss of blood and my broken bones make it difficult to move, even though I want to reach for him.

"Ily?" I whisper, tears well in my eyes. "Eram? Are...are you *real*?"

Ilaris cups his mouth to muffle his sobs as he cries freely. Eram presses his lips together, but I catch a tear dripping down his cheek even though he refuses to show the emotion.

"Dani, I know you can pick locks. Do you have anything on you? Can you get out of these manacles?" Eram questions, his hands hovering over my broken body unsure where he can touch me without causing more pain.

"Y-yeah, but..." I sniffle, trying to stop my tears. "My hands are broken, I... I can't even..." My voice is a whisper amidst the crashing sounds of power echoing beyond my two males.

"*Fuck! Shit!* What do we do, Eram? What do we do!" Ily hisses, hands pulling at his hair as his eyes scan over my body.

"Move!" another familiar voice says.

"Tev?"

"Yes, Sweet One. I am here." His deep raspy voice sends shivers down my spine only for me to gasp in pain as the wounds where my wings used to be shift against the stone. "No, don't move, just bite me. Please?"

Tev presses his arm to my mouth, and without a second to wait, I press my sharp teeth into his skin.

"NO! GET AWAY!" Nyurel's furious screech pierces my ears a second before his power knocks everyone away from me.

But he's too late. I can feel my claim sinking into Tev. The cord that connects us shines a deep maroon as it wraps around my heart, completing our mate-bond.

Everything happens all at once. White snowy magic brushes past my body, black and purple smoke clashes with it. Electric blue power crashes with a boom, like thunder, shaking the chamber. Jerrik's patchwork body flies past me, sizzling and smoking as he slams into the wall. The smoky magic throws Ily and Eram back. Tev and whoever was with him fly into the wall, landing in a crumpled heap. Disfigured beasts lay in broken piles around me.

And then time stops.

Particles of dirt pause in mid-air. My mates halt their trajectories mid-flight. A surge of incandescent energy bursts from within, as if something set my soul alight. The stone altar beneath me cracks with a loud boom, veins of glowing power spidering out in all directions from my core. My body arches, and I scream with pain as my broken bones grind together with the movement, and my raw wounds tug and pull as I twist. The manacles and chains once holding me captive shatter with a clattering shriek.

"Good. Break free, my daughter. Break free and show Nyurel your vengeance." Bassanai's sweet voice sounds all around me.

My body rises in an electric storm of magic, and I spin, trying to find my mother.

"I am not actually here, Dani. But I could feel the barrier shatter and your Demi-Goddess light up the night sky. I'm proud of you. Let no one hold you down again. You are strong. Just like your father," she says, warmth spilling from her words, and washing over me.

"Where are you? What's happening?" I ask, feeling stupid the moment the words leave my mouth.

Obviously, I finally claimed my last mate and broke the block stopping me from reaching my true powers. But… my body is still damaged. How can I fight if both my hands don't function?

"Dani, stop that right now. You are the Demi-Goddess of Torment, Nature and Devotion. You do not feel stupid for asking questions. It's the

best way to learn, my sweet," Bassanai replies to my thoughts and questions. "You are powerful now, Daughter. Heal yourself."

My mouth drops open. Okay... I can heal myself? Wicked. And my Demi-Goddess title? That sounds badass. A pleased grin spreads over my face; my cheeks hurt from how wide it is.

"I must go. Please take care and use your powers to end Nyurel. He's a stain on our precious land," Bassanai says, her words growing darker as she speaks. "I love you."

My mother is gone as quickly as she arrived. Sound warps around me, sucked into the center of my storm before shattering outward in a deafening shockwave. Time resumes its relentless march with a shriek. Wind tears through the chamber, a spinning vortex of arcane energy. Deep red, forest green and sky blue. Flames that don't burn, lightning that doesn't strike and shadows that move against the light. Wild. Untamed. *Just like me.*

I feel it then, my magic itching to heal my broken bones and open wounds. With barely a thought, it races through me, knitting my skin closed and straightening my breaks. My body heals before I know it. Not whole, even magic can't replace what's been taken from me. But I will get my vengeance.

Then, silence. Everyone in the chamber

frozen, staring in awe at me. Even Jerrik, the putrid worm. My gaze narrows on him, and with a flick of my wrist, that deep red magic shoots straight into his body, sending him into convulsions with a gurgling scream. It's not enough, though. I call on my powers over nature and ask if the earth will contain him until I'm ready.

Eagerly, the roots within the soil and rock around us leap to do my bidding. Jerrik's limbs are pulled against the ceiling and his body is strung tight, suspended above the chaos around me.

With that taken care of, I turn my rage to the God in question. Fury contorts my grin into something malicious, and I've barely had the thought before I've sent my deep red powers into his body. Even the God will fall to my Torment.

Nyurel's skeletal form flails against the dirt floor, shaking and cursing my name. My eyesight is better than ever, and I catch his fingers moving, calling up his dirty smoke, attempting to escape my vengeance.

No.

Fuck that shit. He will *never* leave this island.

My Demi-Goddess powers tell me he can't be fully destroyed, so I will do the next best thing. I let my powers mix and mingle together, creating something new and deadly to those who intend harm. Before Nyurel can attempt an escape, I send my magic, all of it, including my air and illusions, into his body and use the powers inherent to me to create a curse and bind him to this place.

His foul magic burns as I pull it out of him and send it deep into the earth. Sinking a metaphysical chain that ties his body to this island. Nyurel shakes, his skeletal frame rattling with each shuddering breath, his mouth open in a silent scream as searing pain wracks his body, the agony a tangible thing. My heart, encased in ice and fury, has no sympathy for the male. He's committed atrocious acts against hundreds. The stench of his depravity is overwhelming but I will end that. He will torment Saforia no more.

The brightness of my mixed power and the blackness of his magic slowly dwindle until there's nothing left inside the God. He's mundane now, as weak as a human and as frail as the elderly, though he is still immortal. His body drops in a crumpled heap on the ground, and I slowly descend from where I had risen above everything, until my feet touch the broken altar.

The sigh that leaves me is heavy with exhaustion, and I collapse, the cold arms that catch me a stark contrast to my weariness.

CH. 38

Tev

My eyes track Dani's glittering bright form as she finishes the spell, a faint shimmer of light lingering in the air around the skeletal male. Whatever she's done to him has wiped out the malicious aura that surrounded this place.

As she stumbles, weak from everything she has endured, the tall male with silvery white hair catches her. I have to curb my instinct to go to her. I am a stranger to everyone except Dani, but I know most of these males and the statuesque female are pack. My new family.

As a solitary Wildling, it will be difficult to adjust to such a large pack, but for my new mate? I will do anything she asks of me. Dani may be tiny, but her presence is larger than life.

Out of the corner of my eye, I watch the short male Omega. He's pretty in a masculine way, but his scent is delectable. No longer burnt with fear, rich syrupy cherries permeate the surrounding air. My mouth waters with the urge to taste him, but he doesn't know me. Would he even enjoy my presence?

Next, I flick my eyes over to the other male that hovered over Dani. He's tall, slim, with rough, bark-like skin. The antlers reaching high above his head are majestic but strange. I don't know what he is, but I sense a kindred spirit in the male. He's one with nature, just as I am. There's no sexual attraction to him, but I have a feeling that out of all my new family, this male will be a good friend.

"Let me down from here, you monsters!" the piemel screeches from the ceiling.

Everyone in the chamber glances up at the male, wrapped in roots and dirt, squirming as if he has even the slightest chance of escape. His boots kick uselessly, dislodging clods of soil that rain down around him.

Fury tints my vision red. This male has done awful, unforgivable things to my mate, and likely to many others. He deserves pain for his part in all this. Before I can move, a teal Fae crackling with rage and electricity stops below the piemel.

"You have done enough, Jerrik." The Fae's voice is layered with power as he speaks. He doesn't need to shout; the dominance and magic pouring off of him presses against my chest, a warning no one sane would ignore.

The roots shudder, then tighten. Bone pops loudly in the cavern. The male's scream breaks into wet, choking gurgles that curl something pleased and dark inside my chest. The restraints blacken and wither, dropping him to the floor in a cloud of dust.

He barely has a chance to suck in air before the white-striped Snow-Cat charges. Crushing jaws clamp around one leg, shaking and shredding the limb apart. Flesh tears, blackened blood sprays, and the leg comes free with a sound I'll never forget.

The tall pink Succubus is already moving, her short sword hacking down again and again until the other leg parts under her blade.

His screams turn shrill, then thin, as the Wolf rips into an arm, teeth crunching through bone. The two Orc's join in with gleeful brutality, blades rising and falling, carving, slashing and mangling the slowly dying male.

Time stretches, each second soaked in sound and blood, until there's barely enough of him left to call it a body. But, I wouldn't change a thing. This is less than he deserves, after all.

Everyone steps back, and Dani mutters something under her breath as she calls on her forest green powers and lets nature reclaim him. He will soon be nothing, his very essence fading like dust, leaving not even a crumb for any possibility of resurrection.

Movement drags my gaze off the curious male, and I come face-to-face with a scarred, angry Alpha.

"Who the fuck are you?" the purple-eyed male snarls.

"That's Tev. He's my last mate, so be nice, Hagon!" Dani chirps from her perch in the icy male's arms.

"Humph, he doesn't look like much," Hagon's voice, a low rumble, answers her. His eyes sweeping over me with a critical gaze.

I know that in my human form; I look like a regular Alpha, nothing special. My life has been a solitary one. I've always preferred the company of nature over beings. It's why I made my home deep in the Naargeestig forest. There are ancient ruins that lie crumbling inside, and I used some of the better off stone to create a cozy den beneath the ground.

My world has changed so much from

where I once was, and while I know I'll be happier with a mate and pack, it will be a difficult transition for me.

"Hagon, is it?" I ask, trying not to allow my annoyance to show, "I may not *look* like much now, but I did my best to protect our mate while we were both imprisoned here. If you'd like, I can introduce you to my Wildling form? Then we will see who *looks* like much." Aaaand I couldn't hold back my snark. Oh well. I'm ready to fight for my position in this pack.

Now that I've found and claimed my fated mate, nothing will separate us. If that means showing this male that I can hold my own, then so be it.

"Hagon," a sharp voice hisses his name in reproach, "if Dani has claimed him, then he is now pack. At least save your Alpha-male posturing bullshit for when we're home?" The pretty male Omega stops our fight before it has even begun.

The scarred one relents, stepping back with a snarl. I force my shoulders to relax and take a deep breath. Tension still bubbles beneath the surface, but I do not want to upset my new pack any more than they already are. This has been a trying time for all of us.

"Good!" The female Alpha claps her hands, the sound like a crack of thunder in the quiet of this cavern of horrors. “Let’s get the fuck out of here, yeah?”

Grunts, nods and mumbled agreement sound around the chamber, and I glance towards the pale Fae. A silent conversation passes between the orcs and the green Fae with a glance, then the Fae turns and heads for the exit. As my new pack sets off, I trail behind, feeling left out, while two orcs wait at the mouth of the dark tunnel.

A glint of something shimmering in one of the Orc's hands catches my eye; I snarl and snatch my pixie's wings free. How dare they touch my mate’s broken wings?

“Easy, friend, we saw em on our way in an knew ye wouldna want ta leave anythin behind. They’re yours.” With a gesture intended to soothe, the other Orc raises his hands.

Muttering a low growl, I cradle Dani's wings and walk past, reminding myself to avoid a fight. I should stay near Dani, anyway. This has been a hard day.

The last thing I expected to find in this hellish place was my Goddess-given mate. To have her taken from me and injured, while I was powerless to help, is unbearable.

Remorse and guilt beat down on me. Why would the Goddess permit this? Have I done something so heinous in my life that I deserve to end up here? No, there has to be another reason, and I'm sure my new pack will fill me in when they feel like it.

Our group follows the dark tunnel, passing bloodstains in the dirt and the door to my cage. Finally, my eyes catch a faint light ahead of us.

Freedom.

When I emerge from the passage into the gloomy cloud-filled sky, I have to stop. My eyes slip shut, and I inhale, reveling in the open air. I did not imagine I would escape. Those males had my death written all over them.

But, along came a tiny Goddess in soft pink and changed my life in a whirlwind of chaos. I don't regret biting Dani when she demanded it, but I'm unsure of my place in her life. She has all these other gorgeous beings surrounding her in love and affection. What does she need me for? I'm just a gruff forest Alpha that has very little social skills and spends most of his time in Wildling form.

A deep sigh escapes my lips, and I trudge after my new *pack* into small rowboats that take us to a grand ship anchored off the shore of this nightmarish island.

The waves are vicious and rough as we

paddle towards our way home. By the time I climb aboard, I'm soaked from head to toe. At least my filthy skin got a brief wash.

"Come, we've got some clean water you can use while the King directs us home." A pale striped Alpha pats my shoulder with a weary smile.

I stand there, staring at his compassion for a moment too long. He stops walking, his smile faltering as he slowly crumples in on himself.

"Yes!" I say, too loud, making the male jump, his eyes wide. "I mean, yes, please. And thank you." My voice softens to something more appropriate, soothing his unease.

"I... I'm Costen. It's nice to meet you, Tev." He offers as he takes me down the steps to the belly of the ship.

For a fleeting moment, the chilling thought that he's bringing me down here to imprison me once again washes over me, yet I feel strangely indifferent. As long as Dani receives proper care, I'm unconcerned about their plans for me.

But, the genial male leads me into a lavish bedroom, where the rest of our pack and my new mate sit around on cushions washing the dirt and other smears off their skin. The scarred one and the Fae tenderly clean Dani, and that sight alone has my shoulders softening. Good. She needs some pampering.

None of the pack bats an eye at my entrance; I even get a few nods from the medley of beings in this room. Maybe my presence isn't as contentious as I'd assumed. It's possible only the angry Alpha has a problem with me. And I can't blame him. If I'd arrived to find my mate mutilated and near death with a new mate mark, I would be just as prickly.

The room is silent, save for the occasional splash of water as we all do a cursory clean. Someone had taken care and provided us with bowls of warm water, along with rags. I hope when we arrive home, there will be a place to bathe. Time passed strangely while I was in that prison alone. I do not know how long I was there before they brought Dani in.

The voyage to the mainland is faster than expected, and I follow my new pack-mates out of the ship only for my jaw to drop at the sight before me.

Varough. The capital city. While I was aware of its impressive scale, I never expected such stunning beauty. My shock only grows at the fact that my pack heads up the mountainside and into the castle grounds. Did Costen say we were on the King's ship? Fuck. I don't belong here.

My skin itches with the need to shift. In my Wildling form, I feel a primal comfort, a sense of belonging that I don't experience in my human shape. That's how I've lived most of my life. I've never experienced a span of time this long in human form; it's both remarkable and strange. Getting around on these short legs isn't as difficult as I anticipated; however, the requirement to talk is quite disturbing. I cannot hide behind my fur and fangs.

Even with my discomfort, I follow behind my new pack, my gaze peering around with wide-eyed awe. Although my body is honed in on Dani, never letting her move out of sight.

The male Omega slows his pace to walk beside me. He glances at me out of the corner of his eye, with a tiny furrow in his brow. Is he trying to understand me? Is he here to add to Hagon's threats? Or maybe he's just trying to get to know his new pack-mate.

"I'm Ilaris. It's... nice to meet you in less harrowing circumstances," the male offers with a wry twist to his lips.

"Tev. I must thank you for freeing me and helping me to get to Dani back there," I reply, voice gruff.

"Anything for her," Ilaris states, a serious

tilt to his lips, "I uh... Do you have any idea what we should do with those? Do you think seeing them will upset her?" He rushes out, gesturing at the delicate wings I carry.

Fuck. Right.

"No idea," I heave out a morose sigh, my eyes trailing down to the precious part of Dani that I cradle. "I didn't want to leave any bit of her back there."

"Yeah, that's smart. Even though she cursed Nyurel, I'm still uneasy that he's not dead." He shivers and quickly changes the subject. "Maybe Seren will know what to do with the wings."

I grunt in response. Which one is Seren?

CH. 39

Seren

Tension continues to radiate through me even though the danger has passed. My arms ache with a sorrowful weight, cradling my sleeping Pixie. Though her injuries from Nyurel and Jerrik have healed, the mental scars will haunt her forever.

That and the fact that they took such an integral part of my Omega. How could anyone be so cruel? What did she ever do to deserve this kind of torture?

My beautiful mate will not be okay, but I know when she wakes she will lie and say she's fine. Dani is so strong. And incredibly stubborn. How do I help her when she doesn't want any help?

With quick steps, I carry her, and lead my pack down the castle halls to our wing. I think a bath and a long nap are necessary right now. The urge to clean Dani and remove any remnants of those foul males from her skin beats at me. My inner Alpha snarls with the desire to replace those scents with my own. That will come, but first, a bath.

When my guards open our chamber doors, I turn to Hagon and place our precious burden in his arms with a quiet directive to bring her to our bathing room. The scarred male is as serious as I am and reverently carries her away.

My eyes flick from Lia to Ily, from Eram to Costen and skipping the new male to my friend.

"Tawson, thank you for coming." I tug him into a tight hug. "I don't know that we would have succeeded without you. Now, can I impose once again? I have a favor to ask." Stepping back, our eyes meet and my stoic friend's lip twitches. His form of a grin.

"Anything, Seren. You know that. How can I help?" Tawson replies, crossing his arms and settling into his regular military-like stance.

"I think after some rest my mate will need her sister. The loss she's suffered will haunt her, and I fear without someone there to force her to confront it, melancholy will drag her under. I don't see her opening up to us as easily. Family has a way of getting under your skin," I say, my words grave. A plea underneath the seriousness.

"Of course. I think Luella would castrate us if we didn't bring her here to visit." Tawson smirks.

"But what about Gin?" Brenth asks, a large tusk-filled grin plastered on his face as he butts into our conversation.

"Gin will behave. Luella will make sure of it," Tawson says, his smirk growing a little wider.

I completely understand that grin. Gin is one of the most stubborn and deadly males I've ever had the pleasure of knowing. Yet, he bows to his tiny Omega so quickly. She is the true leader of their pack.

A matching grin spreads over my lips, and I snort at the look on Brenth's face. The Orc knew exactly when to break the grave air. I can understand why fate brought them to Tawson's pack. Those males needed someone like him.

Rafe is good for some comic relief, but he doesn't know when to turn it off. I shake my head, slap Tawson on the back and send him home to his mate. He's agreed to bring his omega here tomorrow.

Once they're gone, I'm left with Ward and Tev. The rest of my pack have gone to join Dani and Hagon in the bath. I scrutinize the Wildling, assessing him, watching for any aggression, but the male just stares at me, an impassive look on his face.

"So, Tev, who are you?" I demand. I'll save my diplomacy for the public.

He recoils in surprise, eyes wide and mouth parting. The movement pulls my eyes down to the delicate bundle he still cradles.

"Ah, right." I sigh, turning to Ward. "Can you take these to the vault? I have a strong feeling that Dani will want to do something with them, but I don't want her to have to see them before she's ready. They will keep with all the rest of our precious belongings."

"Aye, sir," Ward replies.

"Wait! What?" Tev steps back as Ward attempts to take the wings.

"Easy, Tev. We will place them in storage until Dani is prepared to deal with them. I don't want her to suffer needlessly, do you?"

At my patient response, his tense shoulders relax and he stares down at the iridescent wings in his arms. With a heaving sigh, he relents and hands them to Ward. Reluctance lines every inch of his body, but he's conceding, and that's a step in the right direction. Since we're now family, he will have to learn to trust us and lean on us for help. But that will come with time.

"I-I don't know how to do this," Tev says the moment Ward leaves, his eyes pinned to the door as if he can still see the wings.

"That's fine. You think the rest of us knew what we were doing? We're a motley crew that Dani has collected along the way, and we're still learning how to coexist," I reply with a small smile, thinking of how I literally stole Dani from her mates before they realized we were pack.

"But I've been a loner my whole life. I lived in the middle of the woods with no one around for decades!" he insists, his fists clenching and unclenching, eyes darting around the room.

"Great. And I've lived in this Goddess-damned castle my whole life, knowing I would have to be King. Both are difficult paths, and yet we've walked them and come out strong. You just have to learn to relax and lean on us for help," I snark back before I soften my tone.

"I know," Tev huffs, arms crossing. "It's going to be hard, but after what Dani's been through, I don't want to add to her stress. Although I think I'm going to have to fight Hagon. He's not too keen on my being here."

That has a loud snort escaping. "Hagon dislikes everyone and will make you work to prove you belong with our Omega. We've all had to deal with that grumpy male. Don't worry, you'll be fine. Now, would you rather continue talking, or would you like to bathe with our mate?"

Finally, I spy a tiny smile on his face as he nods in agreement. "Let's go see how our mate is."

After bathing, our entire pack piles into the nest. Even Tev, with minor growling from Hagon and, surprisingly, Eram. Costen urges Tev to sleep near him with his beaming grin and soft words. He's nearly as persuasive as Ily or Dani when it comes to getting us to agree to anything.

Waking hours later, I'm not the first one up. Dani stands on the balcony, staring out at the sea. Her gaze somber as one hand reaches back to the now closed wounds on her back. She can't quite reach them, but I know exactly what she's doing.

"Mate," I breathe as I step into her body, catching her as she startles. "I'm sorry we were too late. I'd do anything to save you from this loss. Just say the word and I'll raze the land in search of some way to get your wings back." The offer is genuine, although I doubt she'll take me up on it. My beautiful Omega wouldn't want innocents to suffer.

"No, I… I'll get used to it," Dani replies softly, her chin dipping as she stares down at her hands. "It's just... I swear I can still feel them, but I know they're gone."

She spins around in my arms and meets my gaze, her gorgeous green eyes watery and uncertain. "I don't know who I am without them. They... they were a major part of who I am. Am I no longer even a Pixie? Have you ever heard of a wingless Pixie? I'm just... mundane now." Her voice grows soft as tears splash onto the tunic she's wearing. Another one of my shirts.

"Dani. You listen to me carefully. Who you are is not defined by what you look like. It's in your every word, your every movement. The graceful way you spin and dance as you practice with your swords. Your energetic rambles when you're excited. The loving way you care for Ily and Costen. And the way you allow your Alphas to care for you. Even when you're stubborn about it."

That earns me a watery laugh.

"My sweet precious Omega. Even without your wings, you are the literal end-all for us. Your entire pack would burn the world just to see you smile," I pause, letting my words sink in before continuing, "The journey to healing won't be easy; expect setbacks and struggles, but you are the most fearless female I know, and if anyone can rise above this, it's you."

"Thank you, Alpha." She sniffles and buries her face in my chest. It's not enough for me, so I pick her up and cradle her in my arms, needing her close.

"Seren, I... I know this will pass, but... Goddess, it hurts. I keep expecting the light hum of my wings when I speak, but this silence is unnerving. How do you wingless beings do this? They were such a big part of my expressions." She peers up at me, eyes red and lips turned down into a devastating frown.

I don't have an answer for her. I've never thought about it before. But I know Luella is coming today, and she will help Dani where I can't.

"I don't know, Sweet Pixie. But, I have someone special coming to visit you today, so how about a bath with me before I help you dress?" I try to add some brightness to my words, a subtle way to cheer her up.

"Luella!" Dani perks up, and even with her eyes still leaking tears a grin slowly grows over her lips. "Yes! Thank you, Alpha. Let's get ready!"

With a soft smile, I carry her inside and towards the bathing chamber.

One small step at a time.

CH. 40

Dani

With a fresh bath and a pretty dress, I'm ready to face the world. Okay, no, that's a lie. But I am ready to see my sister. My pack is wonderful and overly affectionate right now, which is normally amazing, but I just don't feel like myself.

Their constant attempts to coddle me are grating on my nerves. I can feel the tension building with each unnecessary gesture. The harsh words and curses I hurled at my mates echo in my ears, leaving me feeling terrible.

Wandering the halls of the castle aimlessly, I pause at an open doorway. It's a staircase leading up to one of the towers. Curiosity pushes me to explore. Anything to ignore the phantom sensation of my wings at my back.

Throughout my errant drifting, I sense a couple of my mates shadowing my steps. I don't snap at them this time though, because it's actually kind of nice knowing they're there.

A hollow ache echoes in my chest, mirroring the emptiness behind me. Should I jump back into my sword practice? Work on my hand to hand? Attempt to wrangle all the new powers burning inside my core? None of it sounds appealing. I kind of just want to wallow in my misery, and I know that's stupid, but I feel useless from the loss.

The spiral staircase winds upward, a seemingly endless climb. My legs burn, breaths are shallow, and sweat beads on my brow. Did I use my wings so much that without them all my muscles are weak as a lamb? It's as if I've started over from scratch and Bernon has just begun my training.

Fuck. This *sucks*.

I think I'm afraid to go to the practice arena. Before, I was deadly and precise and wowed my mates with my skill. Now... *Now* I'm pathetic and weak.

Frustration bubbles inside me. What if they don't want a frail mate? I can't protect them anymore. I haven't even attempted to look at my bag full of steel. The thought almost makes me ill. I'm a failure.

A gasp escapes me as I reach the top, and a breathtaking view opens up before me. The whole tower is open to the air, and I can see for miles in every direction. The endless sea to my right, a faint landmass in the distance, sends shivers down my spine. That's where Nyurel held me. I turn away, pushing down the anger and fear. To my left, forest and grasslands stretch over Saforia. I swear I can almost see the desert that leads to Banell.

Twisting a little more, my eyes land on a thick forest I haven't yet learned the name of and past it there's a dark mar against the green of grass. What is that? I remind myself to ask someone when I feel like speaking again.

Squinting my eyes to see even further, the start of the marshlands and their low fog lying over the land. That's where... hmm, I close my eyes trying to remember the name of that village. Lia says that's where she grew up. Low... L-La... No... Lowleaf! That's it.

One day, when I'm less fragile from my loss, I will convince Lia to take me there. I want to visit every corner of our land. There's so much to see and experience.

Even though Seren says I'm now Queen of Saforia, I think with a shudder, that doesn't mean I'm going to be stuck in this damn castle. As Queen, wouldn't it be wise to visit each village, experience the distinct cultures and meet the beings who call them home?

Another turn and the Mikta Mountains rise above the land. Will I ever cross them again? Do I desire to return to Pekayan? There's nothing there for me anymore. Tears well, but I force them down; only a single drop falls from my eye. I'll find time to honor my parents. I know they were just foster parents, but they cared for me and taught me how to live.

Footsteps echo on the cold stone, and I spin to see who's interrupting my moment of grief. My mouth a hard line, ready to spew anger and vitriol.

"Holy shit, Dani. Why the hell did you climb up here? Goddess, my lungs hurt," Luella curses, heaving for air before she turns and swats at someone out of view. "No, no, go away; you can't be here. This is girl time!"

The sight of her crumbles the walls I've built to hold back all the pain from my imprisonment. One harsh sob slips forth, followed quickly by a second. Fuck. I don't want to cry!

"Damnit, Lulu!" I curse at my sister only for her to hurry over and fold me into a tight embrace.

Her scent, sweetened even more with her pregnancy, settles something inside me. The familiar warmth of her arms around me and her murmured nonsense into my hair all work together to shatter the tough facade I've been carrying around since my rescue.

"Shh, shh, it's okay. I'm here, D. I'm here and you're not alone. Never again." Luella hums a soft tune as she reassures me.

We end up sitting on the cold stone, entangled in each other's arms as she cries softly along with my wracking sobs.

"W-why are you crying?" I manage in between my harsh weeping.

"Because I'm pregnant, you ninny! Everything makes me cry, dammit! Or angry. I also get so angry at the stupidest things now," she snarls, and the sound is so unlike my sister that a hoot of laughter escapes in between tears.

Luella glares at me for a moment before she joins me. Now we're sitting here in a dusty tower on the dirty floor, cackling. A shuffle of feet on the stairs has both of us stopping abruptly. The moment I open my mouth to hiss out a warning, Luella cuts me off.

"If anyone dares to step a foot into this tower, I will castrate them."

The steps retreat quickly, and I meet

Luella's eyes with a wide beaming grin. We both burst into howls again.

"Goddess, Luella, that was the best thing I've seen all day!" I nudge her with my elbow, trying to get my laughter under control. But every time I think I've got it stopped, she meets my eyes and we start all over again.

"What is wrong with us?" Luella squeaks out past her mirth.

"Stress relief?" I reply, trying to catch my breath.

"Okay, stop looking at me!" she cries, hiccuping through her giggles.

I stare down at my lap, taking deep calming breaths. The laughter peters off and finally I'm calmer. She gets control of herself with slow steady breathing, and finally I feel like I can speak.

"I'm lost, Lulu. They... they took my wings," I whisper the words aloud, scared that if I acknowledge them, the pain of them getting ripped away will return.

"I know. And those bastards got what they deserved. It's just unfortunate that you couldn't permanently kill Nyurel. But at least he's cursed to live as a mortal and chained to that island." The vehemence in her voice, the anger on my behalf, surprises me. My sweet sister is not a violent being. But I know her own time with Nyurel changed her.

"Yeah. But at least Jerrik the Jerk got obliterated by your mate." My lips twitch with the desire to smile at that worm's true end.

"Tawson told me how angry his power felt the moment his eyes landed on Jerrik," she says with a laugh, "he said there was no other choice but to allow his magic to deal with the slimy male. I'm very, very glad to know he's gone, finally."

The emotion thick in her voice has me reaching for her and dragging her into another crushing hug. It's then that I notice her bump. I grab her shoulders and push her back so I can look.

"Oh my Goddess, Luella! You're fucking pregnant!" I shout, eyes wide with wonder.

"Uhh... Yeah, you knew that?" she asks, confusion crinkling her brow.

"No, but I can *see* it! There's a fricken baby in there!" I point at her rounded stomach as if she doesn't know what I am talking about.

She laughs heartily. "Dani. Did you forget about that awkward conversation your parents had with us when we were teens? That's what happens when a mommy and daddy love each other very much," she mimics the world's most embarrassing conversation my parents had ever attempted.

Another peal of laughter escapes us both, and we devolve into a messy pile of tears and giggles. Goddess, it's good to spend time with my bestie.

We pass the rest of the day in the tower, the stone walls feeling cold to the touch. The wind whistles through the space as we reminisce and reassure each other that we're going to be okay, no matter what.

Faceless males push food into the room at odd intervals, ensuring we're fed and watered. Luella or I would snarl a warning that no one better enter this room while we're here. I wasn't ready to face my pack yet, and I think my sister just needed a break from overprotective males.

"Dani," Luella puts a hand on my arm as we slowly descend the stairs, our time hiding out in the tower ending as the sun sets. "You know you're not really different now, right? Just because they did something so heinous doesn't mean you're not still *you*."

Her words penetrate deep into my inner wounds, and I try to pull away, but the staircase is narrow, and she digs her claws into my arm to hang onto me.

"Stop! You can't know that!" I shout at her

calm words.

"Yes, I can, because we just spent an entire day in a dusty old tower and the same sassy Pixie joked and laughed with me like we used to," she insists, not letting go, "Dani, you are still the same stubborn, filthy-mouthed, energetic female that I grew up with."

"But I can't *fight* the same. My muscles are *weak*, and my agility is *hindered* with the loss of my wings!"

"Yeah? *And?* Didn't you have to *work hard* to get to that point? Can't you do it again? I saw a really nice practice arena when I arrived. I doubt any of your mates would tell you *no*. And if they do, just cry," Luella says with a casual shrug.

Laughter bursts from me at her suggestion. Crying isn't something I ever allow anyone to see, except Luella.

A curse and muffled '*I knew it*' sounds from further down the spiral staircase. I meet Luella's eyes with a snort, and we both devolve into giggles again.

"I just... I don't feel *right* anymore. My balance is off, and I swear I can still *feel* them wanting to flutter, but... they're not there," I whisper after the laughter has trailed off.

"I know. But you have a pack of very willing mates that just want to love you. Lean on them when you falter. They adore you, Dani," Luella's reply has me sniffling again.

I nod my head. Yeah, I've been pushing them away for long enough. It's time to face my fears.

CH. 41

Costen

My feet can't stay still as I pace around the base of the stairs. I listen for the sound of murmured voices and light footsteps to tell me my mate is finally coming out of hiding. It pains me that I can't do anything to ease her listlessness.

Those monsters took something integral to who she is, and I don't know how to help her. I pray to the Goddess that Luella can give her some kind of comfort. But what can her sister do that I can't?

Finally, the faint sound of them descending reaches my ears, and I pause my anxious motions to listen. Is she happy? Sad? Angry? How do I act when she comes down? Will she want a hug? Will she let me hold her?

My hands tug at my hair as my mind whirls through what I should do when I see her. Does she even want me anymore? I know I'm a burden, but she seemed happy with me before all this... Maybe I'll be too much for her now. She has enough scars; she won't want my neediness on top of that.

Just as I turn to leave, bright laughter echoes down the staircase. The sound unwinds something in my chest, and I feel like I can breathe again. Thank the Goddess, she sounds a little less sad. I know it won't be instantaneous, but it's good to hear that spark in her voice.

"Costen!" Dani says, her voice brighter than it was yesterday. "Were you waiting here all day?"

I don't want to answer that. It makes me sound clingy and weak. But when I meet her eyes, only curiosity and affection shine back at me.

"Y-yes?" I hesitantly answer, "I... I was worried about you. Is... Are... Are you okay? I mean, you're not but... are you feeling even a little better?" I want to hit myself. That was pathetic and stupid. Of course she's not okay.

"Costen." Her sharp tone has my head snapping up to her face. She stands, hands on hips, with a furrow in her brow and the cutest little crinkle of her nose. "Are those voices bothering you again?"

She means the voices of my past. The ones who hurt me, who put me down and made me feel terrible about existing.

"Sort of... But, I'm more concerned with you right now," I reply, my voice a little steadier.

Dani crashes into me, her arms a vise around my chest, the pressure painful but sweet, a sensation I'd gladly endure forever. When she hugs me, the world melts away, and I feel all my scattered pieces fall back into place with a comforting click.

My nose presses into her messy hair, and I inhale her sugary sweet scent. It's a balm to my frayed nerves, and my entire body releases all the tension I've been carrying since she went missing.

I'm careful as I wrap my arms around her tiny body. I used to be so careful not to crush her delicate wings with my clumsy hands, but now I'm terrified of touching her scars, afraid that I'll cause her more pain.

I should know better. My mate is a Goddess. No, a Demi-Goddess, and she's stronger than I give her credit for.

"It's all right, Sweet Snow. I'm... not okay,

but I will be, in time. As long as I have you and the rest of our pack, everything will be just fine," Dani murmurs into my chest, her voice muffled against my tunic.

"Okay," I whisper back, not wanting to break our peaceful moment.

"Okay," she replies quietly, a smile in her voice.

Dani's hand, clasped in mine, pulls me into the dining hall. The rest of our pack and our visitors chat noisily around the long table. Until we walk through the door.

Silence falls over the room, and every eye turns to our arrival. Ily fidgets in his seat, the need to come touch Dani and reassure himself that she's okay thrumming through his veins. I understand that, and I don't know why he doesn't just come to her.

Seren, Eram, Hagon, Ward, Lia and Tev all watch our Omega with unwavering attention. I can sense their need to come and touch her, but none of them want to overwhelm our little mate.

Dani snorts at the attention, her gaze landing on Luella, and the two females burst out in loud amused laughter. It's contagious, and I join them after a moment. It isn't long before the rest of the room is also chuckling.

"Okay, okay!" Dani huffs, waving a hand in front of her as if she can wipe away the mirth, "one, I am okay. Two, stop staring at me like you're studying a manuscript. And three, I'm hungry, let's eat!"

She drags me along as she marches over to the two empty chairs. Once we settle in, she piles her plate full and nudges me to do the same. It's hard to tear my eyes off her, but it's just so nice to see her smile again.

"So, let me get a few things out. Thank you, Luella and your Elite mates, for coming to my rescue. I'm not sure we'd all have gotten out of there without you," she says softly, her gaze steady on Luella, shifting to each of her mates, making sure they know how grateful she is.

"It was the least we could do," Alec says casually, a small smile on his lips.

"I mean, if we hadn't gone, I'm pretty sure our mate would have banished us from the Keep," Rafe adds cheerfully, a smirk playing over his face, his eyes watching Luella.

"Goddess, Rafe! You don't have to be such a nuisance!" Luella shouts before turning to the Orc sitting next to Rafe. "Please slap him on the back of the head."

"Ow! Okay! I'm sorry... But, I'm not

wrong!" Rafe mutters, rubbing his head from the Orc's hit.

The entire scene sends Dani into peals of laughter, which gets the entire group going again.

This is perfect. I'm beyond thrilled that Dani is in such a playful mood. Her bright smile and joy has the itching need inside me to coddle her, settling down a notch. It's in the moments in between, when the joke is over, that I see the pain swimming behind her eyes.

Dani excels at masking her loss, but I know my mate, and I'm watching her closely because even through our bond she still aches. Oh, she's trying to hide it from all of us, but I have no other skills, so I spend all of my time focused on my Omega.

I'm actually quite surprised that none of my pack-mates can sense it. Although Ily isn't looking as chipper as usual. I should check in with him after dinner. He's a sensitive soul and needs a lot of reassurance, just like me.

Dinner passes with plenty of chatter and jokes, the room a happy medley of voices from both packs. I get to know Luella's males much better and understand why they're called the Elites.

Eventually, yawns spread through the

room, and Seren calls it a night. Offering rooms for Pack Foreastra to stay so they won't have to make the long trek home in the dark.

"Please stay in our guest rooms. It will save you a walk through the cool night, and I know my mate would love to spend a little more time with your's."

"As long as there's a nest for our mate," Tawson replies, arms crossed and face set in stony impassivity.

"Whose castle do you think you're in?" Seren asks, with a cheeky grin on his pale face.

"I don't even care if there's a nest! As long as I can get into a comfy bed, someone take me there now, please?" Luella cuts in, her voice sharp but sleepy.

"Of course." Seren turns to the guard outside the room. "Dralton, please take my guests to their room."

"Goodnight, Dani." Luella shuffles over to my Pix and squeezes her in a tight hug. She leans in and whispers something in my mate's ear, too quiet to hear even with my Cat's sharpened senses.

As their pack heads off, my own gathers around the two Omegas, and we herd them towards our rooms. Our instincts are still on edge, and our Alphas urge us to keep our mates in the center where they belong.

No one will ever take my mate again.

CH. 42

Tev

My sleep was rough and uncomfortable. They shuffled me toward the very edge of the nest, as if I posed a threat to either Omega. I can sense through my bond with Dani how much the male Omega means to her. Nothing in this world could ever force me to harm either of them.

But, the dominant Alphas that my Sweet One has mated are cautious and suspicious of me. On one hand, I can understand that need, but on the other, they can feel me faintly through Dani; they *know* I belong here. They *know* I mean no harm to any of them. But the Alpha bullshit has to be dealt with first.

Today, I mean to make it happen. These

Alphas will push me to the edge no longer. My Wilding snarls violently in my head; he craves blood and demands we force them to submit. But I'm not sure I'm strong enough to dominate all of them. Definitely, the scarred Wolf, the Snow-Cat and the Earth Elemental. But the Succubus and Winter Fae are both formidable.

Those two are going to beat me to a pulp, but I'm still going to fight them; I can feel the adrenaline pumping, the anticipation of battle. It needs to be done to settle the hierarchy so these Alphas stop being so damn suspicious of me. I want nothing except to love and care for my damaged Pixie.

The moment arrives when both Omegas, hand in hand, head towards the ornate bathing chamber, their hushed whispers hinting at shared secrets and affections. They're cuter than I'll admit. I look forward to getting to know Ilaris.

"Where is the fighting arena?" I turn to the pack, my tone vibrating with a growl.

"What?" the Snow-Cat, Costen, asks dumbly.

"We're really doing this?" The Elemental questions skepticism thick in his tone.

"Outside," the Winter Fae states, already heading for the door.

"This should be interesting," Lianis, the tall, slightly unhinged Succubus states, a curl of mischief in her words.

"I do not need to test myself against him," the Beta cuts in, Ward, his name is Ward, "I will stay with our mates and settle their worries when they find out what you're doing."

His disapproval is strong, but he doesn't understand; he does not have our Alpha instincts demanding we resolve this. I *need* to establish my place, or I will forever be on the outskirts of this pack.

That is unacceptable to me. I want to reach for my mate whenever the desire strikes. Without getting into a fight with the rest of my new pack.

The group leads me outside through a winding hallway towards the back of the castle. The bright morning light sears my eyes as we exit the obsidian stone. I'm still healing from my extended stay in the pitch dark those monsters kept me in.

It takes a few moments for the burning to subside, and I can finally see the large sandy arena laid out in front of me.

"Hand to hand?" I ask, "No shifting and no magic. Just sheer dominance, right?"

"I think that sounds perfectly fair, don't

you boys?" Lianis purrs, her pink tail swaying happily behind her as she struts towards the fence and casually leans against it.

"Fine," Hagon grunts, shedding his tunic and doing a few stretches.

"Do we have to fight?" Costen asks, staring at each of us wide-eyed, "I don't really want to, plus I'm not very good… I like him anyway, why would I want to fight one of Dani's mates?"

"No," I cut in before anyone else can respond, "no, we do not have to battle for dominance. Do you concede I am stronger?"

My feet carry me over to the pale, striped male. I hold a hand out to him, and he stares at it for a moment before he grins.

"Oh yes, I can tell you're much stronger than I am. Plus, you protected Dani the best you could under the circumstances! Even with her loss, she's more settled with you around." Costen grabs my hand, giving it a vigorous shake.

His honesty is refreshing, and I can't help the little grin that tips my lips up. Forgoing a handshake, I embrace the male. A silent purr quickly replaces his surprised yip, a soft, warm vibration felt only by me, increasing my admiration for him.

I can understand why Dani chose this Alpha. He's not the strongest, but he carries a warmth so unlike most males. He's… sweet.

"Thank you, Costen," I murmur before pulling away and turning towards the true fight.

Eram waits just inside the fence, a fierce scowl pinned on me as I hop over the railing, landing with a puff of dust. The tall, slim male doesn't appear very strong, but I know determination and the possessiveness over his mate will add strength behind his hits. This one will count on being underestimated. But I've already pegged him. He can fight; he knows how to throw a punch, but I don't think he's had proper training.

Stripping off my shirt, I toss it at the fence without care and settle into a proper fighting stance. After Eram, I have three more battles ahead before this pack will settle down and accept me properly.

"Let's keep this clean and fair," Seren says from the sidelines, "above the waist and don't fight dirty."

Eram throws the first punch; I duck it easily. He telegraphs his moves. This male requires more training.

My fist catches the edge of his jaw, sending him stumbling. Blood leaks from a split lip, but anger burns brighter in his gaze. Eram straightens up, mirroring my posture. I don't mind if this little dominance fight helps him learn more; all the better.

We trade blows until he falters, exhaustion slowing his reflexes. I don't want to go easy on him, but I know if I injure him too much, my Omega will be very cross with me.

"Do you yield?" I ask, panting a little at the exertion.

"Fuck. Fine." Eram curses, dropping his fists. "I'm wiped. I concede you're stronger than I am. For now. I want a rematch after I've had more training," he adds with a small grin.

"I'm always up for a good tussle," I reply, wiping sweat and dirt off my face.

"My turn!" Lia purrs brightly, "I've had a little more training than our gardener." The Succubus nudges Eram as he passes, earning a little snarl.

She throws her head back and laughs; the sight is bewitching. I shake my head. I'm not into anyone but Dani. What the hell is wrong with me?

"Lia!" Hagon shouts, "we all agreed no powers!"

"Ugh, spoilsport. Fine." She does something, and it's as if her presence dims, and I eye her cautiously.

I hadn't even noticed that she was using

her magic. It's so subtle. Damn, she's powerful.

No more words are spoken as she gets into position. Her tail sways eagerly as she grins, flashing her sharp little fangs at me.

We circle each other warily. I observe her posture and footwork and see that she received proper training. This fight offers a greater challenge. But I still think I can win.

After a few more minutes of eyeing each other up, she moves faster than I expect and lands a hard hit on my ribs. An "Ooof" escapes me as she knocks the air out of me, but I recover and block her next punch.

Damn, she's good. I finally hit back and catch her low back, making her stumble. Advancing on her while she's recovering, I throw a flurry of punches towards her face. Lia blocks most of them, but a couple catch her jaw.

Back and forth we each land some solid punches before I catch her with an uppercut and send her flying back. Lia lands with a thud on her back, and everyone pauses, listening for her breathing. Concern flashes through me. I don't actually want to hurt her; she's my pack-mate.

"I'm fine!" Lia slurs, her lip swollen, "I concede. Tev packs one hell of a punch, damn!"

"I'm glad you're not seriously injured," I say, holding a hand out to her, helping her off the sandy ground.

"Nope, I'm pretty tough, but I will admit that you have more dominance than I do. And more training," Lia adds with a small laugh.

She heads back to her place along the fence, and Hagon stomps over, a furious glower marring his face, pulling his deadly scars tight. This male I am uneasy about fighting. His anger is a palpable thing, a bitter taste in the air, each scar a stark white line in the sunlight, a roadmap of hard-won victories, its raised surfaces catching the light.

No words pass between us. We settle in and watch each other. He's got the advantage, having observed two of my fights already. I'm leery of this battle; I don't think I can win this. Despite being tired, I refuse to stop now. I *need* this. *They* need this.

Our pack won't function properly until we figure out where I belong with them.

CH. 43

Hagon

A loud, furious snarl rips from my throat, and I charge at the outsider. The male that claimed my Menace, who was there when I couldn't be. He doesn't deserve her! He doesn't belong in our family.

My body crashes into his, taking us both down to the sand. A thrill of triumph surges through me; the element of surprise is mine, and his stunned silence is my sweet reward. He plants his foot with brutal force in my gut; the impact knocking the wind from me as he throws me over his shoulder. The jarring thud as I hit the ground sends a jolt through my body, but it's nothing I can't handle.

I rise with an earth-shaking growl and my

Wolf. Enraged by the ease of his counterattack, fights me for control. The few seconds I take to push him down is all Tev needs to launch a flurry of blows.

With arms raised high, I deflect most of the hits, but a few still land on my face. With a sickening crunch, my nose breaks, blood gushing down my face, and I grin at Tev, the red a horrifying mask.

Nothing seems to rattle the Wildling, and it only irritates me further. We settle into a tiring dance, trading punches. I do not know how long we fight for, but slowly we both grow exhausted until our hits are clumsy and glancing.

We're both a bloody mess, covered in sweat and sand. The rest of my pack make their way over to stand around Tev and me.

"I think we can call this one a draw. Tev has more dominance, but Hagon, you are one hell of a fighter," Seren remarks casually, arms crossed as he stares down at us, eyes flicking between Tev and me. "Tev, do you still feel the need to fight me? Can we call it here?"

"No, I'm good," the Wildling pants out, "Hagon, are we okay? Do you still resent me?" He aims the question my way.

"Hmph," I grunt out, my jaw aching from too many hits, "yeah. You're fine. But don't expect me to be too friendly." I have to make sure he knows that while I accept him, he's *not* my friend. That shit takes time, and I have far too much pride to concede so quickly. He will have to earn my kindness.

Our group slowly heads back to the castle. Eram, Tev, Lia and I all limping, our bodies aching from the exertion. A hot bath is called for, and Seren's rooms boast a massive tub large enough to fit all of us.

The pale Fae leads us through the winding halls, the guards stationed throughout having difficulty masking their surprise when they catch sight of the four of us. Only the King remains unharmed. I give Tev a modicum of respect for not pursuing that fight.

When we push through the doors into our rooms, both Omegas gasp at the sight of us. Dani's shock dissolves into amusement. She's well aware of the need to fight and is surprisingly conscious of the Alpha hierarchy.

But my Ily is softer and still carries the scars from his past and, as his eyes trail over each of us, cataloguing the injuries, they water. *Fuck.*

"Baby Boy, everything is fine. Just some hand to hand practice is all." I try to breeze past how bad we look, but my Omega isn't having it.

"What the fuck have you all been doing?

Why do you look like you went three rounds with a horda beast? Is your nose broken? Again, Hagon?" Ily's words have all of us shrinking down, shame for even attempting to hide this dominance fight from him.

"I'm sorry, Baby Boy. This was important. If we hadn't done this, then Tev would have continued to be pushed to the edges of our pack, and that would have hurt Dani. Which is completely unacceptable." I try to soften my gruff edge and move into his space.

Ilaris glares up at me the entire time but eventually melts into my filthy embrace with an exaggerated sigh.

"I know. I just like to keep you on your toes, Alpha." My cheeky little Omega smirks.

"Oh, you're just asking for it, aren't you?" I return, my smile growing.

"Go get cleaned up, you four are a mess!" Ily says, spinning out of my arms and turning to Seren, "and why aren't *you* covered in dirt? How did you avoid this tussle?"

"I *am* the King, you know?" Seren smirks, arms folding over his chest. "None of them felt the need to tangle with my power."

It is the last thing I hear as the four of us head into the bathing chamber. I hasten to fill the tub with steaming water and shuck my dirty trousers. More clothing joins mine on the floor as my fellow Alphas follow my example.

A hiss escapes as I settle into the boiling water, but it feels amazing on my sore muscles. Lia, Eram and Tev all slip in, spreading out around the large tub. My eyes slit and I watch my pack-mates wincing and swearing as the water stings the many cuts and abrasions on their bodies.

Luckily, our Alpha healing will take care of these simple injuries very quickly. We'll be good as new by the time morning rolls around.

"So, are we... okay?" Tev asks, hesitantly.

"Of course, Hun! We're Alphas, and getting all that raging aggression out in the sands is all we need before everything is hunky-dory in our world," Lia purrs brightly.

Her eyes close and head leans back as she slips deeper into the water. Her purple hair soaking as she rises from the tub. I've never seen her hair down before. It's always up in a fuzzy pouf. But it's longer than I expected.

Shaking my head out of the daze, I turn to Tev. Our newest pack-mate. I'm still unhappy about this addition. Why does Dani need eight mates? Is it because we have two Omegas? What the fuck was the Goddess thinking? Shouldn't Dani's mother oppose her daughter having so many mates? Damn, this is giving me a fucking headache.

"Yeah, yeah. We're fine, Tev," I grumble, leaning back and closing my eyes. "I'm going to keep an eye on you, though. You're still a stranger. And a damn Wildling."

"What does being a Wildling have to do with anything?" Tev asks, a furrow in his brow when I open my eyes to peer at him.

"Wildlings are loners. You're not pack material. Where were you living before being captured?" My tone is harsher than intended, but I *need* to protect my mates.

"Well… I had a den dug under some ruins in Naargeestig Forest… But, before that I was chased out of Doebra and forced to live alone. I guess they had the same prejudice as you," Tev replies, hurt and anger adding bite to his words.

"Wait a minute," Eram cuts in, "you're telling me you didn't choose to live alone? Why didn't you go to any of the other villages?"

"Yeah, I'm curious about that too," Lia adds.

"I-I did. But none would allow me to stay. They called me a jinx and refused to let me make a home inside the village. I figured at that point that it'd just be easier to go live alone." Tev shrugs, eyes cast down into the steaming water.

If I hadn't been watching him so closely, I would have missed the tears dripping into the bath. He hides his pain well. His voice remained steady, devoid of any tremor as he spoke.

"Hmph, superstitious assholes. There's no such thing as a jinx. They just want someone to blame for any misfortune that arises," I toss the words out carelessly, but my eyes betray my nonchalance, glued to Tev.

The moment what I said sinks in, his head jerks up, eyes wide and mouth parted in surprise.

"W-what? No, they just... They're like everyone else. Wildlings are a curse, not a Shifter, not a plain animal. We're a mix, an abomination, and we don't belong. I don't understand why the Goddess would force Dani to be stuck with a monster like me," he argues weakly, old pain visible on his face.

Ahhh fuck. He fits with us. We're a mess of trauma and old wounds, and this male truly belongs with our pack of misfits. I think the only male in our pack that doesn't have some serious damage is Ward. Even Seren, the damn King, has some fucked-up shit in his history.

"Damnit! Now I can't hate you," I mutter darkly, "Tev, listen up, that's just bullshit superstition that you're repeating and not something you actually believe, is it?" I wave a hand to clear away the question and continue before anyone else speaks.

"Nevermind that; it's dumb, small-minded rubbish. Wildlings are just another type of being that live in Saforia. Just like Wolves, Fae and Humans. The only abominations that I've ever seen are the ones made from black magic that attacked us on our trek here. Now those were fucked up. But you belong. And no matter how much shit I give you, you are pack."

My long-winded tirade slows, and I let my face settle back into a scowl. I have to keep up this grumpy mask or they might think I'm nice, or some dumb shit.

Eram, Lia and Tev all stare at me, jaws dropped and brows raised into their hairline. For fuck's sake, it's not that shocking that I comfort pack. Is it?

"Hagon, have I ever told you how much I love you?" Dani's sweet voice, thick with emotion, startles me, and I whip my head around to the doorway.

The rest of my pack crowds into the small entrance, staring at me with pride and affection. A pink blur dives into the bath with a splash. My tiny but fierce Menace wraps herself around me in a tight embrace.

"Thank you, my brave Wolf. You never cease to amaze me," Dani whispers, planting kisses over my jaw before her lips meet mine.

I take over the kiss, earning myself a light purr that vibrates her chest, pressed tight against mine. Goddess, I'm so glad she's okay. I truly thought we'd lost her when we crashed into that cave. Her body, so still on that stone slab, covered in blood. Her eyes were dull and hopeless. Thank fuck Eram and Ily got Tev over to her before shit got too bad.

Breaking the kiss, I press my face into her neck, nuzzling my mark and drinking in her slightly burnt sugar scent. I have a feeling that her scent won't return to the regular tooth-aching sweetness until she's fully worked through the loss of her wings.

My poor Omega. But she's stronger than anyone I've ever met, so I know she will overcome this, too.

CH. 44

Dani

After months of self-doubt and confusion, I have finally accepted that I'm now only half a Pixie. Anytime I move, the ghostly feeling of my wings flexing fills me with a pain unlike any other.

But now after some harsh training and long days of meditation, I feel almost normal. I know my scent has finally returned to the saccharine, spun sugar that it's meant to be. Ily has been my personal cheerleader throughout my recovery.

Although my pack-mates are supportive, my connection with Ily is unique and irreplaceable. My Alphas and Beta are excellent. There's an undeniable sense of peace and calm that they bring me, but only my Omega centers me. It's a feeling of contentment that surpasses all others.

Luella spends the entire first month of my rescue at the castle, with me and Ily. She calls it *'Omega Time'* and states it's essential for my well-being. We spend hours eating sweets and telling stories. I can see how good it is for Ilaris, but I hadn't noticed how much this time is actually helping me until one day I'm heading down the hall towards the kitchen and I catch myself smiling.

My sister knows her shit well. Luella inspires me to sew again. She demands maternity clothing because, and I quote, *'I'm growing a damn Alpha in here and nothing fits me anymore!'* Luella's belly is truly massive. Eventually her Alphas force her home because she's getting close to her birthing time.

I'm glad she has such attentive and adoring mates. I promise her, as soon as she sends word that the youngling is coming, I'll be up on a horse and rushing to her side. None of my pack protests. They understand how important our relationship is.

All my time meditating is helping ground me, and I've come to understand my Demi-Goddess powers. I started seeing blue threads that stretch between beings, some reaching off into the distance. I swear I'm losing my mind. But after two days of meditation, I discover that it's one of my new powers.

I can perceive mate connections between beings. Once I understand this, I walk around in a daze, staring at the castle staff with awe and scaring the shit out of everyone. It brings up giggles at how much it affects the guards. They think I'm some freaky Seer. I mean... in a way I am except I can see where their other half is, generally speaking.

My mind settles as I situate myself in the sand and prepare to meditate again. Three of my mates stand against the circular fence around the practice area watching me. They are a tad overprotective after being stolen from this very spot, but I don't mind.

Honestly, the first time I came back here to practice my magic, I froze as fear surged through my veins. I felt like I was going through the pain of losing my wings all over again. This was where it started, and I couldn't bring myself to walk in here voluntarily.

Eventually, after a lot of baby steps, I grow brave enough to be here. But, having my Alphas surrounding me is what truly helps. I will never tell Hagon, but Tev's presence curbed my fears. If Tev is here, that means that he's not waiting for me in that underground prison. It means that the nightmare is behind me and I'm going to be okay.

Deep inhale, count to four, slow exhale, one... two... three... four. I let my mind settle, and I sink deep inside my core. The mess of colors dancing inside me grows frantic for a few moments before it settles down.

Royal purple, translucent white, maroon, forest green and sky blue all twirl and twine together. Each color is a representation of the power I contain. Illusion, wind, torment, nature and devotion. It still amazes me I am a fucking Demi-Goddess.

How in the world did I come from Bassanai? Luella, I can understand; she's delicate and sweet, and with her changes after the barrier broke keeping her natural form in hiding, she's basically a smaller version of the Goddess. But me? I've always been too much. Too loud, too rough, too dirty, too energetic. I've heard it all my entire life. And now I'm supposed to believe that I'm a representation of the Gods and Goddesses that created our world? Wild.

One at a time, I pull on the strands of magic and practice my power. An illusion of a thick jungle and marshy grounds littered all over swallow up the base of massive trees. Strange and colorful birds sing and swoop through the branches. Imaginary critters add their odd, rustling sounds to the natural music of the wilds.

The smell of the marshlands rises around me, a damp and earthy aroma. The illusion, rich with the scent of the woods - decaying leaves, new life, still waters and hidden animals - feels solid and true, just like the sand beneath my legs.

As quickly as that illusion appears, I wipe it away with my wind whirling around me. It kicks up sand and leaves all around me, lifting my hair playfully as I control its direction. A small cyclone dances over the sand, growing taller than the walls surrounding the castle grounds. The wind is such a playful, fun power; it's always eager to do my bidding.

My next power, torment, still frightens me with its strength. It's the one that helped me strip Nyurel of his magic, to live as a human and never be able to leave that island. This power, however, has far greater potential. With a thought, I can cripple anyone, leaving them to writhe in agony as pain explodes through their nervous system. The things I can do now fill me with a sense of dreadful awe. I do not toy with this magic for long before moving on to my power over nature.

This is one power that I take great pride in. I've always felt close to the forest, and now I understand why. Being able to create life and encourage plants to grow brings me such joy and serenity. Seren has seen what I've done to his garden out front, but he hasn't said a word about it.

My King just smiles and nuzzles me with a purr. His pride flowing through our bond, settling me even more.

I can even speak to plants. It's not a language that I've ever encountered, but if I close my eyes and place a hand on one plant, I swear it speaks to me. Mostly, they ask for things like water, sunlight and fertilizer, but sometimes they'll bring me news from afar. All of nature is interconnected, and each plant can speak across vast distances. I've heard whispers of things moving in Naargeestig forest, and I'm afraid that Allista will soon have a visit from her horrible ex-mates.

But I have kept this news to myself. The Elves protect her well, and I am sure the Corrigan, with their shadowy magic, will not be able to reclaim her. Allista is stronger than anyone gives her credit for.

Lastly, I call upon my power of devotion. Behind my closed eyes, the pretty sky blue magic blooms. The moment I open my lids, I know strands reaching between beings and stretching off into the distance will bombard me. The thickest, brightest connections are between my mates and me. It just shows how strong our pack is. How perfectly we all fit together.

Relief and pride rush through me at my ability to turn this power on and off. When it first manifested, I had no control over it. There was a sea of blue everywhere I looked. It gave me such a headache. But after weeks of practice, I can call it up at will, and I've already helped so many of the staff find their mates.

When I connected Dralton, one of the King's guards, with his sweet little female, the sight of their excitement and happiness filled me with such delight. With a light push, a rush of warmth floods me, like sunshine on my face. My heart feels ready to burst with joy. This is my favorite power. Being able to bring cheer to everyone is a balm to my pain. It's one of the things that has helped me heal so much.

My missing wings still torment me, but the ache has grown further away and less painful. My pack helps when I'm having an off day. I don't think I'll ever truly stop grieving my loss, but at least it's easier to manage.

Lately, Lia has been whispering mischief in my ear. I haven't been as bouncy and excitable as I used to be. Which means I have not been up to my old self, and I haven't been playing jokes on my pack. But her encouragement has been piquing my interest, and I think I might finally be ready to do something fun.

Hagon, Eram and Seren won't be as excited about this as I am, but I know they won't say a word. My happiness is more important to them than stopping my antics.

What has brought me so much joy is seeing how my pack has finally accepted Tev. They don't think I know about the fights, but how could I miss them returning to our rooms covered in sand, dirt and blood? It doesn't bother me though. I completely understand the need to just fight it out, plus I know they seriously needed to figure out the pack hierarchy. I don't fully comprehend the hierarchy, but I know it has something to do with dominance.

Regardless, I'm happy they've stopped pushing my newest mate to the edges. Even Hagon demands Tev's help occasionally. Although he doesn't smile or stop grumbling the entire time.

I find it cute. But anytime I tell Hagon he's cute, he gives me such a glare. I save that for when I'm feeling needy, because then he spanks me and leaves me lost in ecstasy.

There's still *that* title hanging over my head. Queen. Seren has had some tutors spend time with me, teaching me all the ways a Queen should behave. I don't feel prepared for this, but I'm his mate, and, regardless of how much I don't want the title, I've got it.

Seren is passionate about Saforia and all its subjects. It's actually very inspiring. It makes me wonder how he could have let himself fail so badly for so long. But he's doing everything he can to fix his mistakes.

My King has already sent out some of his warrior packs to each corner of Saforia. Their job is to check for Omegas and ensure their well-being. If they find *any* abuse, they have full leave to be judge, jury and executioner. The rescued Omegas will be brought back to the castle, where Ily and I will tend to their wounds and help them overcome their emotional distress.

Once they're recovered enough, Lia and Hagon have agreed to help me teach them self-defence so they have some way to protect themselves once they decide to leave this place and set out on their own.

Maybe I won't make such a bad Queen after all.

EPILOGUE

Allista

Banell has been such a balm to my injured soul. The bright, clean air, nature all around and the calm teachings of Healer Wick have all been instrumental in mending the mental scars from my forced bonding.

It doesn't hurt that Zenik is absolutely *gorgeous* and has shown me that not all Alphas are terrifying and cruel. Same with Shoha and Tenil. The Elves have all been so welcoming and patient with my soft heart.

Shoha isn't one of Zenik's warriors, but he's one of his best friends. The male is an excellent cook, and his home has one of the escape tunnels that lead out of Banell. He showed me in case something happens and I need to flee.

Also, Shoha has one of the prettiest gardens I've ever seen. The Elves have such beautiful nature magic, but Shoha insists that his garden is so lush because he puts in the physical work too. Solely relying on magic has its limits.

Tenil is one of many warriors and hunters who protect Banell and the Chief. He has spent time with me, showing me proper self defence. Although I think I'm too gentle to use the moves he taught me. The idea of hurting anyone is a heavy weight on my conscience.

Ideally, I'll be safe at Wick's place, creating herbal remedies, when my former bonds appear. And I know they're coming. The Corrigan hasn't stopped plucking at the bond between us. Each time one of Pack Dewal sends their glee or yanks on the cord connecting us, my heart lurches and nausea swells in my gut.

I've lived with fear for a long time. The fleeting glimpses of happiness that I've found here with the Elves seem so limited. As if it'll be ripped away from me at any moment.

I have no doubts that Zenik and his warriors can protect me, but how do you guard against a malignant shade? Corrigan possess the ability to become mist at will, allowing passage through barriers. They prey on fear and torment anything that crosses their path.

Many times I've asked myself, '*Why me?*'

Why did they choose me? There were plenty of other females in Rodera. Even another Omega! From the moment Damenor saw me, my destiny was forever altered.

Each male started showing up anytime I left the house or the healers. They would ask me questions, feign interest in my life and follow my every step. I thought nothing of it until one day they laid hands on me. Muffled my shouts of surprise and fear. Forced me into their home on the edge of our village and took turns, biting me and… and… I can't even say it in my mind.

The horrible nightmares still haunt me. I haven't been the same since that day. Dewal kept me inside, away from anyone else, and barely let me speak. For years, I hadn't uttered a word, and the quiet was deafening. My spirit was beaten down one cruel taunt at a time. One trip to the bedroom at a time. Each moment they touched me killed a part of me. The side that smiled in the sunshine, that sang as she walked down the roads of home, and the bit that pined for a pack of my own.

Before Dewal, I'd wished and prayed for Alphas to love me. The idea of a pack was supposed to be care and adoration. Mutual respect. Kindness and cute moments with each member of my new family. But all those fantasies were stomped down and crushed under the heavy foot of the Corrigan.

Even with Zenik showing me how an Alpha is supposed to behave, there's still a hesitation holding me back from accepting his sweet gestures. I'm scared.

A sharp pang of longing turns my face towards the west. My brother, Eram, was so hesitant to leave me after everything, and regardless of how much comfort his presence brought me, I knew if I ever wanted to move on with my life I had to do this alone.

I miss Dani and Ilaris too. While I hadn't been with them for long, they brought me such comfort and a sense of safety that had been missing from my life. Especially Dani. That tiny female is the strongest Omega I've ever met, and her courage, attitude, and resolve taught me I don't need to conform to expectations.

Ilaris showed me that strength isn't always obvious. It lies within our perseverance, our fight to survive, and the belief that we'll find happiness again after enduring hardship. Watching him pull himself together day after day while we raced through the mountains as Dani lay dying in the cart was eye-opening. His tenacity pushed me to do better.

The two Omegas gave me the strength to stand on my own again. Plus, Eram was becoming increasingly frustrating. Watching him push his fated mate away again and again because of me hurt more than anything Dewal ever did. My brother deserves happiness, but he was cutting himself off, punishing himself for failing me, and I couldn't be the reason that he lost out on the love of his life.

It was time for me to regain my independence. Plus, I really think I could make a beautiful life here with Zenik. And maybe a couple of other sweet Alphas that have caught my eye. I'm not sure when or if I'll be ready for anything physical again, but with their patience and Wick's teaching, I know I'll be okay.

"Allista!" Shoha's deep timber draws me out of my muddling thoughts, "Allista! Do you have time to come help in my garden today? The peppers are ready, and the tomatoes need some support. I thought maybe we could work together to steady them. Or if you have plans with Wick, would you want to come by later?"

A bright grin spreads over my face as I stare at the sweet Alpha, rambling about gardening. I make him nervous. It's cute.

"I've got a lesson with Wick right now, but I would love to come play in the dirt later," I reply, my grin growing wider, making my cheeks hurt as a pretty red flush tints Shoha's cheeks.

"Y-yeah, that sounds good. Would you care for an escort to Wick's home?" He holds an elbow out to me, and it's my turn to blush as I accept his arm.

This is one reason I appreciate Shoha so much. He's always careful to ask before touching me, and he's so mindful. Plus, seeing a tall, handsome Elf turn so shy is endearing. The male could complete all the gardening in half the time without me, but he enjoys my company, and each time we kneel before the rows of vegetables, he's careful to stay close but ensure my comfort.

That, and he smells like rosemary. With each inhale, I take in his presence: crisp, clean and invigorating. His scent brings me to a bright forest after a rainfall mixed with freshly cut herbs. Sweet with an undercurrent of mint and lemon. It's warmth and comfort. Everything I need to soothe my turbulent mind.

We chat about the new sprouts, and which vegetables are almost ready for harvest. Shoha goes into detail about the dishes he's planning, and my mouth waters at the thought of his cooking.

Shoha pauses, gripping my hand gently, as the Healers' home comes into view, and faces me, his expression shy.

"I look forward to our date in the dirt later." He bends into a bow and places a kiss on the back of my hand. "Say hello to Wick for me."

My cheeks burn a fiery red, and words get

stuck in my throat at his gallant gesture. A joyful smile spread across my face, admiring his natural charm.

"Yes, thank you!" I squeak out, nodding rapidly.

Shoha stands and, with one more sweet grin, he turns and heads off. I stand and watch his backside as he strolls away in a daze. That Alpha has a tight butt, and his hard work in the garden really shows.

"Admiring the view?" A voice teases from behind me.

"What!" I jump, spinning around to face Wick's devilish grin. "Don't sneak up on me like that! Wick, you scoundrel!"

"I did nothing of the sort. You were just too mesmerized by Shoha to notice anything around you! I probably could have grabbed my lute, and you wouldn't have heard a thing," Wick teases as he stops beside me.

His words make a giggle bubble up inside me as giddy joy tickles my chest. As soon as they escape my lips, Wick joins me. His laughter is a low, warm sound, a perfect accompaniment to my glee.

Six months ago, I couldn't have imagined I would ever feel such joy in my life. In the darkest of times, I contemplated ending it all to escape those monsters. Thankfully, Eram got me out before I could go through with my plan.

Now, I can feel that everything I've always wanted is finally coming together. Wick is teaching me how to be a proper healer and has become one of my closest friends. I'm surrounded by deliciously sexy Elves.

The air tastes sweeter now that I'm out of their hands, away from those beasts that forced me out of the life I'd strived for, and I've even stopped having so many panic attacks. I know the Corrigan are still coming for me, but for once I'm not afraid.

When they get here, they won't find the scared, timid mouse they created. No, they will face my righteous anger and an entire village of pissed-off Elves.

Bring it on.

THE END

Also By A. R. Lines

Thank You So Much For Reading!

Please consider leaving a review. They truly help.

Dani's story has been freeing to write. She possessed a formidable strength and a fiery spirit, yet she was tender toward her mates. Her love for them is boundless, and they return the sentiment with equal measure. I feel bad that I had to put Dani through some horrible things but I knew she was strong enough to overcome anything.

Next up will be Allista's story, it will definitely be less chaotic and more cozy fantasy. BUT before I get to her book I have a dystopian book that's been nagging at me to get written, so keep your eyes peeled for updates on that!

A big thank you to all my readers. As always, I couldn't do this without you. My goals with writing are mainly just to create a fun world to dive into and find that momentary escape. I wanted to write a book that I would like to read so I can only hope it finds others out there that also enjoy this kind of story.

A shout out to my beta readers, Ashley and Meaghan, and my absolutely amazing editor, Andra. This book wouldn't be the polished story you see before you without their help.

Some days, an idea sticks in your head and

the only way to get rid of it is to write it.

- A. R. Lines

About The Author

AR Lines is a daydreamer, crocheter, nerdy gamer, and avid romance reader. She has been reading the romance genre since she was a teen and has always been interested in writing. As a little girl, she even wrote a terrible children's book and had it published in her elementary school library. AR Lines lives in Vancouver, Canada, with her husband, enjoying the mild coastal weather, beautiful beaches, and mountainous nature hikes. She also has two demons masquerading as cats that she adores, even though they are evil little gremlins that destroy nice things.

Find her online for updates on what's next!

Instagram: @author_arlines

Facebook: AR Lines Readers Group

TikTok: @author_arlines

Signup for her newsletter for sneak peeks of current projects, character art and what's going on in her weird mind - Here

www.ingramcontent.com/pod-product-compliance
Lightning Source LLC
LaVergne TN
LVHW050917080826
845145LV00001B/107

9781738340576